Something Due

Dear Ada,
I hope you enjoy reading my
second novel. Thanks for your
assistance to me this year.

Something Due

Jack Seville

Jack Seville

Library of Congress Number: 2003090173
ISBN :   Softcover   1-4010-9125-3

This book was printed in the United States of America.

To order additional copies of this book, contact:
Xlibris Corporation
1-888-795-4274
www.Xlibris.com
Orders@Xlibris.com
17667

DEDICATION:

TO MY COURAGEOUS AND FAITHFUL FRIENDS OF THE
GREAT SIOUX NATION

Chapter 1

Tukten To'kcca

The waitress stood staring across the dusty street. She listened to the idle chitchat in the room. A diverse gathering of ranchers and truck drivers was drinking coffee at various booths in the little café. She lit a cigarette as she extended her break from serving the men. Those who frequented this godforsaken little dump that passed for a restaurant were folk who didn't know any better, couldn't afford more, or didn't give a damn. They talked of everything as though they knew it all. Every day was the same as the one before: politics, cattle, roads, and the weather. In the winter, only high school basketball replaced politics and seemed, at times, to even preempt the weather in importance to these buffoons. She could hardly stand listening to them.

Word had gotten around shortly after she moved to Kadoka that she was alone. So for the first year, she sought to fend off every pass both the married and single males made at her. Sometimes, one would pinch her rear as she walked by. She would turn menacingly with hot coffee pot in hand and threaten to give the aggressor a bath with the scalding brew if ever he tried that again.

She had intentionally adopted a butch appearance. She never wore a dress. People usually saw her around town in baggy cords or torn blue jeans and a wash-worn blouse or sweatshirt. Her hair was black and cropped to give her the appearance of being a man from the rear. And her accent, noticeably big city, gave her conversation an edge. This kept any local bachelors at bay. Especially since most of the women in town had spread rumors that they thought this new resident was as lesbian as they come.

She kept her distance, put in her eight hours a day, then walked back to her apartment above the only hardware store for fifty miles in any direction. No one knew anything about her except that she called herself Jenny. Jenny Craig. She had ridden into town two years before. She did not do much of anything, except live there and serve as a waitress at the café. People often speculated what she might be living on. But they never asked her.

The local Methodist minister, a young bachelor just out of a theological seminary and unsure of his calling, visited her once to learn if she was interested in attending church. Her answer was that she was an agnostic and hadn't darkened the door of a church since she was fifteen years old. The pastoral call was so uncomfortable for the minister that he gladly left, taking her at her word, and never bothered inviting her to church again.

"Hey, Jenny," one of the men called her out of her daydream. "You got any of them jelly rolls, darlin'?"

"All out," she snarled. "There won't be any more 'til tomorrow."

"Whoa," said his sidekick, who was sitting among the four men at the counter. "You must have the rag on today." Every man in the place laughed aloud.

She recoiled in anger, but said nothing to them. This was their way of starting the day, and she was accustomed to it by now.

"I didn't know her kind had menstrual seasons," said a truck driver as he lifted his cup to his lips. The men laughed anew, one of them smacking his knee.

"If that's supposed to mean something, I don't know what it would be," she yelled back at him. Suddenly, stillness overtook the dirty little café. Even Steve, owner and cook, leaned through the serving window, awaiting a scene. Life in small towns seems always on the edge in ways that she had never expected when she agreed to come here. She had felt that being in this little town in the middle of nowhere, a hundred miles from South Dakota's second-largest city, would fit finely. Lately, she had to admit to herself that it was getting so boring that she almost welcomed these mental wrestling matches with the intellectual lightweights who frequented the café.

"Well," the truck driver stalled, "you know, you being queer and everything."

No one had ever said this aloud to her. She was glad to hear it. It told her that her little act was definitely working. She saw this as the time to confirm her new identity and thus, put people in this stupid little town at a greater distance.

"Look," she said in her best imitation of an angry Bette Davis, "just because I like women much more than I care for you assholes doesn't mean I am not a woman myself. And as for your analysis, smart-ass, I am not having a menstrual period right now. But if it would be helpful to you, I might consider placing a notice on the bulletin board in the doorway for you so you can keep track of it!"

All the men chuckled as the truck driver stood up and took his wallet from his hip pocket. "Lady," he said with a snarl, "I don't have to take that from no butch bitch!" He hurled two dollars on the counter as he began to walk past her.

"Does this mean we won't have the pleasure of your company any morning soon?" she asked now, as though she were Scarlett O'Hara, her eyelashes fluttering and a broad smile upon her face. The truck driver stomped from the café, sputtering as he went, while the men, including Steve, rolled with laughter. Try as often as they could, none of them could get the best of this woman. Each day's attempt seemed to entertain them, though. And, she had to admit, as painful as it was at times for her, she also looked forward to getting things off her chest in this manner. There really was nothing else to do here in Kadoka.

Having lived here for two years, she had been to Rapid City often. She rode the Jack Rabbit Bus west, once getting off at Wall and walking around the drug store before boarding a later bus to

Rapid. Another time, she went to Rapid City when the horse races were in town. She tried her luck at this track where the managers were undecided whether to feature thoroughbreds or quarter horses, even racing them against each other in shorter races. She never got the hang of how to pick winners at this track. Her former life was filled with frequenting racetracks. They were real ones: Aqueduct, Saratoga, Gulfstream, Hialeah. The racetrack in Rapid City sat in a little valley southeast of the city. An interesting mix of Indians and what would have passed for poor whites in other places patronized the track. The horses looked skinny and hungry. Some thoroughbreds had so much liniment rubbed on them that when they walked by in the post parade, she wanted to get some fresh air if only she could have found a more vacant space by the rail.

The jockeys also struck her as a motley crew. A curious mixture of scraggly, bearded, old men and nubile teenage girls climbed upon what horseflesh was here and galloped off to glory before several hundred adoring and wager-frenzied fans. It was a joke. She vowed never to go back. Once was enough. But it was the only excitement in town on Saturdays in summer.

Rapid City struck her as little more than an excuse for a town. Had it not been surrounded by the only mountains for miles and offered an opportunity to camp, ski, fish in Rapid Creek, and venture into some of the West's most legendary hills, she doubted if anyone would ever go out of their way to visit. Simply left to the flatlanders who lived in South Dakota, the Black Hills would have been untouched, except for summer respites. The good city fathers who, like their predecessors in the nineteenth century, spied gold in "them there hills." Rapid City was awash with neon at night and cluttered by ridiculous billboards hawking just about every pleasure and adventure a human being ought to pursue. Lately, word was spreading that the hills one day would be the new Las Vegas. She had decided that it would be best not to be seen often in Rapid City, if that were the case. She did not want to run into any old pals.

So, Kadoka was her home for now. Waiting on café tables was

her new profession, though she really did not need the money. And time, which can never truly be wasted or used up for it doesn't really exist except in human constructs, just ticked by as Jenny Craig, lesbian waitress from some other place, went to work, went home, watched TV, and went to sleep. Each day was like its former, season after season. Life upon the South Dakota prairie moved relentlessly on amidst a mixture of Arctic winter cold, graced at times with Chinook winds, as today, and blistering summer heat, cooled only in the aftermath of ferocious thunderstorms that seemed to come from any and all directions. This was to be it for her. Her new life. Jenny Craig, a waitress in Kadoka, South Dakota, stood by the window and gazed up and down the snow-dusted street as the men, one by one, got up to resume their daily chores. She cleaned up after them, in the hour which usually lacked any patrons before lunchtime brought local store owners and business persons for whatever lunch special Steve had cooked up the night before.

Life here had a rhythm all its own. She had spent two years learning it. If it took her the rest of her life, she knew she would never really fit.

Chapter 2

Tu'we Wan'cadan

"Congratulations," the doctor smiled at the young woman lying in the hospital ward before him, "you've got twin girls!"

Dread crept across the room and sat right smack on top of the new mother with a thud. What was she going to do? Single. Not much going for her, except her body, and now, she wondered what that would be like after bearing two babies at once and having to suckle them for God knew how long.

She considered giving them up for adoption. That's what the priest in town had suggested. He knew she wasn't going to be successful as a mother. He'd heard her confessions. Her secrets were safe with him. But now, there were three where months before, there was only one mouth to feed. What was she to do? She wondered to herself as she lay waiting for the nurses to bring her babies to her.

Her parents didn't want her back. Not after what she'd been doing for a living. She could hear them rant and rave about not protecting herself from such a circumstance, or from disease itself, as she slept with whoever paid the fare to her and her keeper. Even though these babies carried their blood through their little veins and arteries, they'd not be a welcome sight at her parents' house in West Texas.

Her keeper said he'd see that the baby got a good home just as soon as she weaned it from her breasts. But how would he react to two? There simply was no telling how he would see this.

He was not a reasonable man. He was good enough to keep her fed and sheltered. But his concern was economic, not domestic.

What was she to do? Tears filled her eyes as she thought of how she had screwed her life away. And now, she had brought two more mouths to feed into God's world. She wished she had died during the difficult labor which began last evening and didn't let up until just moments ago. *I need a miracle*, she thought, just as the parish priest walked into her room.

"Hey, Sadie," he said as he scanned her unkempt appearance, "they tell me you had twins!"

"Yeah, Father, it wasn't easy," she said limply.

"How are you feeling?" he asked sincerely.

"Oh," she sighed, "none the worse for wear." She liked this man of the cloth. He had been the only male recently involved in her life who neither wanted anything from her in return for kindnesses, nor expected anything to come of their relationship, except her starting a new life. She wanted that also but didn't really see a way to gain it.

"Two baby girls," he said with a smile. "They sure will demand a lot of a mother."

"I hadn't thought about it much," she lied. Since the doctor had told her just moments before, nothing else occupied her mind, except how she was going to care for two babies at once.

"Oh," he replied.

"No, I'm too tired right now, Father," she said again very quietly. "I guess we'll manage somehow."

"Look, Sadie," he began in earnest, "there is no way you or those babies will make it unless you get yourself out of here as soon as you can. You've got to make a new beginning. God has given you an opportunity to start again."

"Hah!" she interrupted him. "That's a good one, Father! I think God has one hell of a sense of humor if He thinks this is the way for a woman like me to make a new start in life."

"That so?" he replied raising his eyebrows, which suggested that he just might have something in mind that would interest her. She waited anxiously as he continued to talk.

"Just might be that God has shown me a way to help you. You've been on my mind and in my prayers, young lady, and I don't mind telling you that my knees are getting tired petitioning the Almighty on your behalf."

She turned toward him and listened more attentively as the priest continued to talk to her in a parental fashion.

"There's a monastery near Round Rock that needs a housekeeper badly. The Sisters of Mercy are looking everywhere for a person to prepare food, clean clothes, and do other light housework at their small house in the country. There are only twelve of them and they are all nearing seventy years of age. They spend most of their time praying and preparing to meet our Heavenly Father. It's a nice place. You and your babies would do just fine there," he concluded with a smile.

"Father," she asked incredulously, "do you really believe that those women who have spent their entire lives in holy service are going to welcome a street-walking mother of two infants as their housekeeper?"

"They aren't picky," he said, "just needy. There's a difference."

"Oh," she turned away from him, starting to weep.

"Now, Sadie," he spoke sternly, "don't you put God to the test. You are a mother now. You have two babies to care for as only a mother can do and there is no reason in this world why you can't care for those sweet old nuns in Round Rock too!"

She laughed. How like a man. No idea in the world what he was talking about. Just trying to be heroic in the face of some of the most challenging odds the Creator ever placed before a creature.

"What are you laughing at?" the man of God wanted to know.

"You," she said as she turned once more to face the priest. "What is it about you people that gives you such a sense of optimism? You never tire of believing in me. Why?"

"Isn't that obvious?"

It wasn't to her at the moment. All that was clear to her was she was agitated with this man's lack of insight into her dilemma.

If she could have gotten up and walked out on this man at this moment, she would have done so. But she was tired. She was a mother of two. And any minute now, they would be brought in to her room to be fed.

"You are a child of God," the priest seriously intoned as he studied her face for some clue as to what she might be thinking as he spoke. "You have a right to happiness, the same as any of God's children. And so do your babies."

She cried. Great tears fell from her eyes as her body shook uncontrollably before him. She wanted to scream at him and his God at this moment. But all she could do was cry.

The priest sat down beside her and took her trembling hand in his. "Sadie," he continued, "God wants you to care for your babies. God is giving you a way to do that. I have spoken with the Sisters of Mercy on your behalf. They'll be expecting you in about a month. Until then, members of the parish have agreed to take you and your babies in and care for you while you regain your strength."

She looked up at him between her tears. This dear man whom she hardly knew was paving a way for her out of her former life that she never dreamed she'd find. She cried tears of joy as she struggled to speak.

"Father, I'm not even a Catholic," she heard herself whisper, "why are you doing this for me?"

"Sadie," he said quietly, "the Mother of our Lord wasn't a Catholic either and she faced what you are facing. She, too, courageously brought a child into this world when it looked like everyone, her betrothed and her community, was turning against her. She was poor. She was in need. She was with child. And the whole town whispered against her. How could the Church, which prays to the Mother of Jesus, turn its back on you in your need, my child?" He stroked her tear-stained hair as he continued to reassure her. "God has given you something far more precious to care for than the sexual needs of men. Now it's up to you to face that gift with courage."

She looked deeply into his steel-gray eyes. This old man had sat behind a confessional screen and heard her pour out frustration after frustration as she longed for a new beginning. This priest, who found her kneeling in the sanctuary at Saint Agnes Church one cold and damp night in Houston seven months before, when she had gone into God's house seeking forgiveness for what she was about to do with her secret, now sat beside her, offering to give her a second chance at life as an adult. This man, who knew nothing of the kind of life she had led until now, was promising to stand beside her as she took whatever steps were necessary to see that her babies were cared for in ways that would spare them her pain. Sadie loved this man, who sat next to her and waited for her babies to arrive, as she had loved no man in her life. She loved him as she would never love another. He was the brother she never had, the father she never knew, the presence of God she had only fantasized. He was really her friend. She would find the courage. She would start anew.

He saw it in her eyes. She said nothing. Her face relaxed. Her eyes softened as the tears ceased. And a smile of agreement crossed her countenance.

"Good," he said, "it's all settled."

A month later, Sadie, along with her twin daughters, moved into the Sisters of Mercy Monastery, located on a rural route near Round Rock, Texas. The names of the children had been suggested by the French couple with whom she had stayed as she recovered from childbirth: Jacqueline and Marie.

At first, it was a struggle. Sadie was feeling better with each passing day. The twins were not as much trouble as she thought they would be. But the cleaning and cooking for a dozen rapidly aging women, in addition to caring for the babies, were definitely a challenge. Her knees soon developed calluses from scrubbing floors. Hands, formerly manicured to attract attention at a glance, now wore scars from grasping too many hot pans from overheated ovens. And she lost so much sleep the first twelve months that she never seemed to quite wake up.

The Sisters loved seeing and hearing the little girls grow up in their midst. Each was eager to be of help to the young mother and her daughters. Month after month passed and soon, the holy family celebrated first birthdays with Sadie and the girls by ordering cake and ice cream from a nearby confectionery in Round Rock.

Both Marie and Jacqueline were walking and jabbering by the following Christmas. Now able to appreciate the sights and sounds of the holidays, the girls were a delight to all as they helped decorate the tree that graced the foyer of the monastery.

As years passed, one by one, the older religious women passed on to their reward. It was difficult work for Sadie. Just before their deaths, each elderly sister needed hospice care in addition to Sadie's labor on her behalf. It was like having an additional baby to care for as each nun became incontinent and unable to care in any way for herself. And the community didn't stop and wait for each to die. Sadie was working harder than she had ever worked in her life. And she was somehow loving it.

The routine, once the girls were out of diapers, never varied. Up at 4:30 A.M. to prepare breakfast so that by 6:30 A.M., immediately after morning prayers in the chapel, the nightly fast was broken with oatmeal, toast with marmalade and butter, and hot coffee. Once a week, on Sundays, the sisters expected eggs cooked over easy, with bacon and grits. By 8:30 A.M., her girls were awake, needing feeding and care. By 9:30 A.M., Sadie was making her rounds of rooms to tidy up, to gather soiled clothes for washing, and to offer daily words of cheer and gossip with the sisters. Day by day, the routine was the same.

As her girls grew, they loved to toddle from room to room in the monastery and jabber with whomever was present. There were more laps to crawl onto, more stories to hear, more cookies to find, harbored in closet drawers and on dresser tops, than any two children had a right to expect. The sisters eagerly greeted them as they entered the cubicles. Open arms, broad smiles, loving words surrounded Sadie's girls every day of their lives. It was a pleasant place to rear her children. Father was right. God had placed a new way of life squarely in front of Sadie at Sisters of Mercy. She was more grateful than anyone could have guessed.

By the time the twins were five years old, there were only eight women left in the monastery. Not one new member had come in during all the time Sadie and the girls were there. They were a small family. They hid nothing from one another. Joys and frustrations co-mingled as Sadie cared for their every need and want. She read the fear in the eyes of each as death approached to claim her. She sought to comfort them as best she could with homespun humor and what little bits of gospel she had learned as a child and still believed in as an adult. The good news in her life was far different from that of the sisters. Sadie knew that to be true. Nevertheless, she would remind them, each one who lay at death's doorway, how in her darkest moment, God had surprised her with the opportunity to live in a different place, a safer place, a place where she and her girls could start life anew. "Maybe heaven is just like this place has been for me," she would say with a smile as she left their rooms. Smiles and tears filled frail faces, which followed her every movement until she was gone.

The day following the twins' sixth birthday party, Sister Margaret spoke with Sadie about the future of the monastery.

"This is holy ground, consecrated to the service of God that we Sisters of Mercy have offered since its founding in 1902," she said as Sadie sat before her, hands folded and eyes alert to whatever message she was about to hear. "And as you can see, we are all getting so much older. I don't believe there is one of us fit to tend the garden this spring and summer."

Sadie listened with rapt attention, afraid that Sister Margaret was about to tell her the monastery would close.

"I think we should hire a caretaker, Sadie. You can't add to your duties here and we can't keep up with the land and garden any longer."

"I think that is a good idea," Sadie responded, relieved that the monastery wasn't closing and she would not have to find a new home for Marie and Jacqueline.

"There's a man nearby who is out of work right now," Sister

Margaret continued, "and I think he is just the person for the job. He was a hired hand for several years but the agriculture around here is going into recession. No wonder so many have simply given up, sold their land, and made a way for Austin to continue to grow in our direction."

"Yes," said Sadie, "it is remarkable how many new developments there are between the capitol and us. Every time I drive to the supermarket, I see another new house going up."

"The man's name is Juan," Sister Margaret continued as if she hadn't heard a word. "He is Mexican, has a family of five to support, and is used to hard work. I think he'll help us get through this spring and summer."

Silence crept across Sister Margaret's desk toward Sadie. It communicated that something more needed to be said. Sadie waited while Sister Margaret sought for the right words. When they came, they stung.

"He's your age, Sadie," she finally said. "I don't know if you have fully embraced your new life here or not. So I feel I must say this to you. No fraternizing with the help."

"What?" Sadie asked, stunned.

"Just that," Sister Margaret said abruptly. "I want no involvement between you and Juan. He has a family."

There it was. Sadie had wondered when it would come up. Not until now had anyone dared refer to her life before she and the twins arrived here, six years before. Now that there was going to be a man on the monastery's land, no doubt, all who still lived and knew Sadie's past were thinking exactly what Sister Margaret implied. They just weren't sure Sadie had changed that much. Six years of scrubbing floors and pots and pans, cooking, changing beds, and praying with them had not addressed their initial concern about who she had been before she came. Like the scarlet "A," Sadie wore her past here as surely now as on the day she arrived.

"Sister Margaret," she began hesitantly, "I would do nothing to jeopardize my privilege to stay here with my girls. This has been the most wonderful place I have ever lived. And God knows, it is the best place for Jacqueline and Marie."

Sister Margaret smiled as Sadie continued to try to reassure her that there would be no involvement between her and Juan.

"I have learned so much about the kind of life I was missing before I came here. I thought a certain man cared for me once. But all he was doing was making sure I was comfortable enough to provide him a profit. I haven't done any drugs or drunk any alcohol since before the twins were born. And I have no interest in breaking up a good man's home. I longed for a good home before my babies were born. My good home is here."

Sister Margaret raised her right hand, as if to say "That's quite enough, my dear," but Sadie continued.

"I, more than any of you here, am quite aware of the risk you took, bringing me and my girls into the monastery. I am very thankful you took that chance with me. You can still count on me, Sister Margaret."

"Sadie," Sister Margaret interrupted, "I believe in you. I always have. But I had to state our policy clearly to you before Juan arrives. He will be spending many hours and days here with us and I sense you, because of your age, my dear, may find him attractive. Please be careful. That's all I'm asking."

Sadie was concerned. Nothing she had said seemed to relieve Sister Margaret's anxiety. It was as if Sister Margaret was reading her mind. Truth be known, until Sister Margaret mentioned Juan was married, her heart had raced a bit with the news that a man was coming to work with them. Sadie knew men. And she knew herself. Having always been attracted to men, every type of man, she knew in her heart that Juan would have to be considerably unappealing not to get some interest from her.

Silence filled the room as the two women stared at one another. Finally, Sadie confessed.

"Sister Margaret," she said quietly, "you are right. It has been a while since I have been with a man. And, God knows, I find just about every man I ever laid eyes on attractive. I will be very careful. Please trust me."

Sister Margaret's face relaxed. "Thank you, Sadie. You know you can come to me any time for counsel."

"Yes," was all Sadie said, dropping her glance to the floor. Their conversation finished, both were looking for a way to end this encounter without it becoming more awkward.

"I'll see you at lunch then, Sadie," Sister Margaret said.

"Yes," Sadie replied and got up to leave the office. As she reached the doorway, she turned and glanced at Sister Margaret, who was now busying herself with random items that lay on her desk. "Thank you," Sadie whispered. And then she left to prepare the noontime meal. She could hear her girls singing to a nun in one of the rooms in the hallway. Assured that they were all right, she hurried past and went straight to the kitchen.

Juan arrived two days later. Sister Margaret walked him through the monastery, introducing him to all of the nuns. Finally, she came to the kitchen, where Sadie was preparing the evening meal.

Sadie looked up into the face of a brown, muscular man in his early to mid-thirties. He smiled. She felt something move within her.

"Sadie," Sister Margaret said rather formally, "this is Juan Lopes. He will be tending the grounds and garden for the rest of this growing season. Juan, this is Sadie Fronteirre."

"How do you do?" Juan asked with a smile and an appropriate accent.

"I am glad to meet you," she replied with a smile, not overdone, as Sister Margaret closely watched this initial interchange with interest.

"Me too," Juan said, more relaxed as he reached out his hand, as if to shake hers in greeting. Sadie started to reach and then quickly withdrew her hand, taking a step backward.

Juan turned to Sister Margaret and said, "Miss Sadie is shy!" Something about the way he said it brought back a deeply hidden memory from her childhood. Just a glimpse, and it was gone, buried where she hoped it would never rise again.

Sister Margaret laughed and replied, "No, she probably has her hands full of cooking oil!" They all laughed as the two women shot one another quick, reassuring glances.

"I will see you around," Juan said as he and Sister Margaret turned to leave.

"You must meet Sadie's children," Sister Margaret said as she escorted the new groundskeeper from the kitchen.

"The senorita has children?" Juan replied incredulously.

Sadie heard Sister Margaret describe the twin girls as they left the room. First encounter accomplished. Sadie sensed that the warning she had received from Sister Margaret was not without merit. He was handsome, sure of himself, and a bit of a flirt. She would need to be on guard around him because from the moment he walked into the room, she was attracted to him. His hair was wavy black, his eyes dark, his skin brown, and his body muscular. *His wife must love him very much*, Sadie thought to herself.

Not having been with a man in nearly seven years, Sadie sensed a hunger within herself every time she looked at Juan. Yes, she would have to be extremely careful around him. She knew she could do it. After all, she had done everything necessary to provide a new life and the best home for her children. They were but twelve years away from graduating from high school and being on their own. No sense messing all that up for them. This was her home. It was to be her home until she saw her girls grown and on their own, she vowed to herself.

Chapter 3

Ta'ku Wowinihan

Sitting alone in her room, Jenny pondered her years at the monastery after Juan arrived. This painful part of her childhood eluded her for years. Most of it blocked from memory until she underwent intensive therapy following her last assignment for the company that employed her from 1970 until 1973. Now that she had her childhood back, she often thought of it as she sat alone at night, in solitude, in Kadoka. *Why couldn't she have been Marie?* she asked herself more than once. *Marie was the lucky one*, she always concluded when she was depressed, as she was this night. Growing up with no father. Having a mother who worked very hard for those who really served as her and her sister's mother was not always what it seemed to be to onlookers. Less than idyllic, the period from the day Marie became ill until the night her mother died unexpectedly now occupied her thoughts constantly whenever time afforded Jenny the opportunity. The terror of this period in her life had now been overcome with the help of modern psychology and more than a little dabbling in various religious studies of her own as an adult.

Looking back, she understood how this dark and unknown period in her life, which lasted until she reached the age of thirty, simply pushed her along the path she had trod before throwing her former life aside, adopting a new persona within the friendly confines of witness protection, and locating herself in a small town in South Dakota.

She sat alone at the kitchen table and looked down upon the one and only business street in this little town. The view didn't change much. Having been here for three years, Jenny Craig, as she was known to everyone in Kadoka, was comfortable for the first time in her life. There was joy to be found in the solitude of this little place in the middle of nowhere.

Once in a while, she wondered who she might have become had she not needed to pretend to be someone she wasn't most of her life, since childhood. She was bright. She might have been a doctor by now, given different circumstances. Or perhaps, a brilliant lawyer like the one who got her past the feds' desire to put her away for a very long time, and into this program, simply for sharing some information. She always liked music. A country and western singer perhaps? Whatever. As she sat and looked down on the street below, she thought of her journey as one somehow coerced upon her from the day when Marie suddenly took ill.

Just before supper, Sister Mary Margaret came running into the kitchen, where Jacqueline helped her mother release muffins from their nestling places atop the oven. Cooling, crisp, brown cornmeal baked, just as the sisters preferred.

"Sadie!" she shouted, "come quickly!"

"What is it?" she heard her mother ask as a mysterious cloud of dread crossed her face.

"It's Maria," the older sister said. The sisters always called Jacqueline's sister Maria. She reminded them of the blessed mother, they explained. So quiet. So thoughtful. Always seemingly pondering what was said to her instead of responding in childlike fashion.

"What's wrong?" Mother asked.

"She's taken ill. Please. Come quickly. We do not know what to do," Sister Mary Margaret said with even more emphasis.

Jacqueline began to cry as her mother dropped the hot pan

holders, grabbed her by the hand, and swiftly moved through the corridor from the kitchen to the room to which the agitated nun led them. Three others crowded the small room where Marie lay upon the floor, eyes staring at the ceiling, perspiration seemingly coming from every pore in her prepubescent body. Random twitching of her limbs and writhing of her body occurred, as though she were possessed by some evil spirit.

Jacqueline's mother bent over her child and tried to speak to her twisting and tortured daughter. "Marie, my Marie," she sobbed, "what's the matter?"

No response. Just more purposeless movement of mouth, eyes, arms, legs and body.

"When did this happen?" her mother asked any one of the sisters, now huddled around her.

"We were singing," said Sister Theresa, "and suddenly, she collapsed and this seizure began."

"Call a doctor," shouted Sadie as she again endeavored to awaken her daughter by gently touching her arms and calling her name. "Marie, Marie, come on, little one, wake up," she cajoled. "Mommy has some nice cornbread muffins, just out of the tin."

No change. Again, Marie's eyes fixed upon something beyond the room and her body responded to whatever it was with even more erratic movement.

"Oh God," Sadie cried out amid God's servants huddled around her. "What can we do?"

Immediately, one of the sisters ran from the room while the others made the sign of the cross and began to pray, lips moving without a sound in the room, except for the child's body indiscriminately scraping and thumping on the floor.

Jacqueline stood, transfixed by the scene.

Her mother bent over her child, took her jerking body into her arms and tried to rock and sing to her, as she often did to both of the girls throughout their lives, seeking to give them a peace she herself most likely had never known. The little girl's body fought the constraint of her mother's arms. Great drops of sweat ran down her mother's arms and began to soak the lap of her mother's dress as the lyrics of "Swing Low, Sweet Chariot" emitted from the trembling lips of Jacqueline's mother. This was Marie's favorite.

"Swing low, sweet chariot, comin' for to carry me home

Swing low, sweet chariot, comin' for to carry me home . . ."

"Ambulance is here," exclaimed a young Mexican novice, who ran into the crowded room as Sadie sang to the unresponsive form in her arms.

Soon, the attendants wrapped her sister in blankets and gently carried her to the awaiting vehicle. Jacqueline noticed the movements of her sister's body beneath the blankets. Chaotic, yet almost like a code. First, an arm, then a leg, then her head, then two legs and the other arm. No sound. Just movement, suggesting that of a puppy just after a bath. Then, a total shudder of virtually every part of Marie's body.

In the hospital in Austin, mother and daughter sat on a hallway bench, awaiting some word from behind the doors where Marie had been wheeled almost as soon as they arrived. People scurried by, glancing in their direction. Nothing was said to them. Her mother quietly cried, wiping her eyes with the hem of her dress whenever the hallway was void of passers-by. Announcements swept across the waiting pair. Not meant for them, they passed, ignored even if heard.

"Doctor Brown, you are wanted in emergency."

"Case nurse needed in room 402."

"Visitors are reminded that parking in front of the hospital is limited to fifteen minutes. Anyone needing more time is advised to park in the parking lot. Thank you."

People and words. None of them helping Jacqueline and her mother cope with whatever was happening to Marie. Like castaways on some deserted isle, they sat, alone with their thoughts of how they got there. Unexpected tragedy washed them up here. Alone. Not knowing what would happen next. Feeling so utterly alone.

The sisters had remained at the monastery to pull together

their meal for the evening and prepare for evensong. Life went on for those who came to the monastery to give their lives in service of a God who, at this very moment, seemed to have forgotten Jacqueline, her mother, and Marie.

In her mind, Jacqueline cursed the God of the monastery as she watched her mother fail to hold back her tears. All the prayers, songs, and services of that place to which her mother had brought them when they were infants meant so much more to Marie than to either Jacqueline or her mother, she thought. Born with some inner cynicism regarding anything this world handed her, no matter how beautiful at times, Jacqueline somehow always knew she would only be able to count on herself in life. She could never go through life as the sisters at the monastery had. Nor could she envision a future for her like her mother's. *Scrubbing floors, cleaning buildings, and cooking for a community are not going to be the tasks that consume my life,* she swore to herself. Taking care of women who didn't seem to have the energy to take care of themselves was not going to be the way Jacqueline would spend her days. She didn't know how her life would evolve. She just knew it wouldn't be this way. So she vowed to whatever spirit wanted to listen to be free of all of this someday. The world owed her more than this. She just knew it.

"Mommy," she said to her mother, sitting beside her. "I have to pee."

Her mother, red-eyed, looked at her and quietly said, "The restroom is down the hall." She pointed in the direction of the entrance to the hospital.

Jacqueline arose without a word and quickly walked in the direction her mother had pointed. As she approached the doorway marked "Public Restroom," Juan passed her almost without noticing her.

"Hi there," he said breathlessly, "where's your mother?"

Jacqueline turned and pointed to the solitary woman sitting along the wall. Juan rushed by her. As he reached that place where her mother sat, she arose and embraced him tightly. Jacqueline watched the two share whatever it was two adults say in such circumstances. They embraced again and then, hand in hand, sat together on the hallway bench.

Jacqueline ran into the restroom to relieve herself. As she studied herself in the mirror after washing her hands, she noted slight curvatures to her body beneath the simple cotton dress she wore. Raising her hands nearly to her armpits, she pressed the dress around herself and moved her hands toward her waist. There was no doubt, her twelve-year-old body was maturing. She could swear she saw little rises where breasts would one day swing. She turned slightly and noticed her behind was also developing. *No wonder the boys are paying me more attention at school,* she thought to herself.

Not questioning where such thoughts were coming from at the moment, Jacqueline stared at herself in the mirror. As she looked, she tried to imagine what she might look like as a full-grown woman. Would she favor her mother? *Mother must have been very beautiful,* she thought to herself. *She still is,* she corrected her thoughts. Her mind recalled Juan's embrace with her mother a few moments before. *Someday, a man will hold me like that,* she mused. And as she did, there was what was becoming a more familiar feeling somewhere deep within her, a warmth and excitement clashing just beneath her consciousness, yet close enough to bring the promise of a pleasantness yet to come in life.

Suddenly, feeling rather silly looking at herself in the mirror, she turned and exited the restroom. She skipped down the hallway just as the doors through which Marie had been wheeled opened and a doctor walked through toward her mother and Juan.

"Your daughter is resting comfortably under sedation now," he said with practiced professionalism. "You may go in to see her in Room 205."

"What's wrong with her?" Jacqueline's mother wanted to know as Juan gently held her arm.

"We are not really sure," the doctor said as though he were acting in a grade-B movie. "We will have to do tests."

"What kind of tests?" her mother asked more seriously.

"Well, this could have been a grand mal seizure. It could

have been an allergic reaction of some kind. Or something more serious," the white coat explained as he was now joined by a compassionate-looking nurse who had strolled through the doorway.

"A seizure?" her mother asked, incredulously.

"Yes, she may have epilepsy."

Sadie gasped. Jacqueline didn't understand. Juan now put his arm around Jacqueline's mother and held her more tightly.

Mistaking them to be married, the white coat now said, "You both may go in to see her. But if in your opinion this may be too difficult for your other daughter, Miss Simpson is here to talk with her while you visit."

"I don't know," Jacqueline's mother hesitated.

It was Juan who settled it. "I think it best we leave Jacqueline out here until we know how Marie is."

That settled, Miss Simpson took Jacqueline's arm and led her back to the hallway bench while her mother and Juan accompanied the doctor through the doorway.

Thus began the separation from Marie which, within three months, would be ultimate. A virulent form of brain cancer had somehow invaded the holy place where they lived and achieved its singular intrusion into the lives of a trinity which was beloved by the sisters, not any less than that one believed by the nuns to be the Godhead. The Sisters of Mercy, upon hearing the news the first time, wept. After that, they presented themselves to Sadie and the girls as very caring and compassionate religious women, trying their best to identify with the mother of a dying child.

Marie came home from the hospital two weeks later, head shaved and turbaned with a fanciful towel, looking like a starving and wan desert chieftain. Weakened by both surgery and radiation, her voice no longer sang hymns with the lilt of imagined angels. Rather, she could barely be heard above the whisper of a nun's prayer.

Sadie watched over her as carefully as she could, given her daily regimen. Jacqueline was assigned times to sit, play, read, and even sing to her sister, although Jacqueline lacked any real talent at singing.

Marie's eyes lifted whenever Jacqueline sang to her. A smile crossed her face as she listened to Jacqueline's serious attempts to make melody with a voice not easily given to finding any place on the musical scale to rest painlessly to human eardrums.

As days passed, there was no improvement in Marie's plight. Ever weakening, eventually, she struggled to lift her head from her pillow in the morning and she needed longer naps each afternoon. Jacqueline helped as best she could to lift Marie from the bed each day. Often, the sheets needed changing due to sweat or nighttime soiling that Marie simply could not control.

Confined to a wheelchair, she delighted in Jacqueline's pretense to be driving her from place to place in the monastery. As they swerved into each nun's room to say "hello," Marie seemed pleased to gaze at each sister, who spoke words of assurance that God would take care of her.

Then one morning, nearly two months after her sister had come home from the hospital, Marie whispered to Jacqueline, "I'm dying." Jacqueline nearly dropped her sister back onto the bed from which she sought to lift her into the wheelchair.

"No!" Jacqueline shouted at her sister, now lying limp in her strengthening arms. "You are not dying."

"Yes, I am," Marie whispered.

"You can't," Jacqueline said to her. "Does Momma know?"

"I think so," Marie said so quietly that Jacqueline wasn't sure she had spoken. A tear rolled down Marie's face.

Jacqueline lifted her sister into the chair, determined to settle this with her mother. This was a troubling thought. It had never occurred to Jacqueline that her sister might not get well. No one had said anything to give her any clue, other than that God would take care of Marie. This, to Jacqueline's pliant spirituality, was good enough for now.

She said nothing as she wheeled her sister down the hallway toward the kitchen. Anger and fear grasped at her as she walked as fast as she could push Marie's wheelchair.

Her mother was scrubbing pans that only an hour before had been sizzling with bacon and scrambled eggs. She glanced up and smiled as her daughters came into the big room, where she spent most of her day preparing meals the sisters requested from week to week.

"Hello," she said. "How are my big girls today?"

Marie did not respond.

"Is Marie dying?" Jacqueline blurted.

Her mother's eyes filled with tears as she looked down at the withering form in the wheelchair, and then glanced menacingly at the daughter who had asked such an impudent question.

"Who gave you that idea?" There was anger in the tone as Sadie peered, singularly focused, into the eyes of her daughter who raised this question on this Lord's day.

"Marie," Jacqueline said defiantly.

Her mother's eyes now fell on Marie. She walked toward the girls and knelt in front of the wheelchair. She stroked Marie's hair and gazed into her eyes.

"Child," she said as assuredly as she could. "You are not dying."

"Yes, Mother," whispered Marie, "I am."

Eternity slipped between mother and daughter with those words, presenting to each a mirror of the other, caught in circumstances requiring honesty and integrity above all else. It was so present, silence like none other filled the kitchen. *So, this is stillness*, Jacqueline mused, glad for the moment that the focus of her mother's attention now was fixed upon Marie.

Mother reached toward daughter as Marie struggled to lift her arms in a mutual embrace. No other words were heard. Just the muffled weeping of mother and child in their initial goodbyes to one another.

As if to outrun whatever it was that was happening that morning, Jacqueline suddenly wheeled her sister from the room down the hallway as swiftly as she could, out the double doorway and on to the brick patio, which was awash with late morning sunlight and shadowed by various mournful-looking statues of saints who might have told the sisters, if only they could speak, what awaited both of them in the weeks that followed. But these forms remained as silent as the space that now enwrapped Marie and Jacqueline in their own interior needs.

Jacqueline tried to sing better to Marie after that morning. Totally unselfish, she cared for her sister from that moment on, no matter how gross the bed sheets were each morning, nor how demanding Marie's eyes got toward the end. Jacqueline loved her sister and didn't want her to go to wherever it is people go when they die. She couldn't conceive what a day would be like without her. Taking care of Marie's every need became Jacqueline's life.

There ought to be some reward for this, she angrily cried in her mind in God's direction. *I'm doing everything to make her comfortable,* she imaginatively shook her fist at the Almighty. *What the hell are You doing?*

Sisters came, one by one, when Marie could no longer be lifted from her bed. Each told her how well she looked that day. *They'll spend an hour in confession for that,* thought Jacqueline. They'd pray as Jacqueline watched. Then, as swiftly as they came, they left Sadie's daughters to be alone with each other on this course upon which some master plan had directed them.

Sadie came into the room more often toward the end. She sat stoically in a chair and watched her daughter, who could now barely whisper a "hello," slip from her forever. And forever is a very long time. A very long time.

Jacqueline watched her sister take her final breath. It didn't seem so hard to die, after all. The struggle against all things in life which holds us down and keep us from being whoever we wish to be, wherever we wish to be, whenever we wish, ceases. *That is really what happens,* she thought as she looked at her sister's lifeless body. *But what happens after that?*

Jacqueline imagined her sister's spirit lifting from her body as her breathing ceased that morning. She envisioned it gently walk around the room, filled with Mother, Juan, nuns, and a doctor, embracing each person one last time. Then finally coming to Jacqueline, her sister's spirit kissed her upon the cheek and whispered in her ear one final *Goodbye, see you later.* And she was gone. Sisterhood ended for Jacqueline in one gentle kiss.

"Marie, oh, Marie," Jenny quietly sobbed as she gazed upon the street below. "Where did you go so long ago, my sister?" Tears coursed down her face as she sat thinking of that quiet morning long ago, when everything changed forever.

Juan attended the funeral and seemed to comfort Sadie by his presence. He stood between Sadie and her living daughter, holding each one's hand as the priest spoke at the graveside of promises to those who believe in God and the Catholic Church.

At the conclusion of the prayer, all but she and her mother crossed themselves. Then, everyone left the graveside and walked toward waiting cars.

The day was beautiful. The sun shone everywhere. A gentle breeze rolled past the cemetery toward the city of Austin. *Summer,* thought Jacqueline, *you died in summer, my sister. What am I to do?*

Juan was everywhere, it seemed, that summer. Nearly every day, he came by to say "hello." He helped her mother with her chores as often as time afforded. He ran errands for her and stayed until the last evening dish was put away. He seemed so solicitous of her mother's well-being.

But Sadie was depressed. Juan at first didn't seem to be able to bring her to any resolution of her grief. She cried every night after he left. Throwing herself upon the bed, weeping until exhaustion transported her to sleep, Jacqueline's mother never seemed to notice how her remaining daughter would later slip into the bedroom, cover her with a blanket, and lift her shoes from her splayed feet.

Jacqueline, who earlier had cared for a dying sister, now cared for a barely living mother. There was little difference, she noted. Like Juan, Jacqueline threw herself into assisting her mother so the day's work would be done. Like Juan, Jacqueline was with her mother most hours of the day.

One evening, about two months after Marie passed away, as Juan and Jacqueline stood in the doorway, gazing upon her mother, Juan quietly said, "And you, little sister, how goes it with you?"

No one had asked until then. Jacqueline nearly cried as she turned and looked into Juan's face.

"I . . . ," she hesitated. A tear rolled down her face.

"I can see how hard this is for you," Juan said in a comforting way.

"I . . . miss my sister," Jacqueline said at last and fell into Juan's arms, sobbing.

"There, there," he gently said as he held her, "it's okay to cry, little one."

They stood there in the doorway to her mother's bedroom for what seemed like a year as Jacqueline's tears rolled forth across both of them.

Eventually, as she regained some composure, Jacqueline began to release herself from Juan's embrace.

"Anytime," he said as he let her go. "You can cry on my shoulder any time."

Something in the way he said it seemed disconnected with the moment. But Jacqueline lacked the maturity to interpret the intent. She noted a smile on his face that also communicated a message which was alien from consolation. But again, she was not sure what this meant.

Gradually, her mother came out of the depression that had gripped her soul for four months, following Marie's death. She began to sing in the kitchen again as she worked. She greeted the sisters more positively. She took notice of Jacqueline.

"My girl," she said one late fall day as Jacqueline came into the kitchen after school had ended, "you are becoming a woman. I'm sorry I hadn't noticed."

Jacqueline blushed.

"Now I don't mean to embarrass you, Jacqueline," her mother continued. "It's just that, with your sister's death and all, I haven't taken note of how you are starting to fill out your dresses."

"Mother!" Jacqueline wasn't sure she wanted to have this talk with her mother. It made her feel odd or queer to be talking with her mother about growing up. The girls at the junior high school compared notes all the time. Each knew when which girl started her period, what training-bra sizes each was wearing, how each had suddenly jumped to teen-dress sizes over the summer, and how all noticed the boys really weren't that well tuned in on their growth.

"I guess it's time you and I had a talk about the birds and the bees," her mother said with a smile. "You need to be more careful about your feelings and the boys at school," she continued.

"Please, Mother!" Jacqueline shouted, "not now." And she turned to leave the kitchen.

"Jacqueline," her mother said in a tone that stopped her in her tracks, "you stay right here, honey. I want to talk with you."

Jacqueline slumped onto one of the kitchen stools as her mother came around the butcher block and sat beside her.

"Honey, I'm sorry if I am embarrassing you. I don't mean to, you know," her mother started the conversation. "It's just that I haven't been myself since your sister passed away. I'm trying to catch up here, Jacqueline."

"I know," Jacqueline said quietly. "I just don't know how to talk with you about these things. That's all."

"That makes two of us, honey," her mother said, seemingly relaxing a bit. "It's important, you know."

"Sex is important?" Jacqueline blurted out inquisitively in anticipation of getting this first conversation of its type ended as soon as possible.

"Yes, it is," her mother said quietly, sensing that both were now in a conversation land neither had found before. "But I guess I was getting at our relationship as mother and daughter."

"Oh," Jacqueline replied.

"You see, as you become a woman, I want you to know that I'll be here for you. I'll answer any question you have, no matter how big, how small."

"Thank you, Mother," Jacqueline said as she turned and looked at her mother's compassionate face as though seeing her for the first time. They embraced. Then Jacqueline arose to leave the kitchen.

As she approached the doorway, her mother said in a tone she had never heard before, "I mean it, Jacqueline. I want to be here for you so that you will never have to go through what I did when I was your age." She turned and noted that her mother was crying.

From that afternoon on, mother and daughter grew to be confidants. Jacqueline discussed each day's activities at school, leaving out few nuances. She discovered in her mother an adult who could simply listen without judgement. An amazing gift. Only later in her life would Jacqueline realize that the world she opened to her mother was one her mother never knew. Hence, her mother was not so much a guide through the turbulence as she was one who simply received reports of it and offered any bits of insight she might have possessed at the time. She began to see her mother in an entirely different way.

Eventually, her mother began to confide in Jacqueline. Longings poured forth from mother to daughter. A mother's past was revealed that was so different from the life in the monastery as night is from day. And, like night is from day, the absence of light in her mother's former life made Jacqueline want to weep.

Juan continued to visit both of them that winter. He said he wanted to make sure they were doing well. Jacqueline noticed her mother blush once or twice when Juan walked into their living quarters unannounced. It struck Jacqueline as odd that he felt so at home in this place. But she assumed this was the way with Mexican men. He was friendly toward them in ways that each of them appreciated.

Then, one spring Saturday morning, Juan suggested he take Jacqueline with him on an errand he needed to run for the monastery. "She'll enjoy riding to Austin," he said to Sadie. Indeed, Jacqueline knew she would, for she hadn't been to Austin since the day Marie was taken to the hospital.

As they were approaching Austin on Interstate 35, Juan broke the silence with which they rode.

"How do the boys like you, little one?"

Jacqueline blushed. She had confided in her mother that she found boys interesting. There was this one boy who played on the basketball team. She confessed she liked to watch him run and jump into the air. She connived with other girls to find out his schedule and to then position herself in the school hallway each day so he would have to take note of her. Sometimes, she told her mother, she felt funny around this boy. Warm all over, she described the feeling.

"It's all right," Juan was saying as he reached across and patted her knee. "I won't tell anybody."

Jacqueline suddenly felt like she didn't belong in the truck with this man. Yet she was intrigued by his attention. So she decided to tell him something.

"Boys are jerks," she said quickly. His hand stayed resting upon her knee.

"Is that so?" he laughed. "Why is that?"

"They don't seem to notice us girls are even around," she said before she could think much about what to say to this man who had been so kind to her and her mother.

He moved his hand up her thigh, and with its movement, her dress also moved, revealing more of her leg than she was comfortable with at the moment.

"It takes a man to notice a woman," Juan said softly as his hand continued to drift up her thigh toward her waist.

She looked at him as he slowed the pickup truck near the edge of the city. He was smiling and gazing upon her legs and waist with a look she had never experienced. It both frightened and excited her. She said nothing.

They stopped at a rest stop which, at this time of the day, was deserted. He gazed at her in silence as his hand now began to move from her waist toward her thigh again and then across her thigh and into her lap. Her breathing began to quicken as Juan simply lifted her dress up to her waistline, exposing her panties. He leaned forward and kissed her upon the cheek, his hand now gently pressing against her, in an area no one but she had touched before.

She felt as though she were going to faint as his hand gently tapped against her and that warm feeling she had experienced before began to focus now in one particular part of her body. She wanted to tell him "There, touch me there," as he kissed her again and whispered to her, "You are a woman, little one."

Suddenly, his hand moved over the top of her panties and swiftly, was inside her panties. She lay her head back upon the truck seat as his fingers moved toward that one place she knew he'd eventually find. His fingers probed her new-grown pubic hair as he slid his hand deeper into her crotch.

"There, right there," she heard herself say.

"Yes, I know," Juan said.

Now he ever so gently rubbed the very spot Jacqueline knew would bring her pleasure. Her girl friends had described it to her. And one night, when she was sure her mother was asleep, she found it herself as she lay upon her tummy. But that was long ago. At least three years before. And this bit of information she had forgotten to ask her mother in their recent candid conversations.

It felt so much better when Juan found it. She closed her eyes and permitted this feeling, whatever it was, to take over her body. She heard herself murmur. Without warning, tension built within her which seemed to threaten her very being. Her body stiffened and then ecstasy swept across her from her pelvis to her head and down her legs, into her toes. Her body relaxed and she opened her eyes.

"You like that, don't you, girl?" Juan said with a smile.

She couldn't speak as he kissed her gently on her lips. This was too intimate. She pushed him away and slid her dress to its proper place just as another vehicle came into view.

"Juan can do that for you anytime you like," he said as he started the truck.

Jacqueline needed time to evaluate what had taken place. She wasn't sure she'd share this with her mother, but she was sure she had quite a story to tell her friends at school. She was fairly sure Juan would not, as he suggested, have the opportunity to do this for her ever again.

The rest of the trip was experienced in silence between them until they had nearly gotten back to the monastery. It was Juan who again broke the silence between them.

"You must not tell anybody what happened today," he said. "Juan would lose his job and your mother would skin you alive."

Jacqueline wasn't sure about the latter. She said nothing.

"What you say we make a pact between us?" Juan now said, a little less certain of himself. "I won't tell anybody if you don't."

She was amused by this man, who now sought some way to assure himself that his experience with her would not come to the light of day. She turned in the seat and faced him as he turned into the driveway.

"I promise nothing," she said with a conviction that came from somewhere deep inside her. "Do you hear me, Juan? I promise nothing."

Juan's face paled as he braked the truck. "What are you saying?" he wanted to know, anger now flashing from his eyes.

"You heard me," Jacqueline said, sensing that such a stance gave her an advantage with this man, who'd been hired to help with the chores at the monastery.

He grunted and said something in Spanish that she didn't understand. Then he gunned the pickup toward the entrance of the building.

As Jacqueline stepped out of the truck, she leaned forward and whispered to Juan, "Don't worry." Then she ran up the stairs and into the building as he drove off toward the barn.

Thus, it continued. The sexual experimentation of Jacqueline Frontierre, daughter of Sadie, sister of Marie, child of the Round Rock monastery. Begun three years before, in the balcony of the chapel late one summer evening, her sister, Marie, tutoring her to the senses with which women are born.

Where?

There, you silly.

I don't see anything!

You can't. All you can do is feel it.

Maybe we're different.

Try.

Oh.

Found it?

I think so.

By the time Juan made his move on her, Jacqueline was ready to learn about men. He was the first of many would-be teachers of fair, young Jacqueline. Little did they know it was she who seduced, manipulated, and used them. Not for sex, but for information about themselves. From each, she learned the nature of all.

She knew, by age sixteen, that men were all virgins, living with the illusion that stolen moments with girls in cars, garages, swimming pools, barns, attics, and even their own bedrooms equaled sexual maturity. Women, she deduced, seem to come into the world intuitively knowing that what men sought in sexual experience was an illusion. Reality lay much closer at hand and could be experienced in a myriad of ways. Not one man, from her first until her last, suspected she had anything else in mind at the moment, save an orgasm only he could produce for her.

"Having a good time?" each would ask her as she writhed beneath, atop, and around them on all kinds of surfaces.

"Oh, yeah!" was her accustomed response as she manufactured moans, groans, grunts, and yells, along with various contortions of her body, just to see how such sounds and movements reverberated in their consciousness. "Oh yeah, baby, that's it!"

It was the last man she sought to know, in the way Biblical writers often referred to, who came to her mind so often lately. He was different. At first, she didn't realize just how different he would turn out to be. She almost sensed it the very moment her eyes beheld him in Pennsylvania Station in New York City that summer not so long ago.

She only knew him for a very short while, but she never forgot his appearance. Angular and tall, soft-spoken and good-looking, uncertain, not cocky, and arms like those a woman imagines every man possesses: arms in which one could die when that time comes. He was intelligent, but not overbearing. He was athletic, but not a jock. He was religious, but not fanatically driven. He was informed and committed to just causes and outcomes.

He was honest. He was fun. He was so good-looking. And he was married!

She remembered wanting to reach out and just lazily run her fingers through his auburn-blonde hair from the moment he stammered to talk to her. She knew she had a mesmerizing effect upon him, dressed and styled as she was that day. Each time she met him thereafter, she sensed she could do anything with this man she desired. He would be clay in her hands.

His eyes were beautiful. Such a deep blue. Sincerity swam in them and leapt toward her from time to time whenever they were together.

She embraced him once. When she did, she knew that what she was doing to him might destroy him. And she didn't want to harm him. He was too good.

Jacqueline knew something else about this last man in her life. She would have gladly gone anywhere with him. She could listen to him talk forever. Despite her cynicism about males of all stripes by this point in her life, she felt drawn to this one, as to no other.

But she had a job to do. She couldn't afford to let him come between her and her assignment. She kept herself under control. But she never forgot him.

Why did I have to meet this one last? She asked herself over and over again at night when work was done and there was nothing more to pretend in the café or on the streets of Kadoka. *Why couldn't we have met when we were twenty?* Her awareness, buried beneath layers of guilt and apprehension, secrecy and pretense, was addressed only four years before with the help of a counselor. Once aware that it was not education, but abuse she had endured those three summers before her mother's untimely and unexpected death, Jacqueline had begun to piece her life together. Once aware that it was not she who controlled her life but a deeper loss of innocence which few children could outgrow, Jacqueline decided to cooperate with the authorities, give them what they wanted in exchange for a certain form of freedom from fear and anxiety by adapting yet one more alias with which to live her life.

But here in Kadoka, on a cold spring evening on the high Dakota prairies, it was easy to see that not much awaited her but the grave. She could spend a decade here while most of her beauty wasted away, hidden beneath overalls and denim blouses, little make-up and heavy jackets. Then, maybe only then, she could go home to Texas and live the rest of her life on her own terms. This kept her going, living a life of regret for the past and longing for the future, pretending to be a lesbian waitress lost near the Badlands of a mostly deserted South Dakota landscape.

Jenny. Jenny Craig sat at her kitchen table as the waning traces of alpenglow sprawled the western horizon and the three street lights of Kadoka winked on, daring to hold back the darkness.

Chapter 4

Ta'ku Waktapisni

The last beautiful landscape seen, in Lark's opinion, was the area of La Crosse. After that, the interstate seemed to get both flatter and wider as he and his family made their way west toward their new home.

He could see them all, riding in the sedan in front of this rental truck that transported all their worldly possessions from Pennsylvania and Maryland to South Dakota and a new adventure. Fran was driving with Walt up front while Leigh Ann and Saul bounced up and down in the back seat.

From time to time, Saul would turn and peer backward toward the truck carrying his dad. Saul waved and made funny faces. Leigh Ann never looked back. She had been the only one reluctant to make this transition in her life. The length of the journey, now into its third day, had done nothing to convince her she was in error about any of her convictions.

Walt constantly chatted with his mother, from time to time gesturing toward to the roadside or to those who occupied the back seat. *Walt is becoming a little professor,* Lark thought to himself as he watched.

Fran, ever the stoic of the family, seemed not to respond at all to anyone in the car. Eyes fixed ahead, she steered the family sedan and positioned it just five car-lengths in front of the truck. This was how they'd decided to make the trip on Monday morning, when they left Lancaster and everything painful about it behind them.

Lark was going to serve a Native American church. He knew little about Indians. He knew even less about South Dakota. The only thing he knew was that, from the time Fran indicated she'd be willing to give their marriage another chance, he was filled with joy to have his family back. If serving a small church anywhere in the world would accomplish that feat, he'd go anywhere God and the church bade him.

They stopped just outside Jackson, Minnesota for supper, having decided earlier in the day to make Kilen Woods their camping spot for the evening. After making sure the parking brake was on and the truck would not roll backwards into some unsuspecting customer's car, Lark joined his family as they headed into the truck-stop restaurant.

"How's it going?" he asked.

"Fine," piped Saul with a grin.

"Dad," asked Walt, "why don't you drive that truck faster? Everybody is passing us."

Fran smiled at Lark and awaited his response, along with the others.

"I'd like to, Walt," he replied. "But the thing's got a governor on it."

"A what?" his older son asked.

"A governor," Lark said.

"What's that?" Walt wanted to know.

"Well, it's a device that only allows the accelerator to go so fast. I guess it's a safety device, in case some people drive the trucks who don't know what they're doing," Lark explained.

"Are you hot in that truck?" Saul wanted to know as they approached the entrance to the restaurant.

"Hotter than an egg in a frying pan, son," Lark quipped. The truck was not airconditioned, as was the family sedan. "That's why I haven't invited any of you to ride with me."

After they were seated and each had ordered a meal, Leigh

Ann looked at her father and asked, "What's it like in South Dakota?"

"You know, honey," Lark hesitated. "I showed you the brochures they sent us from Pierre."

"I know all about that," she responded with a pout. "But I'm asking you what it's like where we're going. I didn't see any pictures of the Pine Ridge Reservation in those brochures. Besides, tourist bureaus only show you the best views, Dad," Leigh Ann concluded sarcastically, reminding him she was growing up now and couldn't be cajoled into any of her father's games.

"Honey," Lark decided to confess, "I have no idea. All I know is we are going to a place called Longvalley. It sounds pretty. From the map, I've learned it's on a main, two-lane road. Highway number seventy-three, I believe it is. But, I've never been there. I have no idea how big Longvalley is, or what's near it, except for Rapid City and the Badlands National Park. We'll just have to wait and see," he concluded.

A dark look crossed his daughter's face as she turned from him and glanced out the restaurant window. Lark wished he could have come a month or so before his family came so he could write to them of his experiences and entice them in ways he felt would win them over to their new home. But Fran thought it best that all shared this adventure together. "It will rebuild relationships," she said as they made the decision following his mother's funeral.

"Dad," interrupted Walt, "is there swimming at Kilen Woods?"

"No, son, I don't believe there is."

"Nuts," Walt said. "I'd sure like to swim."

"We'll get that in tomorrow night in Chamberlain," Fran assured him. "We're staying at a motel which overlooks the Missouri River. That should be fun."

Is there peace beyond the wide Missouri? Lark wondered to himself.

"Daddy," Walt wanted to know, "is the Missouri River really

the biggest river in North America, other than the Mississippi? Is it bigger than the Susquehanna?"

"I believe it is, Walt," Lark responded to the teaching moment. "I've read that it was wild and uncontrollable when Lewis and Clark went north and west in 1804 to discover a route to the West Coast. They really had no idea how long and tough it was when they left St. Louis that summer."

"Did they find Indians?" Saul, now interested, joined the conversation at the table.

"I believe the Indians found them," Lark replied with a wink of his eye. "And from what I've read, the Sioux weren't particularly glad to see them."

"What did they do, Daddy?" Saul asked.

"They stole some of the expedition's equipment and smaller canoes. They tried to keep them from making much headway."

"Were all the Indians like the Sioux?"

"No," Lark replied. "In fact, if it hadn't been for an Indian woman who was married to a French fur trapper and trader, Lewis and Clark might not have ever made it to the Oregon coast."

"A woman!" Walt said, as if to disbelieve his father's rendition of American history.

"Her name was Sakakawea," Fran said quietly to her sons. "Truth be told, many a woman has changed the course of history."

The boys laughed. Leigh Ann sat upright and smiled for the first time in two days. Lark and Fran exchanged warm glances just as the waitress delivered their supper.

When they were finished eating, the Wilsons climbed back into their respective vehicles and drove ten miles north to Kilen Woods State Park. After paying the admission fee and finding a suitable spot for their double-room family tent, purchased with money left over from the sale of things they no longer felt they needed for comfortable living on an Indian reservation in South Dakota, they quickly constructed their resting place. When all were settled, with sleeping bags and pillows where they wanted them, they zipped up the tent, locked their vehicle doors, and walked the park grounds together.

"Lark," it was Fran who broke the silence as they walked, "do you think we'll make it to Chamberlain before dark tomorrow?"

"I don't see why not," he said so all could hear his response, even those campers nearby. "We're only about one hundred miles from Sioux Falls. And, it looks like Chamberlain isn't more than one hundred fifty miles from there. My guess is we'll be there by five or so tomorrow."

"Good," Walt joined the conversation. "I want to go swimming."

"It will be good to have an easier day tomorrow," Fran added. "I don't know about you, but I'm getting tired of driving."

"I am too," Lark admitted. "The scenery lately has left a lot to be desired."

"It's boring," said Saul, thinking he could agree with his mother on her assessment of this day's journey.

"Get used to it," his sister said with no little disdain.

"Now, children," Fran pleaded. "We're all tired. After we're settled, we'll feel better."

"I doubt it," said Leigh Ann.

They walked for twenty minutes until it began to grow too dark to walk without flashlights. The darkness of their mood seemed to crowd out the remaining sunlight. It was time to get ready for bed.

When they returned to the tent, Lark reminded all that the restrooms were only ninety or so feet to their west. "Just follow that path," he said.

"We know," the children said in unison, mocking parental voice tones as they responded.

"It's just anxiety," Fran said quietly to Lark after they left with toothbrushes and face cloths. "They're all worried they won't like living in South Dakota. And they're really worried the Indian kids won't accept them."

"I don't blame them," Lark had to admit. "I'm also worried. I wish I knew more about the place and the people. This is a big risk we're taking."

"No bigger than the risk of reunion, Lark," she said. "Give it time. At least, we're all taking it together. Who knows, maybe this is what God wants all of us to do."

"It's good to hear you say that, Fran," Lark said. "Thank you."

The couple embraced just as the children emerged from the wooded path.

"Now, now," Walt piped up, "There will be no hanky-panky on this outing! No touchy-feely stuff, Mom and Dad."

The younger children smiled as Lark and Fran disengaged and seemed embarrassed to have been caught in an intimate moment.

"You're right, pilgrim," said Lark in his best imitation of John Wayne. "It wouldn't be good for troop morale!"

Everyone laughed. The children crawled into their side of the tent and talked with one another about what each was going to do once they settled in Longvalley. Fran and Lark walked to the restrooms to prepare for the night.

"You see," she said, "they really want to make this work."

"I know," he said. "With God's help, it will."

She put her hand to his and squeezed it as they approached the restroom. He turned and took her into his arms.

"I love you, Fran," he said.

"I love you, Lark," she said as they kissed for the first time since the day of his mother's funeral. "We're going to be fine," she assured him.

He was waiting for her when she exited the restroom. They walked arm in arm back to their tent, climbed into their side, and noted that the children were all now dead to the world.

"Do you want to make love?" Lark asked, after snuggling beside her on the ground.

"Not here, Lark," she said as she pulled his arm around her waist while she lay with her back toward him. "Let's wait until we get to the motel tomorrow night."

"It's a date," Lark said.

He could hardly keep his mind from fantasizing about making

love to Fran. It had been four years since he lay with her. She always fascinated him. He hoped she had missed him as much as he missed her subtle moves in bed. He remembered how, when she wanted him, she seemed to engulf him in passion that was so close to the edge of being uncontrollable that, at times, he worried for their safety. He imagined such a time with her tomorrow night as he finally drifted to sleep.

Chapter 5

Ki'tan'na O'ta

Crossing the border between Minnesota and South Dakota on I-90, Lark could swear the topography took on an entirely new character almost by the mile. Gently rolling rises started to challenge the rental truck's power. The highway itself seemed a bit rougher, suggesting that life here in Dakota might be a bit more challenging. And the billboards came out of nowhere to assault the eyes with come-on after come-on regarding old historic forts nearby to a corn palace in Mitchell, a drugstore hundreds of miles west and a dinosaur park in Rapid City, over three hundred miles west. It was as if the entire state of South Dakota were poised to introduce itself just inside its borders. It was all suddenly very different. Lark smiled to himself as he thought, *So this is home.*

It was a little past one in the afternoon by the time they reached the Salem exit, thirty-two miles west of Sioux Falls. They had decided to stop in that town for lunch since the kids saw it on the map and asked if the name of the town meant the people were peaceful.

The café on Salem's Main street was deserted when the family of five sauntered through the front door. The floor was linoleum-covered, the six tables 1950-vintage-kitchen pinks and whites, with chairs covered with plastic seats. There was a counter with five stools, behind which were assorted glasses on shelves, a blender of some kind, a coffee pot half-filled, and a milkshake mixer. In the wall behind the counter was an opening into the kitchen area, through which a very young female face peered at the Wilsons.

"I'll be right there," the face said to them as they seated themselves upon the five spinning stools at the counter.

Saul spun around several times until he tired of the novelty of it and his sister reached out to stop him, nearly causing him to fall to the floor.

"What can I do for you?" the youth asked as she smiled at the family.

"Do you have menus?" Fran asked.

"On the wall," the young lady Lark guessed to be about fifteen said as she gestured toward the blackboard adjacent to the kitchen window.

"Hot Beef Sandwich and Mashed Potatoes—$2.00
Soup (Knoepla) and Ham Sandwich—$1.50
Hamburger and French Fries—$1.25"

The Wilson kids laughed, then ordered hamburgers and fries. Lark ordered the Hot Beef Sandwich and Mashed Potatoes. Fran hesitated.

"What is that soup, Knoepla?" she asked the young lady.

"Haven't you ever tried it?" the youth asked with a grin.

"I don't believe so," said Fran seriously. "I never heard of it."

"Well, everyone has heard about it around here. We serve it everyday," the waitress said nonchalantly

"What is in it?" Fran wanted to know.

"Milk, dumplings, that's the Knoepla, and butter," the youth responded. "It's really good. If you never ate it, you ought to try it. You might like it."

"Okay. You've convinced me," Fran said pleasantly.

"Coming right up," the young waitress said as she scurried through the doorway into the kitchen.

The meal came in segments. First, the ham sandwich and soup. Then, the hot beef sandwich and mashed potatoes. Finally, three hamburgers and fries. The Wilsons could hear no conversation taking place in the kitchen. And each time something was delivered to the counter, the girl rushed back into the kitchen, only to be seen when she reappeared with more food.

"What will it be to drink?" she asked, setting Saul's hamburger and fries before him on the counter, sweat now starting to show itself upon her freckled brow.

"Cokes all around," said Lark, who had already finished his meal.

Within minutes, the girl reappeared from the kitchen with a tray of five small drink glasses filled with ice cubes and five cans of Coca Cola.

"That young lady is amazing," Lark said to his family after she disappeared once more into the kitchen. "I believe she is the cook, waitress, and bus boy, all rolled into one!"

Lark was impressed with the ability of this teenager, whom he judged to be about a year older than Walt. Never had he seen such a performance. It reminded him of his soda jerk days at Miller's Corner each morning before junior high school in his hometown.

"Well," said Fran appreciatively, "if she made this soup, I am impressed. It is very good."

"Do you see the size of these hamburgers?" Walt asked his parents. "I've never seen such a big burger."

"It's all good," Saul agreed.

Leigh Ann said nothing. She didn't appear to be as impressed as the others. Nor did she seem to be consuming her food very quickly.

"Honey, is something wrong?" Fran asked her.

"I don't feel good, Mom," was all she said.

"Where do you feel bad?" Fran asked her.

"I just don't feel good," Leigh Ann said.

As if sensing their meal was completed, the young waitress reappeared. "How about some pie?" she suggested.

"What kind do you have?" Lark asked her.

"This time of day, not much," she said. "I think there are some pieces of apple, and maybe a piece of rhubarb pie left. Most of it's gone by this time of the day. We normally close around two and don't reopen until six. That gives us time to replenish our desserts."

"I have to ask," Lark hesitantly said. "Do you work here alone?"

"Only after lunch," the youth replied. "My grandmother does all the cooking. Mom and Dad farm just north of here. Mom comes in and helps in the evenings. I help my grandmother in the mornings and through the lunch rush."

"I am impressed, young lady," Lark said.

The waitress beamed but said nothing.

"I'll have rhubarb pie," Fran said. "It has been a long time since I had any and this seems to be my day for adventure." She smiled at the waitress.

"Did you like the Knoepla?"

"Yes," Fran said. "It was very tasty."

The kids didn't want dessert. They excused themselves and ran outside to explore what Salem had to offer.

"I'll have a piece of apple pie, if you don't mind staying just a bit," Lark said to the youth. He glanced at his watch and noted it was nearly two-thirty.

"I don't mind," the girl said.

When she returned with the pie for Fran and Lark, she sat down beside them and ate a piece of apple pie also. "Where you folks from?" she asked.

"Pennsylvania," Fran answered as she lifted a fork full of rhubarb pie to her mouth.

"Back East," the girl said quietly. "I thought so."

"Ever been there?" Lark asked her.

"No," she said. "Never even been to Rapid City. Our family stays close to home. We go to Sioux Falls once in a while, though."

"I see," Lark said. But if he were to tell the truth, he could hardly believe what she was saying to them.

"What part of Pennsylvania?" she wanted to know.

"Lancaster," Fran said.

"They have them Amish people there?" the youth inquired.

"Why, yes, they live in Lancaster County," Fran responded. "They are wonderful farmers."

"That's what we hear," the girl said. "Don't use electricity or modern conveniences at all?"

"No, they don't," Fran said, wondering where this conversation was leading.

"They travel by horse and buggy, do they?" the girl asked.

"That and shoe-leather express," Lark quipped.

"And they live decent, God-fearing lives, I hear," she said to Lark and she turned and faced him. "That's what we try to do in our family," she said with pride in her voice. "My mother says, 'each of us has to bloom where we're planted by the good lord' and I suppose that's what those Amish believe too."

Lark looked at Fran, who was smiling as she listened to this fifteen-year-old philosopher from Salem's only café.

"Some can't do that," Lark obliged. "So they move to where they can."

"And that's what you folks are doin'," the girl said.

"Yes," Lark replied without elaboration.

The girl finished her pie. She stood up and reached out her hand to Lark and said, "I wish you well. May God be with you."

"What do we owe you?" Lark asked her.

"Oh, just add it up and lay it on the counter before you leave. I'll get it when I close."

"Thank you," Fran said to her as she walked toward the kitchen. "It's nice talking with you."

"It was nice meeting you folks," the girl said and then disappeared once more into the kitchen, from which Lark and Fran could now hear water running and dishes being put into an imagined sink.

Lark and Fran emerged from the café just as Walt and Leigh Ann came running down the sidewalk toward them.

"Dad," Walt exclaimed breathlessly, "come see what Saul found."

The four of them walked quickly toward the other end of the street. They spied Saul standing by a fenced yard at the end of the block. When they came to the fenced yard, they immediately saw what had captivated the children.

"What are they, Dad?" Saul asked as he pointed out into the fields which lay just beyond the town.

"They are bison, son," Lark said. "America's buffalo."

"Will we see more?" Walt asked.

"I suppose we shall," Lark said. "Now, we best be going if we are to make Chamberlain by six."

The five of them walked quickly to their vehicles and were on their way back toward the interstate within minutes. For the first time during the trip west, Lark believed the children were starting to get excited about moving to South Dakota. His heart lifted, he sang to himself as he drove onto I-90.

> "Oh give me a home, where the buffalo roam
> Where the deer and the antelope play.
> Where seldom is heard a discouraging word
> And the skies are not cloudy all day!
> Home, home on the range, where the deer and the ante-
> lope play.
> Where seldom is heard a discouraging word.
> And the skies are not cloudy all day."

The sun shone brightly into the canopy of the rental truck as it lumbered west over the rough, tar-striped, and randomly broken concrete roadway known as I-90. The rises and gullies of the land passed by on either side of the Wilson family vehicles as they journeyed toward their new home.

"May it be so, Lord," Lark said aloud as he drove. "May it be so."

Chapter 6

Ta'ku San'pa

Jenny met him in Rapid City, at the races, the first year she
lived in Kadoka. He wasn't particularly handsome. He was
inexperienced. She was always attracted to that in a man. She
found that most men were very inexperienced when it came to
women, especially women of her ability and wisdom in handling
men. He was standing by the rail, tearing up some pari-mutuel
tickets when she approached him.

"Hey, partner," she said in as tough an imitation of a
western South Dakota cowgirl as she could muster at the time,
"looks like if you don't have bad luck, you have no luck at
all!"

He stared at her without responding. He was about five-ten
in height, had brown hair and mustache that needed trimming,
dressed in a colorful, polka-dotted red and white shirt and blue
jeans. The look in his eyes told her he was not particularly
interested in talking to anyone at this moment.

"Say," she continued, "I'm sorry there, partner. I didn't know
you couldn't hear. Guess I ought to use sign language."

A smile quickly crossed his face but still, he said nothing.
He just stared at her.

"Say," she ventured, "what you say we just blow this flea-
bitten bunch of nags for the day and go get us some grub and
coffee, toss down a few, and see what happens?"

He started to turn away from her. She grabbed his arm and pulled him around to face her once again.

"Hey!" he said as he gave her a shove away from him. "Who the hell are you? I don't know you. And I certainly am not your partner!"

She detected a New York accent just beneath the surface of his obviously affected southern drawl. She also noted that he was not as angry with her as he pretended.

"I'm sorry," she quietly responded. "I saw you standing here and you look to me like you need somebody to talk with right now. So I took the chance that I might be right."

"Well," he curtly said and then affected the drawl, as though he were from Kentucky instead of New York or Northern Jersey. "I haven't exactly had a good day. I've dropped about fifty dollars here today and I was debating whether to leave or give it one more try."

"We're in the same boat, partner," she said with a grin. "I've lost all but twenty-five of the dollars I came with here today. I figure, if I leave now, I'm ahead of these boat races!"

He laughed for the first time. And he seemed to relax just a bit.

"Do you come here often?" he asked her.

"This is my first and last time," she shot back. "The way I see it, these horses are merely props for the racing association to run a program so all the owners, jockeys and trainers can eat. Unless you are allowed to sit in on their conversations, there's no way you'll ever get ahead of their game."

"So, you're new here, too," he said with a smile.

"Well, yes and no," she said. "This is my first trip to Rapid City. I don't live here. I live in Kadoka."

"Kadoka!"

"Yes," she said. "Do you know where that is?"

"It's one of those little watering holes along the interstate."

"Yep."

"What do you do there?" he asked.

"I'm a waitress," she said smartly. "But enough about me.

You haven't told me where you're from. Do you live here in Rapid City?"

"No," he said. "I don't."

"Well," she hesitated, trying not to scare him off, "where do you live then? In one of the suburbs?"

He laughed again. He had a nice, easy smile and big dimples appeared on his face each time he employed it.

"Gosh, gal," he said, trying to imitate her speech now, "don't you know there isn't a suburb west of the Missouri?"

She pretended to be a bit embarrassed. She had learned that men liked it when they could make a woman blush and embarrass her just a little.

"You got me on that one, partner," she replied. "So, you live somewhere else. Where?"

"Have you heard of Howes?" he asked her.

"No, can't say I have," she said, determined to check her South Dakota map first thing back in the apartment. "Help me out."

"Well, if you go north on seventy-three, off the interstate, and drive about an hour or so, you'll be there."

"You don't say," she said, smiling at him. "That sounds close to Kadoka, partner."

"Not that far, as they say out here in the great state of South Dakota," he drawled. "Hell, they don't think anything's that far out here."

"I take it you're not from South Dakota then," she surmised.

"Nope," he said, "I was born and raised in Louisville, as in Kentucky, you all," he quipped.

She knew this was a lie!

"Where you from, gal?" He asked her.

Thinking of her new identity and not her real one, she responded, "Enid, Oklahoma."

They talked, without his revealing what he did in Howes, through the next post parade, quarter-horse race, and photo finish to determine the winner. Finally, the two newcomers to South Dakota left together in his three-year-old Ford pickup and drove to a McDonald's near the race track for some burgers, fries and colas.

By six, he dropped her off at the bus station, but not before informing her that his regular day off was Monday and that each Sunday afternoon, he came to Rapid City, for there really was not much happening in Howes. They agreed they'd meet the next Sunday evening at the Native American Museum on the west side of the city.

His name was Mark Whitney. He was just two years out of theological seminary somewhere in Kansas City and already certain that ministry was not what God had in mind for him. In college, he had competed in AAU boxing. His junior year, he felt he was good enough to make the Olympics. But he got knocked on his can at Colorado Springs that winter, and that was that. He still thought he could make it as a pro. The parsonage he lived in during the week was full of exercise equipment and weights. In one corner of the den, Mark hung a punching bag from the ceiling. His parishioners had given him the green light, he said, for they felt he would take better care of himself if he got regular exercise.

Howes, South Dakota, is a small town. Smaller than Kadoka. Being appointed by Bishop Armstrong to this little church in the middle of nowhere on the corner of Highway 73 and Highway 34, about halfway between Pierre and Sturgis, was not Mark's idea of a good place to start his ministry. A less auspicious ending place in ministry, he felt. Ending ministry after only two years of service, however, weighed heavily upon his mind. As much as he'd like to, he couldn't.

He had grown up a Methodist, he confessed. His father and his grandfather had been Methodist preachers in Kentucky, he claimed. Itinerancy was in his genes. He might have questioned the wisdom of the bishop, but not the system. Like most Methodist pastors he knew, he passively accepted his assignment and then aggressively promoted himself at charge conferences with the district superintendent for a new assignment.

Mark's dad had always said the good thing about Methodism

for a pastor was that unlike other pastors of other Protestant denominations, Methodists always had jobs. His grandfather saw it a little differently. But then, his grandfather had never served in any church of more than two hundred souls his entire career.

Jenny understood little of church politics. But after two years of dating Mark on Sunday evenings and Mondays, she knew a lot about one Methodist preacher. She knew that he liked to take risks. And she was as attracted to that in a man as she was to his inexperience with women.

One time, they had gone skiing at Terry Peak after the season was over. The mixture of little snow and protruding rocks was absolutely frightening to Jenny, while Mark seemed impervious to the danger. Another time, he had nearly convinced her to try skydiving but she simply sat on the hood of the car at the Rapid City Regional Airport and squinted at the evening sky as the little dots, far above her, seemed to catapult from the little plane which had carried them aloft, and then bump around the sky for a long time before any parachutes opened and Mark and the rest of the club drifted lazily to earth.

Jenny also knew that Mark truly believed he could make a career out of boxing. Some Mondays, she sat in Chuck Goldy's gym in Rapid City and watched Mark pulverize anyone who dared to spar with him. His blows to the body and head of his erstwhile opponents were devastating. His body seemed impervious to the jabs and punches thrown in his direction. His shoulders and hips moved in opposite directions as his hands searched deftly for the kill.

Jenny also liked this in a man. Brute force only slightly controlled by the social mores of civilization was what always seemed to excite some part of her. She really never understood it. Would she have been a good candidate for abuse in a long-standing relationship? She pondered this at times. But only during the times the brute was absent.

Lately, Mark had talked with fight promoters. He was trying to line up some matches in Bismarck, North Dakota, where prize-fighting was a sport that attracted large crowds on Saturday evenings on the campus of the Bismarck State College. A man named Wiley, he had told her, was lining him up with an Indian from Mandan, North Dakota on one of the Saturday evening cards soon. Even though it would be a six-hour drive from Bismarck to Howes after the fight, Mark was anxious to try his skill once more in the ring. And this time, he would be paid for it.

There was one more thing Jenny knew about Mark Whitney. She knew how to please him in bed. He was insatiable on Sundays, she learned. At times, he seemed ready to have intercourse every five or ten minutes. Then by Monday noon, he was more relaxed around her and she enjoyed these days the most. Just hanging out with him satisfied her. All the rest were tricks of her former trade.

They stayed in different motels, never staying in the same one twice for fear one of his parishioners might see him with her and report it to the parish, or worse, the district superintendent. As far as either of them knew, nobody in Kadoka or Howes suspected them of having anything going on between them. Jenny never spoke to him during the week. She didn't attend church on Sunday mornings. She never called him on the phone.

He drove to Kadoka one day, shortly after they had met in Rapid City, and stopped in at the café where Jenny worked. As she served coffee to the ten o'clock mix of ranchers, truckers, and tourists, in he walked with a gleam in his eye and a swagger to his gait. She was glad to see him, but never let on. He sat at the counter and quietly ordered coffee and some eggs.

As she served him another round of coffee following his breakfast, he introduced himself to everyone in the place. They had all gawked at him when he walked in, he said, so he thought they really ought to know who he was.

"I'm the new Methodist preacher up at Howes," he said as they quietly listened while looking him up one side and down the other, "I grew up in Kentucky. I'm single. And I'm just out of seminary. That ought to hold you for a while."

They laughed uneasily at this stranger who had the brazenness to confront them in their sacred morning space. As he paid his bill at the counter, he turned once more toward the men sitting in the café.

"I repeat, I'm single," he said so loudly that he might have been heard next door if the business which once stood there was still viable, "and I guess I would like to know where a young man like myself might go to meet some nice young ladies once in a while. There aren't any in Howes."

The men stared at him in disbelief. Had they heard him correctly? They looked at one another and shrugged. Then one of them tipped his hat to the preacher and said, "Son, you got balls coming in here like this! Where did you say you're preaching? I just might drive there to hear what kind of sermon comes out of that smart mouth of yours." The men howled with laughter. Mark stood his ground, staring at them like a matador in a bull ring.

Then, one of the regulars stood up and walked toward Mark as he spoke, "Preacher, ain't you got no manners? Why, there's a nice young lady standing there right at the counter and you ain't paid her as much attention as a rooster at a cockfight. Why don't you take Jenny out?" The men laughed again as Mark turned toward her.

"You want to go out with me sometime?" he stammered with a boyish smile. Every patron in the café waited for her answer, for some had bets she wasn't interested in men at all. She had rebuffed every advance which any of them or their kinfolk had made since she came to Kadoka. So the word was, she might be a lesbian.

Jenny smiled at the young man and asked, "Don't you think I might be a little too old for you?"

"I might need a mentor," he said with a grin.

The men yelled from their tables, "Rope her in, boy, rope her in!"

"I don't know," she said to him as he waited for her answer, "but I can tell you where you can meet some nice young ladies if you're interested."

"Told you," yelled one of the truck drivers to the others, "I knew she didn't like men!"

"Step outside and tell me," Mark said to her, "I think these guys have had enough amusement for one day, don't you think?"

She liked his spirit. She took him up on his request and saw him to the sidewalk. Once they were outside, out of earshot of the men inside the café, Mark asked her if she would like to meet him on Sunday night and take a drive. She agreed to do it the following Sunday. They would meet at the rest stop on the interstate, six miles west of Kadoka at five-thirty. She would hitch a ride that far.

From that night until this morning, they rarely failed to spend a Sunday night together. She, his mentor, introduced the young Methodist preacher to almost everything known to the writers of the *Kama Sutra*. And he exposed her to the struggles of the soul of a man trying to discern his true calling in life, acting like a pastor throughout the week and a Casanova on Sunday evenings in Rapid City.

The two of them seemed made for one another. Both knew a time would come when their fantasy would end. One day, Mark would be appointed to another parish through whatever wisdom prevailed in the Dakotas Conference of the United Methodist Church. Or she might move on to another place after a fracas with the sterling clientele of the café someday. Mark might get himself killed in a boxing ring. Or parishioners might stumble into a motel room by mistake because the desk clerk carelessly gave them the wrong key and catch Jenny teaching Mark yet one more position for coitus. Whatever fate awaited them, Mark and Jenny made the most of their Sunday nights and Mondays together. And with each passing month, both were convinced neither was in love with the other. But their arrangement relieved them both of the tensions in their lives. For that, they were thankful. To that, they looked with each passing weekday until they could rejoin each other for twenty-four hours at the start of each week.

Mark came out of the shower, toweling his shoulders as Jenny got up and walked past him, patting his ass as she slid by toward the bathroom.

"Keep that up and we'll never get out of here this morning," he said.

"Don't make promises you can't keep," she said to him with a wink.

Once showered and dressed, Jenny sauntered to the bed, where Mark was taking a brief nap. "It's drizzly out there today, Mark," she said as she pulled at his foot, "what do you think we can do?

"Let's get some breakfast, go to Rushmore and have a picnic," he said.

"It'll be foggy up there today," she said, "what's your plan 'B'?"

"Don't really have one, Jen," he said affectionately as he stood up, "the weather forecast for today is good. Let's trust it'll be all right to do this."

She rarely fought him. She had learned that preachers just like to do whatever comes into their heads on their days off. At least, this one did. And she had only really known one other preacher. She kind of liked him, but she only knew him for a brief time. And that seemed like years ago now. So she would do whatever seemed to bring this man happiness. After all, he was the only game in town.

The call came late one Saturday evening in June.

"Jenny," she recognized the voice.

"Yes," she said as anxiety began to grasp at her.

"I'm being moved," was all he said.

"Where are you?" she asked him.

"I'm in Bismarck, you know, for the Annual Meeting of Conference," he said. "The bishop wants me in North Dakota."

"Where?"

"Devils Lake," was all he said.

Devils Lake. It might as well be hell, she thought as she waited for Mark to say more. She knew it was already decided. Mark had hinted he might be moved this time. He had no other choice but to accept the appointment.

"When?" she asked him sadly.

"July first," was the most he could get out, his voice beginning to betray the emotions he was feeling about the closure of their relationship.

"I'm sorry," she said. And she meant it. Mark had been the force in her life which kept her from going completely off balance. He was the one presence in her life who reminded her who she really was before she began assuming a new identity in the middle of nowhere. Now, she wondered to herself what she would do as she awaited some response from him.

"There's one more thing, Jenny," Mark said hesitantly.

"What?"

"I can't see you again."

There it was, the word she dreaded to hear. It was over. It was over forever. And forever is a long time. Just one more unexpected ending. She knew there was more to this than Mark was sharing at the moment. She just knew.

"I thought we'd get together one more time, whenever this day came," she said as a tear ran down her face. "Can't we, Mark? July first is over a week away."

"Jenny, I don't know how, but somehow, the bishop has learned about us. He has warned me not to see you again or I might be in trouble. I'm not sure whether this is why I am being moved so far from you, or if it is not. All I know is, he has made me swear I'll not see you again."

Fear gripped her heart as she listened. What did the bishop know? How did he learn it? What will he do with the knowledge?

"God, Mark," she stammered, "I knew this would end one day. I never dreamed it would be like this."

"I know, Jenny," Mark quietly replied. "I'm sorry. I'm so damned sorry."

"Mark," Jenny asked seriously, "can I ask you something?"

"Sure," Mark said confidently.

"Don't think I'm being silly," she warned.

"Jenny, go ahead," he said, "try me."

"Did you ever feel anything more for me than you would feel for a friend?"

"Now, Jenny," Mark hesitated, "where are we going with this?"

"I think you know," she said. "I've never been in love with anyone in my life. So I wouldn't know unless someone explained it to me."

Jenny could really act when she wanted to act. This might have been an Academy Award performance if anyone had seen it.

"Jenny," Mark said at last, "I really care for you. You know that. We had some really good times together. But as for love, hell, I don't know what that is any more than you do. All I do know is, my heart is broken right now. But I have no choice but to listen to the bishop."

"All right," Jenny said quietly. "That'll do for now, partner."

"Goodnight, Jenny," Mark said, getting ready to hang up.

"Goodbye," Jenny said as she cradled the receiver in both hands and slammed it onto the pedestal.

Assured that Mark would be as glad to forget about their relationship as she, Jenny was not overly anxious about this sudden turn of events. Still, she had cause for worry whether those others who knew about them might harbor some curiosity. Digging around in her past might get them nowhere, but one never knew. *What was it the federal agent told her?* she asked herself as she crawled into bed.

"You won't have anything to worry about, Jacqueline," he said as he handed her a folder. "From now on, you are Jenny Craig. You come from Tyler, Texas. You didn't graduate from high school but got your GED while you did odd jobs in Tyler. Your new Social Security number and credit record are in that folder," he pointed to the folder she now held in her hand.

"Where am I going?" she asked him coyly.

"A place called Kadoka," he said with a sardonic grin. "It's in Western South Dakota. We got you set up as a waitress in the only café in the town. We got you an apartment there, too. It isn't much but it will do."

"A waitress?" she asked. "I've never worked as a waitress in my life."

"We know," he said. "We think it is great cover for one with your history. It's right out in the open, but you'll never be seen for what you were before you got yourself into trouble."

"How do you know?" she asked him seriously.

"Well, for starters, hardly anyone but the locals have anything to do with Kadoka," he assured her. "It's on an interstate but it's not the place people stop for anything. We've checked it out."

"How big a town?" she wanted to know.

"I don't know," he continued. "It's really small. We think you'll find the role we've set up for you to be perfect for hiding anything about your past."

"Oh," she paused. "And what role might that be?"

"Well, as far as we know, you'll be the only lesbian in the burg," he chuckled. "That'll keep the cowboys off you. And with the new hairdo, body build, and clothes which are in that bag over there, you'll pass for the role."

"What if somebody finds out about me?" she asked anxiously.

"If you ever suspect that anyone is on to you, you call this number right away," he handed her a card as he spoke. "Anytime. You understand?"

"I think so," she said hesitantly.

"Jacqueline," he continued, "you've been a big help to us. We won't let anything happen to you if we can help it. But you've got to be careful for a while. Don't do anything foolish."

"I understand," she said. And she did. She had turned evidence over to the FBI, and God knew what other federal agencies, in return for reduced time and the relative security of its Witness Protection Program. They in turn had kept their promises of a brief time of incarceration, a new identity, and a new appearance. Now, it was all up to her.

Hence, Jacqueline Frontierre, alias numerous other personas, convicted for extortion as a strawberry-blonde professional call girl in service to underworld hoodlums, doing business with political parties out to keep their positions of power, became Jenny Craig, a dark-haired, slightly overweight lesbian who was jailed for possession of a controlled substance and now, down on her luck, was thankful for a waitressing position in some godforsaken place called Kadoka, where she would get another start in life.

"Here's your bus ticket to South Dakota and one hundred dollars," the agent said as he handed her an envelope. "I repeat, don't do anything stupid. Don't think you can drop this identity in a month or so and just get back into the swing of things. The people you worked for rarely believe the stories we concoct about their traitors dying in prison. They will look for you. They have a score to settle with you. Don't step out of character and we're confident they will never find you. Good luck."

"Thank you," she said.

The bus ride was tortuous. Every stop brought great anxiety as Jenny wandered through bus stations, trying to notice if anyone were on to her disguise. The great thing about bus stations, she discovered, is everyone is anonymous. She fit right into the scene.

Still, she worried at every stop. Would someone recognize her? Were the people she worked for really looking for her? But worse was, could she endure the new identity of the life that lay ahead for her?

Three days later, the Jack Rabbit Bus stopped at the Cenex station in Kadoka in late afternoon. Jenny was greeted with a gust of hot August wind, mixed with the strong smell of diesel fuel as she stepped down from the bus and waited while the driver retrieved her duffle bag from the luggage compartment. She, the lone occupant of the bus, was now leaving the driver to go on to Wall, and then to Rapid City.

"Here you go," the driver said as he placed the bag on the sidewalk in front of her.

She picked up the bag and glanced up and down the absolutely deserted mid-afternoon main street of Kadoka. She saw the café, the hardware store, the bar, the post office, and what passed for a grocery store, all in one glance. Two dilapidated car-dealership garages and several vacant storefronts filled out the block. She peered into the gas station and saw one lone pair of old eyes looking back in her direction.

She could only imagine what she looked like to whomever was staring at her through the shaded window of the gas station. Dressed in sneakers, jeans, sweatshirt and baseball cap, she was anything but the attractive woman she once saw reflected from fancy big-city storefront windows or posh hotel mirrors. Nevertheless, she'd been warned that anyone who isn't from a town in the Dakotas will get the "treatment." That's what a passenger a couple of hundred miles earlier had told her to watch for when she got to Kadoka.

"They'll give you the treatment," the older woman said as she chewed her gum and talked non-stop for forty to fifty miles once she learned Jenny was new to the territory. "Every stranger out in these parts gets the treatment."

Jenny laughed to herself as she stood in front of the station and soaked up the "treatment" while turning this way and that, stretching and taking off her baseball cap to let the breeze tousle her short black hair.

Then she walked toward the hardware store. There was a new landlord and a new apartment awaiting her. After showering, she thought she would go to the café for supper and meet her new boss so she would be ready for work at six the next morning.

As she drifted off to sleep, she thought of Mark and another preacher she knew once, not too long ago. She found herself thinking, as she often did when she was with Mark, of the other preacher. Where was he? Whatever became of him? Could he ever forgive her for the way she ruined his life? If there was anyone from her former life she wished she could see, if only for a moment, so she could beg his forgiveness, it would be Lark. The Reverend Lark Wilson was on her mind as sleep overtook her.

"You'll have to do this one day," the voice said to her as she

stood at a graveside, surrounded by people she did not know. She looked in the direction of the voice and there was Lark! Her heart pounded as she gazed at him. He repeated his comment. "You'll have to do this one day, Jennifer."

"What?" she asked him, oblivious to the others nearby.

"Die," he said firmly.

She awoke with fear clutching at her throat, heart pounding in her chest, and sweat forming at her temples. The room was crypt-like in its stillness and darkness. She looked up at a starless ceiling and wondered if she had not already died.

Chapter 7

Ta'ku Wa'pisni

The Monday crowd at the Kadoka Café was no different than it had been for years. There were Mel and Charlie in one corner booth, talking about their weekends. This was a Monday morning ritual with the two men, who appeared to be pushing sixty years of age somewhere further over the hill. And Scooter (why he was called that Jenny never learned) with his friend Oh Yeah were astraddle two stools at the counter. Jenny didn't know his name either but she gave him the nickname because he said very little to Scooter and the only intelligible sounds he seemed to make were "Oh yeah," with differing intonations of his voice, depending upon the content of their conversation. And at the table, which seated as many as gathered for the mid-morning card game and coffee break each day, sat, this morning, Bill and Matt and Sic 'Em. His name was really Slocum, but everybody called him Sic 'Em.

With this crowd every Monday morning came enough testosterone to stop any menopausal woman in her tracks, but not quite enough to get any younger woman's motor running. Jenny had gotten used to their habits, their swearing, their bragging, their put-downs, and their tastes. Without a word, as each entered the café, she would nod to Steve, owner and cook, and he would start cracking eggs and putting bread into the toaster.

"What'll it be?" she yelled at each one as he came through the door, "the usual?"

She was lucky to get any audible response from these worn-out cowboys. A nod of the head was the answer some days. Most days, nothing. They'd eat whatever she put before them. She knew that. As long as it was bacon or steak, eggs all ways, and toast with the usual bottomless cup of strong, black coffee, these men were happy. They paid her little mind after a few months of her arrival in Kadoka. And she didn't bother them much.

This morning, the topic was Wounded Knee again. Over the years, Jenny had learned to keep quiet and listen to these local experts as they devised better ways to deal with just about everything, including the unpredictable South Dakota weather.

Three different groups of men, seated in three different places in the café. But all close enough, due to the size of the place, to enter and exit conversations as they chose.

"If'n it be up to me," said Scooter, "I'd hang that sonofabitch and be done with it."

"So you think Wild Bill was right," shouted Mel from the corner booth, "when he said this is the man?"

All nodded. Jenny had learned that Wild Bill, who was the attorney general when the killings of FBI agents on the Pine Ridge Reservation took place a few years before, was absolutely convinced that an Indian activist from North Dakota was the lone killer of the agents. He had vowed to bring him back from wherever he was hiding in the world and put him on trial for murder.

"Damned right," snorted Scooter, "sonofabitch walked right up to them as they pled for their lives and shot them. Point-blank range. No mercy. He don't deserve none either."

"You were there! You saw him do it!" Charlie laughed as he got into the conversation. Charlie, always the antagonist no matter the discussion, was eager to get Scooter going this morning.

"Oh yeah," Jenny thought Oh Yeah said from the stool next to Scooter.

"Go to hell, Charlie," Scooter said. "I have my sources."

"Must be that squaw I heard you were bangin' in Rapid,"

Mel shouted while every one of the men snickered. "I heard she's a big talker!"

"Yeah," entered Sic 'Em, "she's a good source, all right! That damned woman doesn't know her ass from a Badlands sinkhole, but she's always on top of things. Ain't that right, Scooter?"

"Oh yeah," Jenny heard Oh Yeah repeat, along with some other unintelligible words that only Scooter seemed to understand at the time.

"Well, if you ask me," Matt, the youngest of the regular crowd, snarled, "those *federales* were stupid for chasing those bucks as deep into the res as they did."

"Oh yeah," Oh Yeah agreed.

"Those eastern boys don't really understand our Native Ameericuns," Bill chuckled. "If they'd just waited outside the reservation, them boys would have come out for more booze sooner or later."

"Yeah," Sic 'Em agreed. "Then they could have grabbed them one by one. It ain't like they got much to do down there but drink and screw around."

All laughed but Scooter. Even Oh Yeah chuckled as he punched Scooter in the ribs and mumbled something else only Scooter could decipher.

Jenny squirmed at the racism that drifted through the room like a low-hanging fog, making everyone's vision less clear and dampening whatever spirit of goodwill the sun might have brought with its rising.

"Huh," began Scooter again, "I don't care. I'd hang that sonofabitch as soon as I'd get my hands on him."

"Be careful now, Scooter," it was Matt who spoke again, this time a little more seriously than before. "We do believe in due process in this country, don't forget. A man's got to have a trial."

Then, as if they'd rehearsed it, all but Oh Yeah joined in unison and said, "Then hang him!"

Eventually, each man was served. Mel and Charlie walked to the table and inquired how many were good for a game of cards this morning. Scooter obliged, as did Sic 'Em, Matt and Bill.

"You gotta go then," Bill said to Oh Yeah as he ambled toward the door.

"Oh yeah," was his response, and he left.

The men played draw poker for toothpicks. Jenny never figured out whether these were only symbolic or whether the score, which Matt always kept in a little spiral-bound pocket notebook, was settled at some point in time with one or the other buying lunch or breakfast? All she knew was they played in earnest. That was obvious from the fierce arguments that were likely to break out on any given day or play of the cards. Sometimes, the arguments got so heated that one or more would suddenly get up and swiftly exit the café, swearing as he or they left the game.

Conversations at the card game were less serious and more difficult to hear. Jenny only heard bits of them as she made sure the men's coffee cups were kept half-full to full at all times while they played.

Once in a great while, a few women would enter the café during the morning hours. They never came in groups of less than three. Most times, they numbered four or five. They always sat in the booth in one corner or the other. Unlike the men, the women were discreet in their conversations and solicitous toward her. Jenny always believed they treated her nicely because she was the only other female in the room.

Over the first few months of serving them, Jenny learned that every one of these women was either presently married to, or divorced from, the men who frequented the café every morning Monday through Friday. Once in a while, the women came. After a while, it was rather easy to see who was on good terms with whom. Watching the non-verbal communication that took place whenever the women walked into the café, Jenny knew who belonged, for the moment at least, with whom.

The tension was evident throughout the café whenever the women were present. Territoriality, boundaries, and secrets were all guarded tenaciously in Kadoka. Jenny found a comfort in this fact for it promised the same to her, she believed.

No woman came this morning, however. By eleven, the card

game was over and the men walked to the counter to settle their bills. They chatted usually about what their plans were for the rest of the day as each waited his turn to pay her for his breakfast. After paying, each man, after bidding farewell to the others, went outside and jumped into his pickup and drove away.

Matt was last this morning. He smiled at her as she handed him his change.

"I hear that preacher up in Howes is leaving," he said.

"Is that so?" she said crisply. "I guess I wouldn't know about that."

"Yeah," Matt went on as he watched her closely, "I hear he's a boxer. Some of us went up to see him fight in Bismarck a while back. Real puncher."

"You don't say," Jenny said as she leaned across the counter and pretended to be interested in learning about the man who only once graced their little café. "I hardly remember him," she lied.

Matt stood silently before her, scanning her face as though for some clue. Jenny stepped back from the counter. Finally, he spoke.

"Well," he drawled, "I guess you wouldn't think of him much seein' as how you're not wired like most of us."

Before she could answer him, he turned and strolled out of the café, his well-worn boots making a scuffing sound on the dusty floor.

Did Matt know something? Jenny worried about the conversation as she rehearsed it several times in her mind while sweeping the floor and clearing the tables in order to be ready for the senior citizens' arrival around noon. *Why would Matt think she cared one bit about the preacher up in Howes?* She would worry more about this conversation. But there wasn't time. Napkins and silverware needed to be placed on the table and in the two booths. Glasses needed to be filled with ice and water and left standing on the tray, awaiting the lunch crowd. Coffee, decaffeinated, needed to be brewed. The special of the day needed to be written on the chalkboard behind the counter. The regular crew of seniors could be quite critical if everything just wasn't right when they came for lunch. She hurried as she thought some more about Matt's words. *Did he know? How? Had he seen them together in Rapid? They were always so careful. Maybe they slipped up once?*

By twelve-thirty, all nine senior customers had arrived and eaten the special of the day, which was meat loaf, mashed potatoes and gravy along with peas and a roll, after grumbling about the meal being the same as the previous Monday's and every Monday before that, as far as any of them could remember.

When Jenny first came to Kadoka, there had been an even dozen of them who came to lunch every day. But age serves the gods of attrition. One by one, the ranks were depleted. The town grew smaller. Profits shrunk. Morale withered.

First, it was Sarah, wife of Will, who got sick about three months after Jenny's arrival. "Cancer," they all whispered to one another as the ten of them sat having lunch. "She doesn't have much time," they said as they ate.

And she didn't. Sarah died a month later. She had been eighty-two years old. She had lived her entire life in the Kadoka. She and Will had met in high school, married a year after her graduation, and settled down on a ranch five miles north, where they reared five children.

Will, grief-stricken and heartsick without her, died only two months after she did. His pickup rolled on a turn on the old gravel road that went out to their place, a road that Will had traversed for sixty-four years in all kinds of vehicles and weather, just simply got the best of him one night. It was nearly twelve hours later that they found his pickup, over a hundred yards off the road, on its top in a ditch. His body was lying, crumpled and stiff between the road and the ditch.

"Wasn't wearing his seat belt," they all whispered to one another as they ate that day. "He always did," they agreed. "In fact, he was rather religious about it," they concurred.

Two South Dakota highway patrolmen who investigated the

accident talked quietly to one another earlier that day as Jenny listened.

"Looked like he was movin' pretty damned fast," said the taller of the two.

"Yeah," agreed his partner, "are you thinkin' what I'm thinkin'?"

"Uh hum," the taller officer grunted. "He wanted it that way."

"Yep."

Jenny never shared this with the seniors. Somehow, she sensed it would be old news to them.

Two months before this morning, old Sam was found dead in his garage, his car still running. His wife, Jackie, screamed as they carried his body from their newly purchased home in town. It was rumored that Sam was a first-class alcoholic and that he was abusive to his wife of forty years. But whenever Jenny saw the two of them together, whether in the café, or on the main street of Kadoka, he always seemed to treat her nicely. Nevertheless, the whispers endured about him until the morning Jackie found his body, slumped over the steering wheel of their car in the garage. The rumors were buried with him. Now, all talked of him to Jackie as though he were a candidate for sainthood.

Now, Jackie, newest widow of the group, vied for the attention of the two lone males left in the crowd: George and Stan. Neither of them had ever married but women never seem to give up the idea that men simply cannot live without them. So each woman treated this pair of bachelors as though they were the last two men on earth.

"How are you feeling, Stan?" one of the widows wanted to know.

"Yes, I heard you were under the weather recently," said another.

Stan blushed and glanced at George, as if to ask for rescue from these over-solicitous females. "I'm all right. Just a little cold," he confided.

"Well," said a third widow, "you stay out of that night air, Stan, and you'll be fine."

"Next time you're feeling poorly," said Jackie, "why don't you come over to my place and I'll fix you some hot tea with lemon?"

"I just might take you up on that," Stan smiled. But everyone except Jackie knew he wouldn't.

By one-fifteen, all were gone and headed toward their afternoon reveries. No doubt, their dreams might converge somewhere within that stream of the human unconscious. But Jenny knew nothing would come to any of them. Like the passengers on the *Titanic*, they were doomed to ride along the waves of life in Kadoka until the bell tolled for each of them. Jenny perceived herself to be along for the ride as well.

After clearing the tables and helping Steve with the dishes, Jenny again set the tables. The evening clientele were less predictable. Nevertheless, the café needed to be prepared before she and Steve would indulge in some rest or other pleasure while the café was closed from three until five each weekday.

Sometimes, only one family would come in for supper. Other times, the café was abuzz with the younger crowd, teenagers mostly, who had come to town to get something quick before a basketball game or a baseball game or a rodeo.

And the weather seemed to matter little at all when it came to the evening crowd. The bitterest snowstorms might produce a raucous teenage gathering, anticipating victory in a high school game. The most beautiful summer evenings might produce only a romantic younger couple, bashfully sitting and trying to talk while awaiting a hamburger and fries.

It was two-thirty when the door to the café opened and a family of five walked in, looking hungry. Steve saw them first and nudged Jenny. She quickly dried her hands and walked from the kitchen into the dining area of the café.

When she saw him, she stopped, frozen in fear. How could it be? *I must be dreaming*, she thought to herself as she turned away from the family, who now sat quietly at the table in the center of the room. She walked to the counter, where the menus lay askew, and gathered up a handful of them before turning to face the family anew. *Please God, this isn't happening,* she prayed as she walked toward them.

It was happening. The one she had never forgotten was there. *This must be his family,* she murmured to herself as she neared their table. *That must be Fran. She's pretty,* she thought as she handed each of them a menu. *So far, so good. He doesn't recognize me.*

Jenny stood silently next to the table. Suddenly, she was aware that she hadn't even greeted these strangers to Kadoka.

"Howdy," she said with all the cowgirl imitation she could draw up from within her very frightened self.

Steve leaned through the opening between the kitchen and the dining area of the café and spoke to Jenny.

"We ain't got any specials left, Jenny. If these folk want anything other than dessert, it'll have be hamburgers and fries," he said.

Fran looked at the children. "Will that do you until we get to Longvalley?" she asked them.

She has a nice voice, thought Jenny.

"Yeah," the older boy responded.

"It's just right," said the younger boy.

The girl didn't look too happy about it.

"How about you, Lark?" Fran asked.

Confirmation! It wasn't a dream. It really is him, Jenny thought as she looked at him and waited to hear him speak. Then she would be sure.

He nodded his head in agreement.

"What would you folks like to drink?" Jenny asked, again affecting a cowgirl drawl.

"We'll all have colas," Fran responded.

Jenny turned quickly away from the family and walked unsteadily toward the kitchen. "Burgers and fries for the five of them," she almost whispered to Steve as he glanced inquisitively at her.

"Losin' your voice?" he asked her.

She didn't respond. She walked back behind the counter

and prepared the colas for each of the surprise patrons. Once done, she walked slowly toward the table where they were sitting and placed a cola to the right of each of them. When she leaned over the father's shoulder, her left arm brushed slightly against him. For the first time since they had entered the café, he looked up at her.

"Sorry," she drawled.

"That's okay," he said as he stared at her.

Does he recognize me? She walked around the table and returned to the counter to await Steve's completion of their meals. She glanced at the family. He was not looking her way but was talking with the children and his wife.

"We don't have far to go now," he said.

"I bet," the girl said sarcastically.

"Now, Leigh Ann," her mother quickly shot her a disapproving glance.

"Oh, Mother," the girl complained. "I'm sick and tired of this trip. I just want to get there and get it over with."

"I can hardly wait to see more buffalo," the younger boy joined the conversation while his father amused himself by glancing around the small café and taking in whatever ambiance could be mined.

"I want to go horseback riding," the older boy added.

"You two kill me," the girl said with such feeling that her father stopped just short of looking at Jenny and addressed his daughter instead.

"That'll be enough, Leigh Ann," he said strongly. And it was.

A few minutes later, after all had fallen into an uneasy silence, Jenny delivered their burgers and fries to the table. Fran thanked her and they ate appreciatively as the tension among them seemed to ease.

Jenny watched them from the kitchen as she continued to help Steve with the cleaning. They wouldn't get away from the café until around three-thirty, since the family had come for lunch so late. Steve didn't seem to mind. He continued to whistle some nondescript tune as he placed utensils where they'd be needed in a couple of hours.

"Who are they?" he asked Jenny as she folded some dish towels in preparation for placing them in the drawer next to the silverware.

"I don't know," was all she said.

"Nice young family," Steve continued, "probably on vacation."

Jenny hoped they were. In fact, now that she had seen Lark with his family, she hoped she'd never see them again. It was frightening seeing him. Not at all like she imagined it would be these past few years. Last she had seen of him was the night she slipped him that drug in her apartment in Lancaster five summers before. He had passed out immediately. She had an awful time awakening him. He seemed so disoriented when he left that night, mumbling something about committing an unpardonable sin. He hadn't done anything. She knew that. But he didn't.

She felt sorry for him as she watched him walk down the stairs and out the door. It took him a while to get his car started. In fact, it took so long she nearly went outside to see if he had passed out again. This drug hit him harder than she had ever witnessed anyone under it. She could have done anything with him, she felt, and he never would have known.

Shortly after he left, her phone rang.

"Did he come?" the voice asked her.

"Yes," she said.

"How did he do on that drug?"

"He was out like a light in a minute," she shared. "I had trouble waking him up forty minutes later. How much of that did you give me to give him?"

"The usual," was all her caller said.

"Now what?" she wanted to know.

"You best be preparing to go back to New York City. One of our agents will contact you at your apartment."

"How many more of these do I have to do?" she asked. "Tonight wasn't very easy."

"You aren't getting soft on us, are you, Jacqueline?"

"No," she spat. "I just wanted to know, that's all."

"We'll talk about it when you get back to New York," the voice on the other end said, and then there was nothing but a dial tone.

She left the next morning on the 7:00 A.M. train to New York City and to her rendezvous with her agent.

"I think they might like dessert," it was Steve who broke her daydream as she stood staring into the café dining area.

"Oh," Jenny said, and she walked back to the dining area.

"Would you like some pie?" she asked the family.

"How about it, kids?" Fran spoke, "you want any dessert?"

"I'm stuffed," said the girl.

"Me too," the older boy said.

"I'll have some blueberry pie, Mother," the younger boy said.

Lark simply looked at her, as if trying to decide what he wanted to say.

"We don't have blueberry pie," Jenny said quickly. "All we have is apple and cherry."

"Oh," the younger boy said. "I'll take cherry."

"How about you, Lark?" Fran said to her husband as he continued to focus on Jenny.

What is he looking at? Jenny thought to herself. *Does he suspect anything? How could he? I've put on ten pounds, at least. My hair is dark and straight. My clothes are all too big for me. Even my eyes . . .*

"Do you have any cookies?" He stayed focused as he awaited the waitress's answer.

"Yes," she said nervously. "I think we have chocolate chip and oatmeal raisin."

"I'll have one of each," he replied as he smiled at her.

Jenny wanted to run from the table and never come back. His smile, just the way she remembered it, wormed its way into her psyche and she truly wasn't sure what she would say or do next.

"How about you, Fran?" He turned toward her, inquiring as to her taste in dessert.

"I'll have a cup of coffee and a chocolate chip cookie," she said.

"Make that two coffees," Lark chimed in as he turned once more toward Jenny. "Black."

Jenny turned to walk away when Lark's voice stopped her in her tracks.

"What's your name?" he asked.

She turned and faced the family. For the first time in a long while, her fingers trembled and her legs seemed to weaken beneath her. *He knows who I am. Oh God, how could he?*

"Jenny," she said. "Jenny Craig. Why?"

He stared at her now more deeply than he had before. Fran turned and looked inquisitively at him, as if to say *What are you doing?*

"You remind me of someone," Lark said as a smile crossed his face anew. "Are you from around here?"

"I am now," she said, without thinking of how it might have sounded to him. "I came here a few years ago from Oklahoma. I've been a cowgirl most of my life," she said, regaining her composure and affecting her voice once more so one might think she was born on a horse.

"Is that so?" Lark said as he glanced at his wife. "She reminds me of someone. Does she remind you of anyone, Fran?"

"Not really," Fran said as a frown crossed her face. "We've met so many people on this trip. It's only natural that some of them are going to remind us of people we know back East."

"I'm sorry," Lark said, still looking intently at Jenny, and he obviously meant it. "I didn't want to be nosey. It's just that something about you reminds me of a person I once knew. They say we all have a double somewhere. I guess you are somebody's double."

Jenny turned and walked to the counter to pour two cups of coffee, gather three cookies, and a piece of cheery pie. Once prepared, she returned to the table, where the family was now engaged in remembering friends from the East.

"What did John have to say about our moving west, Lark?" Fran asked as Jenny's heart skipped a beat.

"Not much," Lark replied. "He just said that I might find it more difficult than he could imagine to live on a reservation and become, for the first time in my life, a minority person."

"He would say that," Fran said smartly as she reached for her coffee. "Everything is racial in his mind."

"Everything is racial in this country, Fran," Lark said.

The kids listened as their parents discussed the topic of racism in America.

"Daddy," asked the younger boy, "do you think the Indians will like us?"

"Sure they will, Saul," said his mother quietly. "How could anybody not like you?"

The younger boy beamed at his mother while the other two children looked at one another as if to say, in unison, *Oh brother*.

In a matter of minutes, they were finished with their dessert. Lark walked to the counter, where Jenny was turning off the coffee pot that she had quickly brought back to life when the family entered the café.

"How much do we owe you?" he wanted to know.

She had it all figured out and written on one of the green slips Steve pored over on Friday evenings, after the café closed for the weekend. She turned and handed it to Lark.

"I'm sorry if I embarrassed you a few moments ago," he apologized anew. "It's your eyes that remind me of someone. Please accept my apology."

"No problem," she looked away from him and studied the wall to his left.

He placed three five-dollar bills on the counter. "Keep the rest as a tip," he said.

"Thanks," she said as she looked up and watched him turn and walk away. "That's mighty generous of you."

"My pleasure," he said as he and his family walked out the door of the café.

Jenny followed them to the door, where she turned the "Open" sign around to read "Closed." As she did, she peered out the window and watched the family get into two vehicles: a sedan and a rental truck. *It's true. They're moving west. Where?* As the sedan backed away from the curb, the younger boy, now sitting in front next to his mother, waved at her. She waved back. And they were gone.

Jenny's head was spinning when she returned to her apartment at three-thirty. She threw herself across her bed and recounted the events of the last few days. Each time she thought of Mark, she heard Matt's voice, asking her if she knew he was leaving. Each time she thought of her day at work today, she saw Lark and Fran and their family walk into the café. Each time she thought of Lark, she remembered his look when he left her apartment in Lancaster and heard his voice ask her, "Who are you?"

She could not rest. What would she do if Lark ever came into the café again and announced that he remembered who she was? *Should I call the number?* she asked herself over and over again.

"Now, Jacqueline," the agent said to her the day she left for her new life, "if you ever fear that someone, anyone, is on to you, you must call this number." He placed a small card in her hand.

"And if I don't call?" she asked coyly.

"You will be jeopardizing the entire program," he said professionally.

"Oh, big deal," she laughed.

"You also may be endangering your life," he said gravely. "So remember to call this number any time of any day, if you need to do so. Promise?"

"I promise," she said with a scowl. *These guys are always so damned melodramatic. Whose ever going to find me in . . . where is it . . . Kadoka, South Dakota?*

She arose with a pounding headache at four-thirty. She went to the bathroom medicine cabinet and retrieved a couple of aspirin. After drowning them with a glass of cola, she quickly showered, dressed again, and walked back to the café. It was to open at five for supper. *With all the surprises today,* she thought to herself as she walked briskly toward the café, *who knows, maybe the pope will show up for beans and frankfurters tonight?*

"What are you so happy about?" Steve asked her as she came into the kitchen.

"Do I look happy?" she asked.

"Well, you seemed to be chuckling about something when you came through the door just now, that's all," Steve said.

"Oh," she said, "I heard a joke on the radio this afternoon."

"Well, come on," Steve suggested, "share it with me."

Jenny stood for a moment and tried to remember if she knew any jokes.

Then, one she had heard Mark tell a few months before came to her mind.

"What's the worse thing about American Motors' two-for-the-price-of-one Pacer sale?" she asked him.

"I don't know," Steve said, going along with the patter, "what is?"

"That you might end up with two lemons!"

Steve laughed robustly as she chuckled to herself, proud that she remembered the joke at all.

"Good God," Steve said after his laughter subsided, "where did you say you heard that?"

"On the radio," she lied.

"Well, it's a wonder they don't get sued for stuff like that," Steve said.

The two of them stood and waited for whoever it would be to come through the door and order something for supper. They waited. They waited.

It wasn't until six that anyone came through the door. When he did, he came as quietly as any spirit. It was Mr. Davenport, the local undertaker.

"Good evening, Mr. Davenport," Jenny said as she handed him a menu. "What brings you out to our little café tonight?"

"Well," Mr. Davenport replied, "the missus is in Seattle visiting her sister and I didn't feel like eating alone at home tonight."

"Is that so?" Jenny bantered, "how long will Mrs. Davenport be gone?"

"About a week," he said as he glanced at the one-page, one-sided menu of the Kadoka Café. "She went back for her twenty-fifth high school reunion."

"Well, I'll be," Jenny kidded him, "I didn't think you folks were that old!"

"Oh," Mr. Davenport quipped, going along with the tease, "Mrs. Davenport's much older than I. She robbed the cradle!"

They laughed. It was the best Jenny had felt all day. She enjoyed the small talk with the locals now that she was well established among them.

"Look, how about getting me a cheeseburger and some fries and a chocolate malt?" Mr. Davenport said quietly.

"Coming right up," Jenny said and she walked into the kitchen, where Steve was already putting the fries into the deep fryer. "His usual?" he asked Jenny.

"Yep," was all she said as she sat down and watched Steve flip the burger on the grill. *I wonder which part of old Bossie's rump Steve is frying?* she thought as she watched this middle-aged husband with four children do his magic in the café kitchen.

Once the meal was ready, she placed it on the counter while she mixed Mr. Davenport's chocolate malt. Once done, she carried everything on a tray to him as he sat in a booth, looking out the window at all the inactivity of Kadoka's main street on an early-summer Monday evening.

Lewis Davenport had lived in Kadoka since graduating from embalmer's college somewhere in Chicago twenty years earlier. A man with small stature and mild manners, he was rarely seen in the county, except when he conducted funerals. His wife, Muriel, and he were absent much of the time from Kadoka. Rumor had it that they owned a lake cabin somewhere in Nebraska. Wood Lake would be the most likely spot, most people guessed. An easy summer morning's drive from Kadoka, it was imagined by many in the town that Lewis spent his days in the cabin, reading. He never seemed tan enough to be an outdoors man. Muriel, on the other hand, looked as if she'd spent every waking hour lying in the sun. Yet no one ever saw her sunbathe in Kadoka.

Being the only undertaker in the entire county had its advantages. Lewis could be available whenever he wanted, sometimes holding families hostage to his schedule due to the mysterious vacations with his wife during the summer months and needing to be called back to Kadoka from a far-off vacation in Mexico in fall and England in spring. Lewis was a "regular gad-about," people said. But he never seemed to talk about any of his adventures with anyone. Not even Dorothy, the local receptionist, talked about the couple's travels. She simply seemed to know where to call whenever he was needed for advice and counsel when death occurred. And it occurred, in a small place like this, infrequently enough to allow for the idiosyncrasies of their local undertaker and his wife.

Just before seven forty-five, Oh Yeah, of all people, entered the café and walked straight to where Lewis sat, sipping some of his malt. Jenny watched as the two bid one another good evening. Then she walked to the booth to see if Oh Yeah, who never came to the café in the evening, wanted anything to eat.

"What can I get for you?" she asked him.

He shook his head and muttered something. It was enough to tell her he didn't need anything at the moment.

"If you need me, holler," she said.

"Oh yeah," she thought he replied.

Lewis and this character to beat all characters seemed to be having a one-way conversation, with Lewis doing all of the talking and Oh Yeah nodding his head from time to time, indicating either his agreement or cognizance. After about ten minutes, Oh Yeah suddenly got up and started walking toward the door.

"You call me when you're ready," Mr. Davenport said in a businesslike manner.

"Oh yeah," he said, and walked out of the café.

"Now, I think I'll have some dessert," Mr. Davenport loudly announced.

Jenny walked to the booth and informed him they had two pieces of apple pie remaining. They also had some ice cream, she informed him.

Lewis decided he'd have a piece of apple pie and some vanilla ice cream. But only if she joined him in having some. His treat, he said. There being nothing else to do, she obliged. Within two minutes, she had it all in front of both of them in the booth.

"What was that all about," Jenny inquired, "if you don't mind my asking?"

"Not at all, Jenny," the undertaker said as he shoved a piece of pie with ice cream atop it into his mouth. "He's making arrangements for his funeral."

"He's what?" Jenny said and put her fork down. "Is that galoot dying?"

"Can't say," replied Lewis. "We all will someday. I guess he just wants to get it taken care of since he lives alone and all."

"Well, I never figured him for being so practical," Jenny said as she began to lift a fork full of dessert toward her mouth. *Good pie,* she thought as she savored it. *I'll have to compliment Steve's wife next time I see her.*

"Jenny," Lewis asked with a serious tone, "do you have family?"

"No," she said as she looked into the undertaker's eyes. "My momma died when I was a kid. Never knew my papa. Not much of a family."

"Too bad," Lewis spoke earnestly. "Family is all we have in this world. And when it's gone, we're all orphans."

"Well," Jenny said, "how come you and Muriel never had kids?"

"Couldn't," the undertaker replied, "and it's been the biggest disappointment in our marriage."

Silence draped the pair as they finished their dessert. When the last morsel of pie was consumed by the undertaker, he looked up at Jenny and looked as if he wanted to ask her another question, but was afraid to do so.

"What?" she spoke.

"Oh," he hesitated, "I don't know how to ask this so I guess I'll just come right out and say it."

"Go ahead," she encouraged.

"Well," he hesitated again, "is it really true that you are a lesbian?"

Stunned, Jenny looked at him but said nothing. *What's this all about?* she asked herself.

"I'm sorry," he said. "I guess I shouldn't have asked you that."

"It's a fair question," she said cautiously.

"I have always thought that something happened to you to make you what you are," Lewis said. "I see a beautiful woman beneath that exterior, Jenny. I am trained to look at dead bodies and see what life might have done to them, you know. I can't help it. I look at you and get the feeling there's a life missing. I sometimes wonder what it was."

Jenny was fearful to continue this conversation. She never imagined this man ever paid any attention to her for the two of them had only seen one another a dozen times or less during her time in Kadoka.

"I'm sorry," he continued as if she had encouraged him to talk. "It's none of my business, and I am not a betting man. But if I were, I'd bet you were an entirely different person before you came here."

There it was. *With whom has he shared these thoughts?* she wondered. *Are there others here who see what he sees?*

"I . . ." she was at a loss for words to respond, "I hardly know how to answer your question."

"Hey," he said more casually than before, "it's a secret between us. There's nobody else around here who suspects you are anybody other than who you are pretending to be. Your secret is safe with me."

"Well . . ." she hesitated again.

"Look," he said like a father, "you don't have to say anything, girl. I already have my answer."

Her heart pounded in her chest. Suddenly, this little town was closing in on her. She would have to leave. She couldn't risk being found, or found out. She decided she would call the number the agent gave her. While she was deep in thought, Mr. Davenport reached across the booth table and took her hand.

"Look," he said, "I'm sorry I've frightened you. Please don't worry. All of us have our secrets," he said with a wink of an eye and a smile. "You are as safe here as any place on earth. I ought to know."

"What?" Her surprise was revealed.

"Nothing," he said, "I shouldn't have brought any of this up with you. But I just had to know. Now you go help Steve clean up for the night and don't you think another thought about our little conversation." He smiled as he squeezed her hand.

Jenny left the table with the soiled dessert dishes and the ten-dollar bill Mr. Davenport had given her, along with his words "keep the change." He quickly left the café as well.

When she entered the kitchen, Steve was already cleaning the grill once more and getting ready to close for the night. Jenny put the dishes in the sink with Mr. Davenport's dinner dishes and began to wash them.

"What were you and that weirdo cookin' up?" Steve asked.

"Nothing," she said.

"Nothing?" Steve turned and looked at her inquisitively. "Well, that was the damndest serious talk about nothing I ever saw." He turned back toward the grill and rubbed it down with a paper towel.

When both were certain no one else was coming to the café, Jenny dimmed the lights in the dining area to their overnight setting, turned the sign once more to read "Closed" and walked back into the kitchen to say goodnight to Steve.

"You look a little peaked tonight, Jenny," he said, as though he truly cared for her well-being.

"I guess it's that time of the month," she said.

"Oh," he said. "Well, have a good evening."

"You too," she said.

Jenny walked back to her apartment. *What should I do? I'll call tomorrow. I've got to get out of here.* She climbed the stairs, unlocked the door, walked in and bolted the door behind her, and felt safe once more in the anonymity of existence in this place where no one had ever visited, save the landlord when there was need. She sat heavily in the rocking chair opposite her small television set after turning it on to the one channel she could receive from Rapid City, just as her favorite Monday evening show was coming on air.

The television blared a well-known mystery program while Jenny's mind drifted to an earlier time, a night her mother shared a story about her beginnings in America. Sadie began by explaining this event was buried so deep within her that to recall it seemed to her to be little more than looking at another person's life.

The river was alive with sounds, the current swifter than she had imagined whenever her mother spoke of the trip they needed to take.

"No matter what you hear or feel," she said to the two little girls, "don't let go of my hand. I will get you safely to the other side. We can start a new life there."

Into the water she pulled them, frightened children squeezing tightly to their mother's hands. The water was not cold. It was alive! As they crossed, pulled by their mother's strong arms, the girls paddled at times with their feet, as instructed, while bits of darkness struck them from time to time in various places of their bodies.

"I'm afraid," one of the little sisters said with a startled voice. "Something hit me in my side."

"Hold on, little girl," her mother gently said above the rumble of the river. "We're almost there."

Once ashore on the other side, the mother took a towel from the backpack she wore while crossing and wiped the girls' arms and legs with it. Then one by one, she undressed them and dressed the girls again in dry underwear and dresses, stuffing the wet clothing into her backpack.

"Hurry," she whispered, "we must meet the bus."

They walked for what seemed like an hour. It was totally dark and silent around them. But their mother seemed to sense the direction they should take and soon they stood on a dusty road, awaiting the bus.

Time passed slowly as they waited. The children were hungry and told their mother so. They were told they would eat when they got to town. One sister whimpered. Once more, she was afraid, this time, of the darkness. Mother soothed the both of them with a song Jenny never forgot hearing her mother sing but once.

Si fui motivo de dolor, oh Dios; si por mi causa el debil
    tropezo
Sientus caminos yo no quise andar perdon, oh Dios!

Startled by the sound of her voice recalling her mother's song, Jenny sat upright in her chair, her heart suddenly beating quickly. There was more to remember, but she rarely drifted beyond the song.

"You must forget this journey, my daughters," the little girls were warned as the vehicle approached from the west. "You must never tell anyone of this journey. I will teach you what to say. In time, you will think of this night no more."

She squeezed them tightly to her bosom as she spoke. When the bus reached them, they climbed aboard and found a bench on which all three sat quietly among others like themselves: pilgrims to a new world filled with hope of staying by getting lost deep within it.

"So that is how you got to America, Mother," Jacqueline asked her mother so many years before.

"Yes," Sadie answered quietly as she lay dying. "You, Jacqueline, are a citizen of America. You were born here. Don't ever forget."

"And, your sister," Jacqueline asked seriously, "where is she, Mother?"

"I don't know," Sadie replied weakly. "I lost track of her a long time ago."

Chapter 8

Ta'ku Taninsni

Once they left the interstate and headed south on Highway 73, the land took on a certain asperity and a disheveled appearance. Within five miles, they approached a broken-down and bullet-hole-ridden sign which read:

"WELCOME TO PINE RIDGE
A RESERVE FOR THE GREAT SIOUX NATION"

The Pine Ridge Reservation abuts the Rosebud Reservation and Highway 63 on the east, runs parallel to Interstate 90 on the north, and coils around the southern edges of the Badlands National Park on the northwest, then stretches to the South Dakota and Nebraska border on the south, except for the checker-boarded section which excludes the towns of Martin and Tuthill along Highway 18, east of the town of Pine Ridge itself. The site of the Wounded Knee Massacre, which took place in December of 1890, is located just about twenty miles northeast of the town of Pine Ridge. Longvalley, located at the very southeast edge of the reservation, lay about fifty miles south of Kadoka.

With each ascent of the rental truck and car, the Wilson family expected to see, just over the next ridge, some sign of life. Nothing. Rolling hill after rolling hill to the east and to the west. Grass and sandy-brown earth were all they saw as they drove in the late afternoon heat, the rental truck straining up each hill and rumbling down each decline.

After thirty minutes, they approached a crossroad. The sign read: "West—Kyle, forty-four miles and East—White River, forty-four miles." The highway east and west was numbered 44. Lark chuckled to himself as they passed the crossroad. His older son said not a word, but continued to stare ahead as if in shock at the lack of civilization all around them.

"What are you thinking, Walt?" Lark asked him.

"Where is everybody?" The boy grinned at his father nervously.

"I don't know," Lark replied. "I knew it was pretty sparse, population-wise, out here, son. But I had no idea it was this devoid of people."

The two rode on in silence as the rhythm of rising above and falling upon the prairie floor began to overtake them both in its monotony.

"Shouldn't we be just about to Longvalley?" Saul asked his mother as she watched the rental truck in front of them rumble down a hill they had just climbed in tandem.

"Won't be long now, I think," Fran assured.

"Whoopie!" Leigh Ann mocked excitement from the rear seat of the sedan. "I can hardly wait!"

After an hour of driving, as they proceeded to climb yet another rise of the road, Lark spied a blue, cylindrical tower rising on the eastern horizon. He surmised it to be a water tower. And since there were no other towns on this road, he concluded that this tower provided the water pressure for Longvalley.

When they reached the top of the hill, the land stretched before them. And there, dotted among a few trees and fences, were a dozen or more homes and one church steeple.

"There it is," Lark said to Walt.

"That's it?" Walt said, astonished.

"It has to be," said Lark. "There is nothing else on the map."

Walt said nothing as the truck rumbled down the last hill. When they reached the bottom, Lark turned the truck left into the little village. Another sign greeted them. It simply read "Welcome to Longvalley." Lark saw Fran turn their car behind him onto the only street of the town. It was a dirt street. Dust swirled behind them as they drove its length, about three city blocks in all. They stopped in front of the church building.

Eyes saw them drive toward the church building. Moving out of the shadow of one of the houses they passed, Eyes watched as the family of five got out of their vehicles, stretched, spoke with one another, and walked into the church building. Eyes moved cautiously toward the vehicles and the people who had gotten out of them just moments before. Eyes crossed the street to get a better look at the vehicles. Looking back and forth, Eyes now walked directly toward the rear of the truck.

Inside the church, the Wilson family stared in disbelief at what they saw. Two pews and a smattering of chairs did little to improve the appearance of the room, which was covered with various pieces of linoleum, some of which was not well adhered to the floor beneath them. At the front of the room, on a platform raised about three inches above the rest of the floor, stood a naked, outsized pulpit, perhaps given to the parish by some other congregation, a small table with some artificial flowers protruding out of a used bleach bottle, and an opened Bible. The walls of the one-room building were painted light blue and were adorned by various posters and what looked like church school pictures. On the wall behind the pulpit and table was a large picture of a laughing Jesus and a light affixed to the wall above it, which still had some leftover Christmas tinsel stringing from it.

Lark sat down in one of the chairs, while the children walked around the room, picking up bits of scrap paper and looking at the posters and pictures. Fran stood beside Lark and placed her hand upon his shoulder.

"Not much here," she said quietly.

"Harry said it needed a lot of work," Lark replied. "I guess he wasn't kidding. They've been demoralized here since 1973, according to Harry."

"Well, let's go next door and see what the parsonage is like," she suggested. "We've got all week until Sunday to get this place ready for worship."

"Okay," Lark shrugged, suddenly feeling a bit sluggish.

Neither of them said anything to one another about seeing only a small grocery-store-gas-station combined and nothing else, save a dozen dilapidated houses and the church building in Longvalley. Just these few homes and a church building. Neither of them wanted to alarm the children with even a hint of disappointment. Neither of them wanted to do anything to tip the fine balance between them as a reunited family. So each was committed to a covenant of silence as they exited the church building and walked next door to the parsonage.

The first thing that struck both Lark and Fran about the parsonage was that it had no windows that were not boarded over with plywood, and it had a padlock on the outside of the front door. The house that was to be their home for the indefinite future while Lark served this congregation leaned slightly toward the northeast, and its roof lacked some shingles. Behind it stood a much older and long-neglected outhouse. A good sign, this, for it suggested that the parsonage had running water. What might pass for grass in Longvalley grew to various heights around the parsonage and appeared as though it had somehow been trimmed, in anticipation of their arrival.

Eyes watched the family standing in front of the house. Eyes darted this way and that, suddenly seeing a friendly face approaching the family. Eyes stood and watched.

"Hello," Lark said as he glanced up at the bark of a dog accompanying an elderly Indian man walking toward them.

The man approached them silently. He carried a ring of keys in his right hand and a pot in his left. The dog leapt at the pot he was carrying in his left hand, and the man shushed the dog and pushed it away with his foot.

"Good afternoon," Lark said again as the man reached the spot where the family stood. "I am Pastor Lark Wilson. This is my wife, Fran. And these are our children, Walt, Leigh Ann, and Saul."

The old man looked at each member of the family. His eyes gave no hint whatsoever as to whether he understood one word or cared one whit about any of them. He extended the pot to Fran.

"Woshapi," he said.

"Woshapi," Fran repeated after him.

"It is a berry pudding," the old man continued to speak in a broken, halting, voice. "It's warm. So be careful."

That said, the old man extended the paper sack he carried.

"Fry bread," he said to Fran. "It was made yesterday. I hope it's not too hard. Just dip it in the berry pudding."

"Thank you," Fran said as she smiled at him.

Turning to Lark, the old man said, "Now, I suppose you want to move into the church house."

"Yes," Lark said. "I hope you have a key."

"I've got a key to every home in Longvalley," the old man said. "My name is Ethan Long Elk."

"Nice to meet you, Ethan," Lark said.

"Uh huh," the man said as he walked to the front door of the parsonage and began the process of finding which padlock key from among the many he carried would release the lock, and allow the Wilson family to enter their new house.

"Some of the women cleaned the house yesterday for you," the old man said as he found the right key and the lock opened. "Somebody will come by tonight and take the wood from the windows. We have to do this while the house is empty because the kids will throw stones through the windows when no one is living here."

"Thank you," Fran repeated.

The old man turned to Lark and asked seriously, "Do you speak Dakota?"

"No," Lark said. "But I'd like to learn."

"Mrs. Long Elk and I would like to have you join us tonight for supper," the old man said. "We've invited others to come. We will eat around seven."

"Thank you," Fran said again as the children walked into their new home.

"We will see you then," the old man said. "Our house is that light green one on the other side of the road. You best eat that while it's warm."

He turned and walked away, the dog running up to him and jumping at him as he walked back toward his house.

"Did you notice anything strange about that dog?" Walt asked his father after Ethan and the dog were out of earshot.

"No," said Lark

"I did," Saul got into the conversation. "That dog had blue eyes."

As Saul said that, the dog stopped its jumping around Ethan, turned, and stared in the direction of the Wilson family.

"Must be a different breed," assured Fran.

"Well, let's get at it, gang," said Lark as he walked toward the rental truck. "We've got a lot of work to do and not a lot of time."

The family worked very hard, carrying their belongings into the little wood-frame building, which was to be their new home in Longvalley. The boys would share a bedroom. Leigh Ann would have her own. Fran and Lark took the largest bedroom. They would all share the only bathroom. The kitchen, dining room, and living room combination was smaller than anticipated, but they got nearly everything into it, except for the two end tables. These were placed, one in each of the children's bedrooms.

There was no basement and no storage building for the seasonal things they had brought. Bicycles, sleds, golf and tennis equipment, a freezer, and odds and ends of automobile equipment Lark had collected over the years and used to keep their various vehicles moving all were placed behind the house. A brand-new pair of snow tires, purchased in the East and brought West in anticipation of an early and hard winter in South Dakota, also had to be placed behind the home, in full view of the entire community, until a shed or some other place could be procured in which to store their extra belongings.

By six, the truck was basically emptied of everything, except clothing that had been placed in neat cardboard, upright, temporary closets and placed against the very back wall of the rental-truck bed. Fran unfolded two lawn chairs and invited Lark to rest, while the children each gathered up their bicycles. They had decided it was time to explore the town of Longvalley.

"Well, we did it," Lark said quietly as they sat in front of their new home, catching a little bit of the shade that was creeping eastward across their lawn.

"I'm amazed we got almost everything into that house," Fran said. "It looked so small before we started carrying things into it."

"How do you think the kids feel about it?" Lark asked her.

"Hard to tell, Lark," she said as she glanced toward him. "This is really quite an adjustment for them, especially Leigh Ann."

"Yes, I know," Lark said seriously, "it's going to be tough for all of us. Thank you, Fran."

"For what?" she asked him.

"For coming out here with me," he said as he turned and looked directly into her eyes. "I love you so much for doing this."

Fran smiled as her eyes began to well up, and then she looked to the west. "Lark," she said as she continued to look away from him, "it will take time. But it's not impossible."

"I know," he said.

When the kids came back, they were sweaty and dusty from their bike rides. Each wanted to give her or his impression of their new location at once. Lark sat quietly and listened to them trying to outdo one another in their descriptions of Longvalley, the conclusions of which were that all wondered what in the world they would do in a town so small until school started.

"And," Walt said suddenly, "by the way, where is the school?

We didn't find one. And believe you me, we rode everywhere in this town."

"We'll ask tonight," Fran said to them. "Now, take turns cleaning up for supper." The children disappeared into the home.

"They seem to like it here," Lark said as Fran chuckled to hear him say it.

"You are an incorrigible optimist, Lark Wilson," she said after she stopped laughing. "I think that is what I've always loved about you."

He reached out and clasped her hand in his. "Thanks, ba . . . ba . . . baby." he said, as they both laughed at this little long-standing joke between them. When they entered the little house, their children were sampling the pudding Ethan had brought to them earlier in the afternoon.

"This is really good," said Walt as he scooped the pudding from a bowl into which Fran had placed it with a piece of fry bread and lifted it toward his mouth.

"Tastes like blueberries," Saul said appreciatively.

"Not bad," was Leigh Ann's summation.

"Be careful," Fran said to them with a smile, "that you don't spoil your supper."

The admonition unheeded, the three ate the rest of the pudding and bread with enthusiasm.

By seven, the Wilsons were ready for supper at the home of the Long Elk family. They walked west on the only street in Longvalley until they came to the little light green frame house, in front of which sat the dog. As they approached the front door, the dog arose and walked around behind the house, out of sight.

"Come in," a cheerful female voice bade them enter, "we're all anxious to meet you."

When the Wilsons walked into the Long Elk home, they noticed no one, except Ethan, sitting on one of the two chairs in the living room, smoking a pipe.

"Welcome," he said and he raised his hand in greeting.

Mrs. Long Elk rushed into the room from the kitchen, part of which could be seen from the front door, her hands wet with something, drying them on her apron. She was a short, stout woman who looked to be old enough to be the children's grandmother. As she smiled to greet them, it was noted by all that several of her teeth were missing.

"Ethan and I are happy you can be with us tonight," she said warmly as she reached out to shake Lark's hand.

"Thank you," Lark said. Then he introduced Fran and the children to her while Ethan remained seated, puffing on his pipe. The dog came to the entry way of the kitchen and stood, watching them all make their acquaintances.

"We don't have a lot of furniture," Mrs. Long Elk, whose name she said was Percy, short for Priscilla, said to them as they stood in the living room. "Pastor, why don't you visit with Ethan while Fran and I continue to fix supper."

"Oh," Fran said, "I'd be delighted to assist."

"You kids can make yourself at home around the house," Percy said.

Lark sat down after all vacated the living room. No television, stereo, or radio present that he could see, Lark wondered what Ethan and Percy did to amuse themselves in the evenings. He said nothing. He could hear his wife and Mrs. Long Elk talking in the kitchen. He could hear the children talking with one another in front of the Long Elk home.

"Do you smoke a pipe?" Ethan asked Lark.

"I did a few years ago," Lark answered his host's question. "But I quit when I burned a hole in a brand-new polyester suit Fran had just purchased for me."

"Um," was all Ethan said. He continued puffing on his pipe while the two men sat in silence.

Lark grew more uncomfortable as the minutes passed and nothing was said. He didn't know what to say himself. He hoped his host would lift what, for Lark, suddenly had the feel of a gloomy beginning between them.

The dog wandered into the living room and walked toward the front door. *The children were right*, thought Lark. The dog had blue eyes. Suddenly, the dog stopped, turned, and walked straight toward Lark, and then curled at his feet. Ethan continued to puff on his pipe, as if not even seeing the dog and its approach to Lark.

"What kind of dog is this?" Lark broke the silence with a question as he reached down and patted the dog's head and felt its mangy black-and-white fur.

"A genuine blue healer," said Ethan. "He found us a few years back, in 1973."

"He found you?" Lark said.

"Yes," Ethan said. "It was the morning after the trouble over at Wounded Knee. I went out to the outhouse that chilly May morning, and there stood this dog. He's never left us since. We don't even know his name."

"He doesn't have a name?" Lark said incredulously.

"No, we're waiting to learn more about him," Ethan explained. "Then maybe, we'll know his name."

"I don't understand," Lark said honestly. "Why can't you give him a name? He's been with you for almost four years, hasn't he?"

"Um," was Ethan's only response to Lark's inquiry. And silence once more gained the upper hand between the two men.

Lark glanced at his watch. Seven-thirty. No other guests had arrived for supper. Fran and Percy were talking animatedly in the kitchen about families and life experiences. The children could no longer be heard in front of the Long Elk house. Lark and Ethan sat in silence.

"It was a troubling time," Ethan said as he stopped puffing on his pipe. "It still hangs heavily over us all."

"Four years ago at Wounded Knee?" Lark asked.

"Chief Big Foot and his braves were rounded up and brought here from Cherry Creek," Ethan went on now, as if not hearing Lark's question. "Some of them were still wearing their Ghost Dance shirts. Big Foot himself was ill with pneumonia. Our people were desperate. Sitting Bull was dead. Red Cloud's heart had been buried in a secret stream bed, to await the coming of the new day. We were being crowded out by the white man and his soldiers. We were being killed by disease, as well as bullets. Our young braves were taught to purify themselves: always speak the truth, love one another, and dance the dance that would bring a new earth to our people, an earth that would cover the whites and nonbelievers."

"You are talking about the last century," Lark offered as Ethan went on with his tale of his people, not acknowledging Lark's interruption.

"In those days," Ethan said, "we believed the world would be destroyed, for it had become unlivable for us. We believed the dead would be returned. We believed we could change to more righteous ways. And we believed that only this could save us. So we danced. And we awaited the fulfillment of prophecy. The one who was to come would save us, and our people would be restored."

Lark sat now, listening to this tale told by his host, a tale of an event nearly a century old, told in such a way as though it were a mere four or five years ago.

"That winter on the Pine Ridge our rations had been reduced. Our people were starving. Many were sick with another round of white man's disease. So Big Foot suggested the dance. Our young braves danced north of here, for we knew the white soldiers feared our medicine and we didn't want them to find us.

"The troops searched and found Big Foot and our braves. They brought them and their families to Wounded Knee. Many were still wearing their Ghost Dance shirts. Most believed that by doing so, the bullets of the white man would not harm them.

"The word went out that morning from the white chief that our warriors were to be disarmed. They took everything: guns, axes, knives, even tent stakes. Still not satisfied, they took the blankets and made the braves strip in front of all the people.

"Then Yellow Bird did a few Ghost Dance steps, trying to rally the band to resist the white soldiers. *The bullets will not touch you,*" he chanted in Dakota. *The prairie is large and the bullets will all miss you.*"

"The soldiers found only two guns. They were furious. One of the guns, a new Winchester, belonged to Black Coyote. He refused to give his gun to the soldiers because he had just bought it. He was proud of it. He held it high above his head. And when he fired it into the air, the white soldiers, fearing an uprising, started firing. They shot at everyone and everything. Of our three hundred people, one hundred fifty-three died immediately. Braves, women, and their children all lay in the cold December snow, stiffening by the second."

"This was the Wounded Knee massacre of 1890," Lark said to his host.

"Yes," Ethan said as he smiled at Lark for the first time. "White men will tell you to this day that is wasn't a massacre. They'll tell you that they lost twenty-five soldiers and another thirty-nine were wounded that Christmas season on the Pine Ridge, when the Sioux defied their orders. But all of them were shot by their own people. Our people had no guns."

"And what of Big Foot?" Lark asked. "Did he die that day?"

"Yes, our chief died," said Ethan. "A blizzard came upon the place almost as soon as the shooting broke out. All were left dead in the field until the spring. We found Big Foot's body in April, along with all the others."

"And Black Coyote?" Lark asked.

"Black Coyote died also," said Ethan. "But he never heard the shooting."

"What?" Lark was astonished. "The sound must have been deafening. I've read that the army used Hotchkiss guns at Wounded Knee. How could he not hear the shooting?"

"He was deaf," Ethan said. "He didn't understand a word anyone ever said to him."

The room became quiet once more. There was nothing more to say. The scene was perfectly clear. Two cultures. Both highly suspicious of one another. Illness, pain, disillusionment, and despair, the lot of almost everyone on the prairie that winter of 1890. And a deaf Minneconjou at the center of an event that, to this day, darkens the history of the U.S. Army. Lark saw it all now, as though he were privileged to a revelation.

The end of a struggle between Native Americans and European Americans precipitated by a deaf man, who simply didn't know what was being asked of him that day. Lark thought of all of this as they sat in silence and Ethan relit his pipe. Lark had one more question to ask his host. But he held it for a later time.

At seven-fifty, a knock upon the front door brought Percy once more from the kitchen with a cheery, "Come in, we're expecting you."

A family of five entered the little living room. Two girls and a boy, about the age of the Wilson children, a husband and wife. They said their names were Yellow. Angus and Dolores Yellow. Their daughters were Louise and Phyllis. Their son was Paul. The Wilson children had entered the living room with the Yellows. Hence, the room, which had stood in silence for nearly an hour, save Ethan's retelling of the 1890 massacre, was suddenly alive with human sound.

Lark rose to introduce himself and his family to the Yellow family and the dog rose with him and stood at his side.

"Looks like that old hound likes you," said Angus with a smile. "Nice to meet you, Pastor." The two men shook hands.

After all introductions were completed, Mrs. Long Elk announced, "Now that we're all here, let's go out into the yard and have our supper." Everyone walked out the front door and around the house to the back yard, where Fran and Percy had already placed an oil cloth over a picnic bench, piled dishes at one end, along with silverware and drinking glasses. Another table held the evening meal in various pots and pans, lids still upon them.

"Pastor," said Ethan, "would you offer a prayer?"

"I'd be glad to," Lark replied, as he thought to himself what he could pray among these people he barely knew. The dog came and stood beside him. He looked around. His family, the Long Elks and the Yellows, made an even dozen. A *Last Supper* thought crossed his mind as he began, "Let us pray," and all bowed their heads. "The eyes of all look to you, O Lord, and you give to all your people what we need. We thank You that at our most needy hour, You gave Your only Son to us to show us the way to live among all people. We thank You that You still honor his petition that we might receive our daily bread. And we thank You that no matter where we are, You are here in our midst to sup with us. Receive this prayer in Jesus' name. Amen."

All but the members of the Wilson family repeated, "Amen."

"Now, let's eat," said Percy. "Pastor, you and your family go first. Take anything you see and fill your plates!"

Hesitantly, Lark, Fran, and the children picked up plates and walked toward the table with the food, each feeling self-consciously on display and being tested in their knowledge of customs and mores in this strange new land, among its ancient people.

The food looked and smelled delicious. Each member of the Wilson family approached the offerings on the table differently. Leigh Ann took a piece of fry bread and spread some butter on her dish, along with some salad. Saul took a large piece of the boiled meat, whatever it was, and also a couple of boiled potatoes. Walt took a bowl of the soup that had various heavy cuts of some kind of meat floating among potatoes, corn, and turnips. Fran took a piece of fried chicken and some salad, along with a piece of fry bread. Lark took a little of everything, wanting to make his first taste of Indian cooking a learning experience. Strawberry lemonade and coffee were the two drinks. The kids took the lemonade. Fran and Lark poured themselves a Styrofoam cup of coffee each.

When all were seated, kids at one end of the picnic bench and adults at the other, the conversation ensued the same, as it does anywhere on the face of the earth whenever strangers meet and eat, knowing that they will not be strangers forever. The Yellows engaged Fran in talking about her experience as a teacher back East, while the Long Elks talked with Lark about his college and seminary education. Fran and Lark asked, at times, what seemed to be awkward questions about each of their new acquaintances: occupation, tenure of life in Longvalley, the rest of their families.

Ethan didn't work at all. He was "retired," they said, as the Yellows and the Long Elks laughed. Angus worked in Rapid City in various construction jobs. "Whatever he can get," said Dolores. Percy worked in Rapid City also, as a nurse's aid in the local hospital. "She works four ten-hour-shift days a week," Ethan explained. "Dolores works at the hardware store up in Kadoka," said Angus. As for families, the Wilsons learned that Indian families were among the most extended they had ever known. Two of the Yellows' children were actually a niece and a nephew, as the white man would account. *There is so much to learn here,* thought Lark, as the dinner host family and only other member family of the church to which he had been called revealed a bit of themselves to the Wilsons.

When everyone had finished eating, Percy jumped to her feet and announced that there would be ice cream, with various toppings for dessert. "Would any of you kids want to help me dip the ice cream?" she asked. Everyone of them arose to volunteer! Looking at the six of them, Percy said, "I'll take you, Leigh Ann, and you, Phyllis. The rest of you can clean off the table for us."

The boys and Louise shrugged and set about the task of clearing table for dessert, which soon arrived. Heaping bowls of vanilla ice cream stood in front of each diner and bottles of various toppings were passed up and down the table at request.

"Grandfather," said Paul as he finished his dish of ice cream, "tell us a story."

"Yes, Grandfather," said Louise, "tell us a story."

"Wait, wait," said Percy. "Let's clean up this place a bit while the men build a fire out there beyond the shed. Then Grandfather can tell his story."

Lark and Fran looked at one another in bewilderment. In all of the dinner conversation, neither had heard anything to indicate that these two families were related.

Quickly, everyone had a job to do as Percy gave instructions. She excused Fran from helping, for she explained that Fran had helped prepare the meal. She and Fran would simply sit and advise. Dolores was directed to supervise the clean up in the kitchen. Lark watched as his children smiled at each other, and then did as they were told by their hostess. He also noted that Ethan and Angus had quietly slipped away to prepare the fire. Deciding that Percy's instruction that the "men will build the fire" included him, he walked after Ethan and Angus. The dog arose and walked with him.

Behind the shed was a small fire circle and some logs standing ready. Angus gathered some dry grass and weeds while Ethan stood the logs on end, tilted them toward each other at the top, tepee-like. When all was ready, Ethan leaned down, took his lighter from his pocket, and struck the dry grass and weeds with the flame. In a few minutes, a blazing fire was leaping and crackling.

"That wood must be pretty dry," said Lark as he watched the flames build.

"Everything out here is," said Angus with a wink of an eye.

"Cottonwood makes the quickest fires," said Ethan. "I go up to Cherry Creek and get a load of it about twice a year from along the Cheyenne."

Lark glanced in the direction of an old rusted Chevy pickup that was standing, leaning to one side, near the shed. He wondered how much wood an old truck like that could haul. And how far. As he looked around, Lark saw no visible evidence of the wood being cut on site. Yet, the pieces Ethan had used to set the fire this night were each about eighteen inches long, and all were about the same diameter.

Soon, after the fire was blazing and needed some more wood atop it to keep it going, all were gathered in lawn chairs around the fire's west side, for the smoke from the crackling cottonwood was drifting lowly eastward. The sun had now dipped below the horizon and there was a hint of a chill in the air.

"Now, Grandfather," said Paul, "tell us more about your childhood."

The story that ensued from Ethan's lips was not spectacularly embellished in any fashion. It was simply a tale of Ethan's boyhood, the summer he learned to ride a horse. The year was 1913. Ethan's father, who had walked with a limp all of his life and was known as "Walks With One Strong Leg," was determined his son would learn to ride the same year he did: his fifth year of life. The listeners sat, enthralled by this simple tale of a very young boy's struggle to both please his father and overcome his fear of such a large animal at the same time. Ethan left out no small detail, Lark noted, as he talked of the weather of the day, the sweet smell of the prairie, the rain earlier that morning, and the wet odor of the horse as his father lifted him up on it and instructed him how to hold tightly to the horse's slippery mane.

Lark glanced at his own children. They seemed to be as interested in this story as the Yellow children. Ethan took his time in the telling. Great pauses were taken as he lit and relit his pipe. When he was finished, he simply said, "That's all I have to tell you."

"Thank you, Grandfather," said Phyllis.

"Yes," said Leigh Ann, "that was a wonderful story." She smiled for the first time since they had left Pennsylvania.

Fran arose and asked Percy if there were anything she could help with before going home. Being assured there wasn't, Fran suggested that she, Lark and the children might take their leave, since all were weary from their four-day trip west and Lark had to run the rental truck into Rapid City first thing in the morning. Guests bade one another "Good night," and the Wilsons walked back to their house. The dog walked with them, just two or three steps behind Lark.

"Do you think he is our dog now?" asked Walt as he noticed the animal trailing his father.

"No, he'll go back home," said Lark. "He's just being sociable."

They walked in absolute darkness, save for the moonlight, which outlined the dusty road on which they trod. Longvalley had no street lights, no stop signs, except the one that stood at the entrance to Highway 73, and very few homes were lighted well enough from inside to provide light for walkers at night.

"It sure is dark here," Saul said as they approached their home.

"Yes," said Leigh Ann. "But just look at the stars! I've never seen so many in my whole life."

Fran squeezed Lark's hand. It was good to be entering their new home as a family once more. Lark paused at the door to their home and suggested they have evening devotions in about fifteen minutes, as soon as all were ready for bed. The family agreed.

By ten-thirty, they sat in the living room as Lark opened the Bible to the book they were reading as they crossed the country. He said to them that he felt this was a fitting book to read as they prepared to enter a new country and start a new life. He began reading the chapter for this evening, "'Now faith is the substance of things hoped for, the evidence of things not seen . . .'"

When he completed the chapter, he asked what things any member of the family had learned about faith this day. There was silence. Then Leigh Ann spoke. "Father," she said, "I've learned that faith sometimes means taking a very big risk. Mr. Long Elk taught me that tonight. It got me to thinking about what we're doing here. And I think we've got a lot of faith to come out here, where we don't know anybody or anything. I hope it's going to be a wonderful time for us. But none of us knows for sure. That's where faith comes in."

Fran looked at Lark and smiled. The boys looked at the floor. Fran spoke next. "I learned that no matter how well you are prepared for something, God always has some surprises in it for you. It takes faith to accept them, no matter if they are positive or negative, and to move on."

Saul looked at his mother and said, "I agree with Mom."

Walt spoke up. "Dad, I think you've got a lot of faith. The church you are going to serve has seven members, as far as I can tell. You've got a lot of work to do, for there are more than seven people in this town. You've got a lot of faith, Dad."

Finally, Lark spoke again. "I believe we've just begun to see evidence of things we never saw before in our lives. I believe God has brought us, as a family, to this place and time to learn some new things about faith. Thank you. Let's pray our Lord's prayer."

The family prayed aloud, holding hands and standing in a circle. Then Fran and Lark hugged and kissed the children good night.

Fran took Lark into her arms in the newly darkened living room of their new home after the children were in their beds. "I love you," she whispered. "I love you, too," he responded. They walked arm in arm to their bed room.

"I think I know you," Lark said to the waitress as she stood before him, awaiting his order. The place was dark, except for the table and the two of them. But he was certain he knew her.

"I don't think you do," she said curtly. "I've never met you."

"It's your eyes," he said as he stared at her. "If they were blue, and your hair was blond . . ."

The waitress turned and ran into the darkness. Lark stood up and, within seconds, ran after her, from time to time, catching sight of her in the darkness. She wore blue jeans and a denim shirt. No, it was a skirt and blouse. No, it was a fine red dress. No, it was a ravishing mint dress and hat to match! And she wore sunglasses.

"Jennifer!" he screamed. "Jennifer, come back here!"

"Jennifer," he screamed and sat upright in bed, reaching toward the end of the bed with both hands. "Jennifer, come back here."

"Lark," a startled Fran was awake beside him. "What is it?"

"What?"

"Who were you calling?" Fran asked. "It sounded like you called for Jennifer."

"I must have been dreaming," he said as he noted he was sweating and slightly out of breath. "I was dreaming."

"About what?" Fran inquired. "Or should I ask whom?" There was a hint of concern in her voice.

"Oh, Fran," he confessed. "It's crazy. I dreamed that the waitress we met earlier today was really Jennifer."

"What?" his wife said, astonished. "She was nothing like Jennifer."

"I know," Lark said hesitantly, "and yet, there was something about her."

"What?" Fran asked.

"I can't say," he quietly spoke. "I was uneasy around her. Something about her voice, and her eyes. I don't know."

"Lark," Fran assured, "you're tired. It's been a long trip. We're starting over again. Let's get some sleep. It's just a dream. Besides, how would a woman like her ever live in a place like Kadoka? It's just not possible." She took his hand and asked, "You don't still think of her, do you?"

"Honestly," he said seriously, "I had all but buried her in my mind until this afternoon at that café. There was just something about that waitress."

"So, you've been thinking of her since this afternoon?"

"Yes."

"Well, there you have it," said Fran. "That's why you dreamed of her tonight. I'm sure it won't happen again."

"I hope not, Fran," he said and squeezed her hand as they lay down together once more.

"Fran," Lark said quietly.

"Yes," was her quiet response.

"Thanks for being so patient with me."

"I love you," she assured him once more.

"I love you, too," was his response.

Theirs was an uneasy sleep the rest of the night. Fran was deeply concerned about the tone of her husband's scream. She had heard it before. It sent chills down her spine to hear it anew.

Lark pretended to sleep for nearly three hours after the dream. His mind raced as he asked himself a thousand questions about the possibility of Jennifer's presence just a mere fifty miles north of them. To both of them, Fran's confident conclusion of the impossibility of such a reality was Lark's only recourse short of madness. If it were only his imagination, he surmised, it could be explained by the stress of the trip and the subsequent challenge facing him as a new pastor in a very new world, with a newly reunited family. Maybe, it was only the name of the waitress that triggered this anxiety in him. After all, how far is it from Jennifer to Jenny? But really, rationally, what would Jacqueline Frontierre be doing in Kadoka, waiting tables, when there was money to be made by her in almost any other profession and place in the world? It really was preposterous, he concluded. Just a trick of the mind. Nothing more than that.

Finally, he rolled over toward Fran and grasped her around the waist as she slept. *Thank you God for Fran,* he prayed. Sleep approached him once more. And as sleep was nearly in control, Lark saw her eyes once more. Jenny's eyes were brown. That was it. What was missing were the blue eyes. He breathed deeply. *How could I have overlooked that?* he thought. It couldn't have been Jacqueline. The waitress had brown eyes. He breathed deeply once more and was asleep.

Chapter 9

Iyotan Waaktasni

The crash of thunder rumbled over Kadoka and ran its course eastward across the prairie. Loud, it startled Jenny from sleep. Still early, she nevertheless arose as the early morning storm had its way with the earth. Lightning flashed and booming thunder crashed shortly thereafter, while rain poured in windy sheets, creating pulsating sounds of force upon the roof of the hardware store.

Jenny made her way to the bathroom, relieved herself in the darkened room, illuminated for only split seconds by lightning striking unsuspecting cattle in fields, various hay mounds, bare, dry ground, and listing telephone poles in nearby vicinities.

Jenny stood and reached for the light switch next to the sink and discovered that once more, Kadoka had lost its source of power due to the overwhelming storm now visiting. Her face, hair, and teeth would have to wait. So would a shower. But a cup of coffee could clear the cobwebs from her groggy mind.

She carefully walked into the kitchen area, grabbed the teapot from the gas stove, walked to the sink and filled it with water, then placed the pot back on the stove and turned on the burner. Swoosh, the gas exploded around the bottom of the kettle, just as another crushing blow of thunder echoed throughout the area.

The rain began to let up as Jenny scooped a tablespoon of instant coffee into the cup she had fetched from the cupboard.

By the time she sat in the living room area and glanced out the window, a cup of steaming coffee in hand, the rain had stopped and only echoes of thunder, sounding like distant artillery fire, now assaulted the calm of the early morning hour.

Raindrops ran quickly down the gutters of the building, out across the sidewalk and into the street, where they merged with millions of others and ran swiftly along either side of the main street toward the interstate highway to the south.

Suddenly, a light came on in the bathroom, signaling the recovery of electrical power. Jenny turned on the radio as she walked into the bathroom. The morning disk jockey from a Rapid City station that had become Jenny's favorite was reporting that severe storms had played havoc with much of Western South Dakota overnight, and he predicted that early in the morning, these storms would all make their way to the northeast, and that it would be a very hot day. *Great,* thought Jenny as she straddled the side of the bath tub and turned on the shower water. She turned and looked at her backside in the mirror over the sink. *You still have it, kid,* she said to herself as she admired what she saw.

Stepping into the shower, she relaxed beneath its gently falling stream of warm water. She reached for the soap and lathered her body completely, pausing here and there at sensitive spots of her anatomy, taking pleasure in the feeling which came over her as she did. Rinsing quickly, she stepped over the tub's side, grabbed a towel and dried off quickly, viewing herself full frontally as she raised the towel over her head and pulled it down behind her back. *Those look great still,* she said to herself as she admired her taut breasts. Her eyes fell and she whistled as she looked at her midsection and pelvis surrounding her bushy triangle. *If I don't stop this,* she reminded herself, *I'll forget who I am.*

But the truth was, such moments helped her retain a degree of sanity in the charade that had become her life. She could not help but wonder what or who she might have become had she ever really been free to just be herself. Most of her life a game, Jenny now played the most dangerous game of all. Survival. And, in light of the events of the past forty-eight hours, her success in this game was now questionable.

As she dressed, she debated whether to call the number and seek an escape route. It would be so easy, she had been told. Just let them know. A new place and a new identity would be created in a matter of hours.

Who will I be next time? she wondered as she pulled on her jeans after wrapping her legs with that ridiculous cotton that made them look twice their actual size. *What kind of stupid role will I have to play in the next town?*

Then, the question that seemed to come to mind every time she had ever faced a crisis in her life arose. *What difference will it make?* She was still a young woman. There were times she wanted desperately to just be an average woman, with a husband and two kids to care for as she grew older. Why couldn't her protectors arrange that kind of hiding place for her she asked herself over and over.

It didn't seem to matter in her life for whom she worked. No change ever brought her closer to what she thought of as normalcy. How she envied Fran the day before as she served her, Lark, and their children. How she envied most of the women of this town. Pain-filled though they might be, at least they lost in the game of love in a real world. Not an illusory one, the likes of which Jenny never seemed to escape from since childbirth. God, how she longed for just one good chance at it. No pretension. No role. Just everyday, plain, old normalcy. Yes, that would be nice. And it definitely would be a change unlike any Jenny had ever known.

"If you ever suspect that anyone is on to you, you call this number right away," he handed her a card as he spoke. *"Anytime. You understand?"*

"I think so," she said hesitantly.

"Jacqueline," he continued, *"you've been a big help to us. We won't let anything happen to you if we can help it. But you've got to be careful for a while. Don't do anything foolish."*

The agent had smiled after he said those final words to her four years before. *All I have to do is call*, she said to herself. She walked to the phone in the living area and picked up the receiver. There, taped to the base beneath, scribbled in her own nervous hand, was one of many notes she left herself in various places. She carried the number with her at all times. She had a note in every handbag. She had a note in every room of the apartment. She even had placed one, when Steve was not looking, under the glass on the counter at the café. A simple number. The number was clearly visible everywhere. She had glanced at it innumerable times during her sojourn in Kadoka. She was sure she had memorized it by this time. All she had to do was dial. They would take care of the rest. She'd be safe. Once more.

She replaced the receiver. Fixed herself another cup of coffee. Drank it. Then walked to the café to help Steve open it for another day. The sun was nearly fully over the eastern horizon as Jenny stepped into the café.

"You're late," Steve said as she walked into the kitchen. "I started the coffee for us."

"Yeah," she said, "it smells great!" And it did.

"At least you look better than you did last night, Jenny," Steve said as he peeled potatoes in anticipation of the usual early morning run on hash browns and country-fried potatoes.

"I slept well until the storm," she lied.

"Wasn't that something," Steve exclaimed. "I heard on the radio that some poor rancher lost thirty head to a lightning strike."

"Oh God," she drawled, "that's awful."

"It rained over an inch here this morning," Steve went on about the weather. "We need it, God knows. But does it always have to come all at once?"

"Don't see how we can do much about it, anyway," Jenny rejoined. "'Gotta take it as it comes,' my momma always said." A sad vision of her mother's last words raced across the back of her mind as she said this.

"That's a good philosophy, I guess," agreed Steve. "It keeps a man from worrying too much about things he can't control."

"You got that right," Jenny concluded. "Now I best get the dining area lighted and ready for our breakfast crowd."

"Before you do," Steve asked her, "do you mind if I ask you a question, Jenny?"

"Not at all," Jenny replied. "Shoot."

"Well, I couldn't help but notice that you told that young man yesterday, who came in here with his family toward the end of the afternoon, that you were from Oklahoma."

"Yeah," she said, suddenly realizing where Steve was headed in his questioning.

"Well, I thought you were from Texas, that's all," Steve said as he glanced in her direction. "I guess I'm curious why you lied to him, Jenny."

"I didn't like his nosing in my business, Steve," she lied. "Whenever I feel a man is asking me questions I don't want to answer, I give him a bum steer."

"Hah!" Steve laughed. "That's a good one! I thought he was pushing you pretty hard there with personal stuff. I didn't know you had it in you, girl!"

Lucky for Jenny, Steve didn't know about which man she spoke. She walked into the dining area, glanced quickly at the number beneath the counter glass, then got ready to smile at the first boorish cowboy who entered for breakfast.

The morning passed, as did most, with nary an unsettling moment, and not one surprise. Jenny relaxed as she waited on the usual motley group of cowboys, ranchers, and townsfolk who came in almost every morning for breakfast. Even the card game was uneventful. No one got angry. The men seemed to have a good time with one another. Every one of them stayed for it. They had the place to themselves. No women, except Jenny. They didn't count her as one, anyway.

"You ever been in love?" Sic 'Em asked Oh Yeah.

"Oh yeah," was the response.

"That must have been a mighty interesting relationship," Mel chimed in on the talk.

"Oh yeah," Oh Yeah repeated himself.

"I heard that when she was through with you, she hightailed it to Denver," Bill added.

"Oh yeah," guess who said.

"Look, boys," Scooter jumped in to protect his stool buddy, "leave my partner alone. None of you guys has had any better luck being in love than he."

"Oh yeah," ended that conversation.

By eleven-thirty Jenny, and Steve had the place to themselves once more as they got ready for the seniors to come for lunch. Steve needed some fuses, for two had blown during the breakfast crowd's visit.

"Why don't you run over to the hardware store and see if they still have any of these?" Steve said to her as he handed her what looked like a small stick of dynamite.

"Okay," she said, and she quickly walked to the hardware store.

"Hi," shouted Dolores as she stood up behind the counter. Dolores and Jenny had been friends almost from the day Jenny arrived in Kadoka. In fact, Dolores was the one who showed Jenny her new home, the apartment above the store. "How's it going?" she asked Jenny.

"Great," Jenny said, and she meant it. It was always good to talk with this particular Native American woman. She liked her and often wished she had gotten to know her better.

"What's Steve need now?" Dolores asked.

"We blew some fuses this morning," Jenny said as she handed Dolores a burned fuse.

"One of these days, that place is going to burn down if Steve doesn't bring the wiring up to code," Dolores chirped. "I don't know of anybody in this town who still uses these kinds of fuses. Doesn't he know they're just not capable of handling as much electricity as we use these days?"

"I don't know, I only work there," Jenny smiled. Both women laughed, no doubt, at each one's understanding of the stubbornness of men.

"Well, I'll go into the back room and see if we still have any of these dinosaurs," Dolores quipped. "You can come back with me, Jenny. It might take a bit."

The two women walked into the cavernous back room, where just about everything was stored, Jenny imagined, since the founding of Kadoka. Odds and ends of machinery, pieces of lawn mowers and cultivators, chains and cogs, and boxes, row after row of boxes, with hand-lettered notes as to what each contained.

Dolores spied the box she was looking for halfway down the right aisle and up four shelves on the wall. "Fuses," was all it read.

"Grab me that stepladder over there, will you, Jenny?" Dolores asked as she paused before the shelves. "I think they might be up there," she pointed to the box.

She quickly climbed the ladder, retrieved the box, glanced into it, and turned toward Jenny. "How many does he want?" she asked.

"A couple," was all Jenny remembered.

"Now, ain't that like a man," Dolores grunted. "A couple!"

After getting two fuses and returning the box to its storage space, Dolores clambered down the ladder and the two women walked back toward the storefront.

"We met our new preacher last night," Dolores said quietly as they walked into the store again. "He seems like a nice man."

"What's his name?" Jenny asked as her heart began to race.

"Lark Wilson," Dolores confirmed Jenny's biggest fear. "He has a real nice wife and family. His wife used to be a schoolteacher out East. Their kids are Angus and my kids' ages."

"I see," Jenny said in a hushed tone. "Where did they come from exactly?"

"Lancaster," Dolores said. "It's some town in Pennsylvania."

"I wonder how they'll do in a place like Longvalley," Jenny said reflectively.

"That's what Angus and I talked about last night after we went home from Ethan and Percy's place. This has got to be a whole different world for those people."

"Yes," Jenny said thoughtfully.

"Do you go to church?" Dolores changed the subject slightly.

"No," Jenny said. "I guess folk like me and the church don't get along."

"I see," Dolores said as she looked Jenny straight in the eye. "You mean, because you are a . . ." she paused as she asked, "what do they call it, lesbian?"

"Yes," Jenny said. "The church has always had hard things to say about people like us. I try to stay out of harm's way with this as much as I can. After all, I guess you know, none of us volunteer for this assignment."

"Well, I think you'd be welcome in our church if you ever wanted to come," said Dolores seriously. "We don't have that many members. And believe me, in our time, we've all had to deal with what other people think of us. And we didn't volunteer to be born Indian, either."

The women smiled at one another.

"Thank you," Jenny said. She saw Dolores as being one of the kindest yet simplest persons she ever knew. She respected Dolores immensely.

"Have you always been a lesbian?" Dolores asked.

"Yes," Jenny lied. "I just didn't always know that I am."

"So," Dolores hesitated, "you have known men."

"Yes," Jenny confessed truthfully. "Although I've yet to meet a man I couldn't live without!"

They both laughed. Dolores seemed genuinely interested in getting to know her. Jenny really liked this about Dolores.

"Well," Dolores said, "that will be a dollar for the two fuses. And you tell your boss that we only have three left. He better get that place rewired."

"Right," Jenny said as she grabbed the fuses, "Steve will be over this afternoon to pay you."

"No problem," Dolores said. "See you later."

"No doubt," Jenny smiled, and walked quickly back to the café.

"Steve," she said as she walked into the kitchen, "Dolores said . . ."

"I know," Steve interrupted, "she said I should get this place up to code.

What she doesn't understand is that I don't have the money to do it, or I would."

"They've only got three of those kind of fuses left at the store," Jenny informed her boss. "I get the impression that they may be hard to get from now on."

"Yes," Steve said, "I know. I'll look for them in Rapid City next time I'm there. I'll try to stock up on them."

Just then, the door to the café opened and in walked the first seniors for lunch. Jenny walked into the dining area, welcomed them, and waited upon them, as well as the others who arrived shortly thereafter. The luncheon crowd, like the breakfast group, was the usual cast of characters. Just a little more picky about what each wanted and how it ought to be prepared.

By one fifteen, all was quiet in the café once more. Jenny helped Steve wrap it up and both were out of the café by three. They walked across the way to the hardware store. Steve entered the store and Jenny went to her apartment.

As Jenny ascended the stairs, she heard her telephone ringing. She raced to the door, unlocked it, and ran to the phone.

"Hello," she said, gasping for air.

"Is that you, Jenny?" a vaguely familiar voice said at the other end. "What's wrong? You sound short-winded."

"Who is this?" she asked.

"A friend," the voice said. She thought she recognized him. It was the voice of the agent who last talked with her. Having rehearsed his last words to her many times, she recognized the accent. "I'm calling to see how you are doing."

"I didn't know you did this," she said.

"Yes," he went on. "It is part of the protocol that we check in every once in a while to see how our clients are doing."

The word *clients* bothered her for an instant, but she pushed it out of her mind as she waited for him to speak again.

"Well," he insisted, "how are you doing?"

"I'm doing as well as I can," she said cautiously. There was a long pause on the other end of the line. Then Jenny continued, "Actually, I've had some nervous moments lately."

"What kind?" the voice asked.

"In the past couple of days, there have been some," she hesitated, "developments. I almost called you this morning." Again, a lengthy pause at the other end.

"I see," the voice said quietly. "Why didn't you?"

Jenny really didn't know the answer to this question. She stalled for time.

"Nothing that important," she lied, "I'm just nervous lately."

"What's making you nervous, Jenny?"

"Oh," she paused, "nothing I can't handle."

"Is that so?" The man at the other end of the line wanted more than she was offering.

Why hasn't he scolded me for not calling? she asked herself as silence fell between the two of them. Then she pushed the question out of her mind.

"Is your cover working?" he asked her.

"Yes," she said.

"And you haven't done anything foolish that might break it?" Jenny relaxed when she heard the question for it was exactly what he had warned her originally never to do.

"No," she lied.

"Well, then," he pressed on, "what's worrying you?"

Jenny knew he wasn't going to hang up without learning why she had almost called the number given her to use in case of emergencies. She knew she would have to tell him something. Her mind raced as she struggled to concoct some story that would satisfy his whetted curiosity. It came to her. She would talk about the conversation with Mr. Davenport, the undertaker.

"There's this undertaker in town," she began. As she told the agent of the conversation between her and the undertaker, she sensed the man at the other end was taking notes, for she could hear paper being shuffled.

"And what is the undertaker's name?" he asked her.

She gave the name and then elaborated as she told how Mr. Davenport's questioning her sexual identity made her nervous. She explained that everybody else in town was still buying the act. She omitted any mention of the conversation she had with Dolores earlier in the day. She didn't get close to talking about Mark, nor the fact that one of her *clients* from four years before had just moved to within fifty miles of Kadoka, nor that this *client* and his family had visited the café, nor that this *client* thought she reminded him of someone. *Why don't I tell him about Lark?* she asked herself that question as she talked about Mr. Davenport. Something sealed her lips on this subject. She wished she knew what it might be.

"Well, Jenny," the voice said, "that doesn't sound too serious."

"I guess it doesn't," she agreed, but wondered to herself *Why?*

"You take good care," the voice said. "We'll be talking with you."

And the phone line was dead.

Strange, Jenny reflected as she poured herself a glass of cool water from the refrigerator. *He didn't remind me to call if I needed anything. He didn't even ask me if I remembered the number to call.* She drank all of the water for her mouth was suddenly very dry. For a moment, Jenny Craig, lesbian waitress at the Kadoka café, panicked. Her heart beat rapidly. Sweat broke at her temples and beneath her armpits. *What if this wasn't the agent*, she pondered? Her heart beat even more rapidly.

Jenny had to get a grip on herself. These past few days, her sense of security was assaulted in various ways. *Was there something I was not paying attention to as each surprise came my way?* She couldn't think of any. *Is there someone I can talk with besides the government agent?* Only Lark came to mind.

But how will he accept what I have to tell him? she wondered. *And would it be fair to involve him again in the mess she had made of her life?* Lark seemed happy. Dolores liked him. Their church leaders accepted him. He and Fran were together. *Why involve him?*

The truth simply was that Jacqueline felt terribly guilty for what she had done to this preacher and his young family four years earlier. She had never forgiven herself for the role she played in nearly destroying him, his family, and the church he served in Lancaster. *If I can apologize to him, he will forgive me*, she had said to herself over and over again since that fateful night at her apartment. Something deep within her, something decent which she had all but forgotten, longed for that forgiveness.

Jacqueline's life was one long deception. She had used many persons, men and women alike, to get whatever she wanted. She herself had been used by others to get what they wanted. It was the way of the world, she believed.

Then, on assignment in Lancaster, an assignment, like many others in that time of her life, aimed at knocking a person off balance just enough that anti-war efforts would be weakened in this country, she met one man who seemed to be genuinely committed to serving God. She knew that if she carried out her assignment he would be hurt. Being a professional, she did her job. She staked him out. She manipulated him with her beauty and charm. She drugged him in her apartment. And by doing so, her handlers could convince him and leaders of his congregation, with the help of phony photographs, that he had broken his marriage vows and despoiled his ministry.

It was all so easy. She had done it with others. Politicians, like the congressman she manipulated onto the boat dock so secret cameras could catch her sitting amorously upon his lap. Tabloid newspapers ran a story purporting to reveal his hypocrisy. Civic leaders, like the mayor with whom she pretended to indulge in pot smoking and illicit sex. The cameras behind the mirrors rolled and next day revealed, on television, the dalliance of a popular leader. Religious leaders, like the bishop of one of the most important archdioceses in America, were caught by the camera in less than liturgical embraces with an unknown brunette outside a run-down motel.

It had all been so easy. The money flowed with each act. She was a different person every time: Jocelyn, the newspaper reporter with almost-white blond hair and glasses; Fredericka, the scientist with cold black hair; Amanda, the swimmer with red hair. Character after character, she played it. Unlike her earlier profession in New Orleans, she really didn't need to bed these men in order to be well kept. She just manipulated them to a place in their relationship where her handlers could then convince them it would be best they leave the scene for a while since the "truth" about their behavior was about to be revealed to the world. Jacqueline was more than well paid for her entrapments of known opponents to the Vietnam War. And the "truth" was generally leaked to the media despite the actions of the entrapped for it was always good public relations to show how weak those who opposed the war really were.

It had all been so easy, until she met Lark Wilson. She was Jennifer, the strawberry-blonde with blue eyes, who was coming to Lancaster to be a guest lecturer at Franklin and Marshall College. It was so easy. But halfway through their brief encounter, she nearly walked away from the scene entirely. She was in too deeply. She knew that they would find her. She knew that they would force her to continue. She was afraid. So she did her job one more time. And then disappeared.

When she got off the Broadway Limited at Grand Central Station, Jacqueline hurried to her apartment on the upper east side of the city. The doorman greeted her with a smile as she exited the cab. She rode the elevator to the fifteenth floor and got out at the penthouse she called home.

The usual manila envelope lay on the table just inside her doorway. She opened it. Twenty thousand dollars drawn in a bank cashier's check was folded inside a simple piece of white stationery.

"Thanks," it read, "for a mission successfully completed for our country."

It was signed "Richard M. Nixon." Jacqueline always suspected this was a pseudonym. She chuckled as she handled the check. *If my momma could see me now*, she laughed aloud.

She hurriedly undressed, jumped into the shower, running

the water for ever so long so as to get all of the dirt from her body. She then jumped into bed and slept fitfully until the next afternoon.

It was when she awoke that she knew this kind of life couldn't continue. Her heart raced as she hailed a cab downtown and found herself almost hypnotically walking into a federal building just off Second Avenue.

The board said FBI offices were on the twelfth floor. She rode the elevator aloft and wondered to herself how she would ask for help and whether anyone would believe her.

The agent assigned was a man named Morris. He listened as Jacqueline told her story. He jotted some notes, excused himself, and later returned with another agent named Sally. She asked Jacqueline to retell her experience.

As fate would have it, Jacqueline had walked into the one office of the FBI in America that was presently investigating connections between the Mafia and the pro-Vietnam war forces in the nation. The two agents nodded to one another as Jacqueline told how she was first approached by whomever she worked for in a brothel in New Orleans. She related how many persons she had trapped in various ways over the previous two years. She told them how deeply affected she was by recent assignments that led to religious leaders being disgraced. And she finished with her concern for the most recent case, the one in Lancaster, just ended two days before her appearance in their office.

Soon, four agents were in the little room, listening and talking. She could sense their excitement as they spoke with one another about persons she truly did not know. She sensed that the FBI had actually staked out reconnaissance posts throughout Manhattan and tapped phone lines, recording conversations between known criminal leaders as they talked about "Operation Screw Up." The FBI knew something big was happening. But until Jacqueline walked into their office that afternoon, they had never spoken with anyone who actually was working on the inside of the operation.

They convinced her she could quit once and for all if she helped them with one more case. This time, the trappers would be trapped, they assured her. She would be a hero, they told her. She could make amends for all of those whose lives she had ruined, they encouraged her. And she agreed. One more time. She might not even have to really do anything. Just wait until contacted, and then act as though she were following through. She was to reveal her target to the FBI. They would contact the targeted person and make it look as though, for the benefit of anyone who watched her movements, she was successful one more time.

It worked. The FBI picked up the persons along the line in the community to which she had been assigned. They picked up the courier in New York City. They tapped her telephone line and followed leads. They ran fingerprint checks on documents she received at her apartment Within a matter of two weeks, the ring was broken and its leaders were charged with extortion. Jacqueline was charged, along with the rest, for conspiracy to commit extortion. She was convicted, as were they, and sentenced to prison for fifteen years. Jacqueline didn't last long in prison, however. Two weeks after getting there, she contracted pneumonia and died in a local hospital.

All in all, fifteen persons were condemned and sentenced to various times in federal prison. Jacqueline, who, as far as the world was concerned, was dead, soon became Jenny and rode the bus to Kadoka, South Dakota. Condemned to always be looking over her shoulder, Jenny Craig was created to hopefully live the rest of her life far removed from those who used her previously to bring down others who opposed the Vietnam War.

The same Jenny Craig now sat fidgeting in her living room area above the hardware store. Something deep within her urged her to call the number given her four years before in order to be assured that the earlier call actually came from the FBI. She walked to the phone, picked up the receiver, and dialed the number.

"Hello," said a strange voice at the other end after four rings.

"This is Jenny Craig," Jacqueline said.

"Wait a moment, please," the voice at the other end said.

Jacqueline waited for what seemed like an eternity. Was she being foolish? Would they think she was coming apart? Her legs jumped up and down beneath her as she waited.

"Hello," a more familiar voice interrupted her anxiety. "Is that you, Jenny?"

"Yes," she said. She waited for him to ask her why she was calling him on the same day he had called her. He didn't.

"What's wrong?" he asked.

"Did you call me earlier today?" she blurted out.

"No," was all he said, and her heart sank.

"Oh God," she gasped. Someone was on to her.

"What do you mean did I call you earlier?" the agent asked her. "Did you get a call from someone pretending to be from the agency?"

"Yes," she began to sob. "I thought it was you."

"Listen, Jenny," he said confidently, "you've got to try to remember every word that was spoken between you and whoever it was that called you earlier."

Silence.

"Jenny," he repeated, "you've got to tell me what was said. We need to know."

Jacqueline did her best with what she recalled of the conversation. All the while, her teeth chattered and her body began to shake. If someone knew who she was and where she was, she could be in significant danger. When she finished, the agent was silent for a moment.

"Listen," he said, "is there something you are not telling me?"

"About what?"

"Anything. Anything at all you might be leaving out."

"I don't think so."

"We've got to get you out of there," he said with a sense of emergency to his voice. "We can't take chances with your life or with our continuing operation," he said.

"What should I do?" she asked seriously.

"Go about your business as usual," he said. "I'll be back in touch with you early tomorrow morning. Chances are, we not only might have to move you, but have to establish an entirely different identity for you," he concluded. "I'll call you at six tomorrow morning. Your time." He hung up.

Jacqueline was stunned. How could anyone have known where she was and who she was pretending to be? Had the young Methodist minister indiscreetly disclosed her real identity? Had his church leaders known all along she wasn't who she was pretending to be? Had the undertaker in Kadoka called some of his buddies across the country and talked about her in ways that eventually dropped into the lap of her former employers? Had all of this somehow come together to conspire to reveal her whereabouts to people who obviously had a score to settle with her for her assistance to the FBI?

She began to cry as she sat alone in her living room, looking out the window. Her body convulsed with emotions long stored deep within her psyche. *Is there no one with whom I can talk,* she wondered as teardrops fell across her face and down onto her shirt.

Regaining her composure, she got up and washed her face, straightened her hair, and pinched her cheeks to replace the ruddiness to which she had become accustomed.

Jenny walked outside into the brilliant sunlight of late afternoon South Dakota in summer and hurried across to the café. When she entered the café, Steve was talking with someone in the kitchen. She didn't introduce herself, but went straight to getting the dining area ready for the evening patrons.

"Jenny," Steve yelled as he stuck his head through the counter opening. "Come back here. I want you to meet my new dishwasher."

Jenny walked into the kitchen to see Steve standing there with a squat little man with a big belly and big arms, who she guessed was about fifty years old.

"This is Max," Steve said as the man stepped forward to shake her trembling hand.

"Hello," she said as she nervously reached for his hand and shook it. "I'm Jenny Craig."

"I'm Max," he said with a foreign accent.

"What brings you to Kadoka?" Jenny was curious, for this man looked as out of place as she.

"Bad luck with the ponies," he said gruffly. "I have had four years of bad luck with them hay burners."

Steve laughed. He had been trying to entice several teenagers to do the dishes in the evenings at the café so he could go home earlier. But until this man showed up, Steve had found no takers.

"I think you'll like Max," Steve said sincerely. "He'll give me a break this summer and he might even find the time to help you so you can go home earlier in the evenings, Jenny."

"That would be nice," she lied as she eyed Max for any sign of danger that she might detect.

"Where you from originally?" Jenny asked the newest person on Steve's payroll.

"All around," Max said, a little softer than when he first spoke. "I'm a horse trainer. Thoroughbreds, mostly. My trouble is that I didn't stop at training them. I bet on them, like all the trainers do. Only thing is, I bet way too much. I'm into hock in every track east of the Mississippi."

"Well, I wouldn't know much about that," she lied again, trying to ascertain if Max were buying her act any more than she was his. "I always rode horses back home," she said with a drawl, "never bet on them."

Steve shot her a knowing glance, as if to ask why she were not mentioning her trip to Rapid City and her disappointment with the track and caliber of horses. But he said nothing. He stepped back from his two employees and listened as they introduced themselves to one another.

"Well, you're lucky there, girlie," Max went on with his story. "Gambling has been my downfall in life. It has ruined three marriages and has left me running from revenue men and bill collectors all over America."

Steve laughed. "He's pulling your leg, Jenny." He held up an application form on which Max had written his need for such a job as this.

"He is?" She wasn't sure he wasn't telling the truth about running from the law. There was something about Max she didn't trust. Where did he come from, really? Where is he living? Why did he stare at her so intently when she entered the kitchen?

The two men laughed. Jenny smiled.

"Max is going to be here about a month, Jenny," Steve confided. "He's not as delinquent on his responsibilities as he says. He's really a writer whose doing some stories about small-town race tracks across America."

"Yes," Max said with a grin, "I might even have a novel in me."

The tension between them relaxed as Jenny eyed him and his face broke into a smile, along with Steve's. The two men were proud of themselves. That was obvious to Jenny.

The fact that Steve was a fairly naïve person had already been established. Like most people in these parts, Steve took everyone at face value. He never seemed to question. He was one of those persons who accepted another right out. Then he would listen intently, as if to make sure his initial trust of his own instincts about others were not transgressed in any way.

"All right," she said. "I think you'll get along just fine with some of our cowpokes around here."

"That would be nice," Max now said with an affected drawl of his own. "I like cowboys." He winked at Jenny.

Steve had undoubtedly already informed Max that she was not a woman who liked men. Max was, in his own way, trying to identify with what was probably an on-going joke about town since her first day in Kadoka.

"Be careful," was her only advice to the dishwasher. She turned and walked back into the dining area while Steve and Max jabbered like long-lost friends in the kitchen. She intended to take that advice also.

The evening held its own excitement for the newly formed crew of the Kadoka Café. Halfway through preparation of three hamburgers, three orders of fries, two malts, and one chocolate soda, ordered by three hefty teens who wandered into the café around six, a huge lightning strike and accompanying roll of thunder attacked Main Street without warning. Every light in the café went out. The kitchen's electrical receptacles sizzled for seconds following the jolt from the skies. Both Steve and Max screamed simultaneously with the flash and clap, which seemed to happen at the same time. Jenny ran into the kitchen to witness the two grown men cowering near the stove.

"What the hell was that?" Max asked, still bent down like a soldier hiding in a foxhole.

"I bet we lost every electrical appliance in the place," Steve whispered before Jenny could affirm that she thought the building might have been struck by lightning.

"Damnedest thing I ever heard of," Max swore as he straightened his body to a more manly pose.

"I'll go outside and check our building," Steve said as he walked toward the doorway to the alley behind the café.

"I'm going with you," Max announced as he followed Steve into the alley way.

Jenny walked back into the café dining area. The teens showed no signs of changing their conversations, which basically had been a contest of who each thought was the hottest girl in their senior class.

"Your meal will be delayed while we check out our building," Jenny told them.

"No problem," one of them replied and then rejoined the others in their competitive conversation.

In a few minutes, both Steve and Max walked into the front door of the café and strolled over the counter, where Jenny awaited the meal for the teens.

"Everything looks fine," Steve said with a smile. "All the lights in town are out, as far as I can tell. So I guess we'll serve these guys colas instead of what they ordered."

"I'll tell them," Jenny said as she walked around the counter toward the booth, where the teens, still engrossed in their perceptual comparisons regarding their female classmates, did not yet note that something might have changed their meal plans.

"Boys," Jenny interrupted them, "we've lost our power. So Steve asked me to tell you we can't make malts or sodas. You'll have to settle for colas tonight."

They sat and stared at her for a few seconds. Then the one with the most acne said, "Whatever. We've had to settle for a lot less in this town."

Jenny walked back to the counter. She couldn't have agreed with them more!

Steve pushed the three plates through the counter opening within minutes. As he did, he told Jenny to put the "Closed" sign in the doorway. "No use kidding ourselves about when the power might come back on," he said.

After serving the teens, Jenny went to the door and turned the sign around to read "Closed." Within five minutes, the teens were through. Each threw his money on the counter and then walked as fast as he could out the door. Jenny cursed them under her breath as she cleared a tipless table, then carried the messy plates and glasses into the fast-darkening kitchen.

"I don't think you'll be able to see to do these dishes," she said as she placed them by the sink.

"Baby," Max confided, "I grew up in New York City. I learned how to do a lot of things in the dark."

Steve chuckled to himself, then glanced at Jenny as if to say *He's not as bad as his bark.*

Jenny looked at Max disdainfully and said, "Yeah. Well, did you learn how to make water hot by rubbing your hands together?"

"Oh, oh," Max laughed. "You got me there, girlie. I think we'll get along just fine. You can take and you can give. I like that."

"Look," Jenny started to say, "I'm not your 'baby' and I'm not your 'girlie' or any other damned appellation you might care to give me while you work here. My name is Jenny. Just Jenny."

"Appalachian?" Max was puzzled. "I thought they were mountains in West Virginia."

Steve began to laugh out loud as he listened to these two spar their way toward closing time. When he gathered himself, he said to Max, "You didn't know our Jenny here is educated, did you?"

"Naw," Max grunted. "I sure as hell never suspected that."

Jenny stepped toward Max with something of vengeance in her eyes.

"What are you trying to say?"

"Nothin'," Max, suddenly aware he had offended her in some way, replied.

"I think you are trying to say that because I'm lesbian, I'm stupid."

"No," Max stammered as he looked into her eyes, "I meant nothing of the kind. I'm sorry. I was just having fun with you. I guess I should get to know you all better."

"Good idea," Jenny concluded. "See you two tomorrow." She stomped out of the café and across the street toward her apartment, pleased with herself that she had gained the offensive with the newcomer to Kadoka.

She settled into her favorite chair. Staring blankly out the window onto a fast darkening main street, she thought of Lark Wilson. She owed him an apology. She'd soon be leaving Kadoka. Perhaps, she would take Dolores up on her offer to attend church at Longvalley. Yes, that was it. On her last Sunday in this territory, she would finally tell Lark and his wife she was sorry for the pain she had caused them. It was the least she could do.

After settling this in her mind, Jacqueline felt at peace within herself for the first time in many years. She got up, brushed her teeth, and fell upon her bed and into a deep sleep.

Chapter 10

Anpetuwakan Hanhanna

The phone's ringing interrupted the preacher's thoughts as he nibbled on toast and sipped some coffee while scanning his sermon for the day.

"Hello, Mark Whitney here," he said as he wiped his face with a paper napkin.

"Hello, Peppy," the voice on the other end struggled to say between short rasping breaths.

"Hey, Uncle," Mark said, "how are you?"

"Fine," the older male voice at the other end of the call said, "for an old, fat man."

Mark could see his uncle sitting in the bathrobe he always seemed to wear when at home somewhere in his palatial apartment. He pictured the older man in his mind: unshaven, stooped, and rather unimpassioned. *How misleading*, thought Mark.

"To what do I owe the pleasure of this call on a Sunday morning?"

"I just needed to talk to you, Peppy." This was the nickname Mark's father gave him when he was about three years old. Everyone in the family called Mark "Peppy."

"I see," Mark hesitated, for this was most unusual.

"Do you remember our family reunion at Donatello's in Hoboken?"

"Yes," Mark said, wondering to himself where this

135

conversation with his father's brother was headed and why he wouldn't remember something which took place only five weeks before while worrying about whether he would have time to finish this conversation before needing to be in church next door. "I apologize for my behavior, Uncle Joe."

"No need to apologize," the old man wheezed as he spoke. The word in the family was that Mark's uncle was suffering from emphysema. But Mark's uncle never talked about his breathing difficulties.

"Thank you."

"You were fairly sloshed, Peppy," the old man said. "But I want you to know that you helped us a great deal."

"What?" Mark said, with some curiosity creeping into his consciousness. "I was in an awful state. I'm glad there were no Methodists within twenty miles of us."

"No need to apologize, Peppy," the old man assured him between gasps for air. "You helped us locate an old friend."

A cold shiver moved down Mark's spine when he heard his uncle say the word "friend."

"You remember," the old man continued, "telling your cousin about that waitress you were . . . ," his uncle struggled for air in order to continue. "That young woman you were sweet on in South Dakota?"

Mark was now more cautiously participating in this conversation. He had no idea exactly what his uncle was getting at, but he did know that Jenny was not who she pretended to be. Maybe she didn't want to be found. Maybe she was hiding from members of his very own family.

"You there?" The old man asked when Mark did not respond to his question.

"Yes," Mark said. "I'm here."

"Let's see," the old man said, moving the conversation in another direction, "what is it you call yourself?"

"Pastor," Mark said.

"No," the old man breathed more heavily, "I mean your name."

"Oh," Mark said. "Mark. Mark Whitney."

"Um," his uncle said. "I like that. You made a nickname out of your Christened name. But where'd you get the 'Whitney?'"

Mark smiled.

"Come on," the old man said, "you can tell your Uncle Giuseppe."

"Well," Mark said now with a grin, "do you remember your favorite baseball team?"

"The Yankees?" the old man gasped, "Yeah. What about them?"

"And do you remember what you used to say about the Yankees?"

Silence invaded the conversation between them save the sound of obvious attempts to breathe on the part of the dying man.

"You used to say 'The Yankees were nothin' without Mickey 'n Whitey.'"

"Yeah," the old man rejoined the conversation, "what about it?"

"I just added the 'n' to Whitey."

It was a lie, of course. But Mark suspected his uncle would appreciate the story. The ruse got him through college and seminary. It enabled him to be a person in the world he never could have been had he stayed in New Jersey after his father's unexpected arrest. Mark had even embellished his identity to the point where he could talk with others about a Kentucky family that existed only in his mind.

"I'll be damned," Mark's uncle exclaimed, breaking Mark's train of thought at the moment. "That's a good one."

"Uncle Giuseppe," Mark asked, "how did I help you?"

"Well," the old man seemed to hesitate, "we'd been looking for an old friend we owed some compensation for doing a job down in Pennsylvania. She'd disappeared for some reason. I don't know. We couldn't locate her. At one point we thought she had died."

"And," Mark asked, "how did I help you, exactly?"

"You told your cousin about the tattoo on your girl friend's hip," his uncle confided.

Mark shivered again when he heard the inflection of voice when his uncle said "friend."

"Well," Mark said, trying again to distract his uncle, "I'm not seeing her anymore. My bishop got wind of our relationship somehow and assigned me here to Devils Lake. I'm not even sure she still lives in South Dakota. She said something about leaving last time I talked to her." It was a mixture of truth and falsehood.

"I see," his uncle said quietly. "Nevertheless, Peppy, I want to do something for you as a way to say 'thank you.'"

"You made contact with her then?" Mark asked him.

"Sure," his uncle embellished the truth.

"I see," Mark relaxed.

"Anyway," his uncle continued, "we want to thank you by sending you a new car."

"What!"

"A new car," the old man gasped. "You just tell me what you want and we'll have it sent to you in a week."

"No," Mark said. "I don't want anything from you."

"Now," the old man said with just a tinge of pity in his voice, "remember, my boy, that all any of us has in this world is family. Everything else is a lie."

"I don't have family," Mark said angrily.

"Peppy," the old man said gently. "You know we're all sorry your papa got nabbed by the feds. You just can't trust the feds, you know."

"There are a lot of people in this world you can't trust," Mark snorted.

"I can appreciate your disappointment about your papa," his father's brother said. "There's not a time I go to church that I don't light a candle for my dear innocent brother."

"Sorry, Uncle Giuseppe," Mark stopped him from talking. "I've got to get to church."

"Just tell your Uncle Joe what kind of car you like," the old man begged.

"Look," Mark said as the fear he was feeling might have been revealed in his voice, "I'm a pastor in a little town in North Dakota. Everybody knows the money I make. I can't just suddenly go driving around this area in a new car."

"I see," said his uncle. "I can see that might be a problem."

"Thanks, Uncle Giuseppe," Mark said hurriedly. "I have to hang up now."

"Goodbye, Peppy," his uncle said sincerely, "God bless you."

"Thank you," Mark said. He placed the receiver in the cradle and rushed out of the parsonage and trotted across the street toward the Methodist Church. The bell that signaled the start of worship began to ring as he entered the church building and rushed to his study to put on his robe and stole.

The undertaker was just finishing the sports section of the Sunday edition of the Rapid City Journal when the phone rang. Assuming it was a loved one calling to tell him that a family member had just passed away, Davenport cleared his throat and assumed his most compassionate voice as he lifted the receiver.

"Davenport Funeral Service," he said. "How may I help you?"

"I need to tell you that your cover may have been blown," the voice said from the other end as fear raced down the undertaker's spine at this word.

"What?"

"We have word that an operative may be in Kadoka. We can only assume that, if this is true, you are in danger of being discovered."

"I see," the undertaker said, trying to regain his composure. Never in his wildest imagination did he dream he would ever be found. The plastic surgery, the training in caring for dead bodies, the financial support from the family, all had enabled him to hide in Kadoka for over twenty years.

"Lewis," the voice interrupted his reverie, "where's Muriel?"

"How the hell do I know?" Lewis Davenport answered with a snarl. "She's probably out banging some tennis pro in Las Vegas."

"Can't blame her," the voice went on, "seeing as how you gave up being a man a long time ago and all."

"What the hell has this got to do with why you called me?"

"I'm sorry, brother," the voice continued softly. "I just wanted to let you know that you might want to watch your back until we find out a little more."

"Well, if they're on to me at last, there's not a whole hell of a lot I can do about it, is there?"

"What about going to your cabin for a while until we know?"

"That's a possibility. I guess I could do that," Lewis said as he began to regain his nerve.

"Chances are, they just have a hunch or a lead. There's only one of them there, according to our sources. I don't think they usually make moves with just one."

"Maybe he's just a private dick," Lewis Davenport said.

"Yes, we thought of that too," the voice at the other end went on. "So just make yourself scarce for a bit."

"I can do that," the undertaker agreed.

"Good," the voice concluded. "We'll be in touch."

The line went dead and Kadoka's only undertaker put the phone back onto its cradle. He stared at the phone as if in disbelief that this conversation had taken place at all. Then he walked to the bar and poured himself a tall scotch and sipped it as he tried to steady his nerves. *What would the FBI want with me after all of these years?* he wondered to himself. *It was postwar America. His professors were enthusiastic Communists. It was they who led him to the Rosenbergs. They were all indicted. Why him? Why now?*

Another possibility crossed his mind. More likely whoever was present in Kadoka was not the FBI. A shiver coursed Lewis' spine. *Could it be, they are still out to settle a score?* Lewis Davenport's only recent mood of relaxation devolved to panicky desperation as he thought about this latter possibility.

Lewis walked to the study, drink in hand, opened a desk drawer and studied the revolver lying in it. His plan was to never be trapped. His plan was to kill himself rather than be arrested and tried for treason. His plan! His plan!

The truth was, Lewis Davenport never had much of a plan. He was a smart kid and could have gone a long way in physics. But sexual experimentation in college, what did they call it then? *AC/DC*, led him directly into the arms of those who sought to assist the Soviet Union in its mad dash to gain access to nuclear secrets and thereby, equality with the United States as a superpower.

He sought the relative security of his family in Chicago while he tried to figure what to do next with his life. Never a secure man, the family always gave him odd jobs and courier duty. This worked for nearly two years until one night one of his messenger tasks got wildly out of hand and Lewis then needed to be given an entirely new identity.

Lewis knew that he had to disengage from the family business and the whole scientific world. So with the help of his family and the marriage to his new sweetheart that was arranged by his uncle, he enrolled in embalmer's school in Chicago. Two years later, he relocated to the town of Kadoka and settled down, for a while, with his new wife Muriel in their new town and business.

But his performance in bed was unconvincing. Muriel suspected something but had no proof until she accidentally ran into him coming out of a Rapid City hotel with a younger man by his side. One look at his guilty face told her all she needed to know about what was missing in their marriage bed.

Lewis never denied his attraction to younger men but always protested he actually was a bisexual. Muriel, wedded to the money and free lifestyle that being married to Lewis afforded her, made a bargain. She'd stay and play the role with him, but she needed to be free to find love wherever she wished. She did. He did.

Their *cabin* and *trips abroad* were the times and places each needed to satisfy their physical hungers. When they were together in public, they were a model couple. When they were alone in their home in Kadoka, they barely tolerated one another.

Lewis Davenport's entire life had become one long soap opera. He was weary of it. He assumed Muriel might be also. He always knew there would come an end to this time. So he kept the revolver loaded. When the time came, he knew what he would have to do.

As he finished the scotch, he thought to himself, *I may not have much more time.*

Lark Wilson had given up having many more people in church than those he met his first night in Longvalley. In fact, the teenaged daughters and son of Angus and Dolores never came to worship. This made Lark's children more rebellious than either he or Fran could have imagined. No one else had come to worship for over two months in his ministry. This meant that Lark basically prepared worship for three families, including his own.

After worship, each week, a meal was served. Three times as many people came for dinner as those who came for worship. Mostly elderly, the dinner crowd rarely spoke to the new pastor. They all knew one another and, at times, seemed to enjoy being together. Lark and Fran usually ate at one end of the table. Try as he did, Lark seemed unable to crack the reticence of these people. They were unresponsive during worship and nearly as elusive of the Wilson family during dinner.

Once a week, he and Fran, along with their children, were guests for dinner in either Angus and Dolores' house or Percy and Ethan's house. The parishioners took turns inviting the Wilson family each Sunday morning.

"We'll see you then for supper Wednesday?" Dolores asked as she shook his hand following the church luncheon.

"We're fixing some good Indian food," Percy would say, "and your family's invited to come Wednesday night."

So it went, week after week. Lark walked around the community and knocked on doors. He had been to every house in Longvalley three times. Hardly anyone answered and no one invited him to come into their homes if they did answer the door.

All conversations with the residents of Longvalley took place out in broad daylight.

Eyes walked behind him on his rounds and generally sat in the shade of a tree whenever Lark was lucky enough to find someone at home. Eyes seemed to know just when Lark was going to do almost anything. Eyes walked and watched, always from a distance, as the new pastor endeavored to call the people of the community into the congregation.

Resigned to greeting four or five persons this Sunday, Lark sat quietly outside the little church building, waiting to see if Fran could persuade their children to come to worship on this final Sunday before school was set to begin. Just as Fran emerged from the parsonage next door with Walt, Leigh Ann and Saul trailing behind her, a thoroughly beaten-up pickup truck rumbled up the road and halted at an angle a short walk from the church.

Stepping out of the truck was the waitress from the Kadoka Café, along with the driver, Dolores! The waitress reminded Lark of someone. But he hadn't thought much about her in recent weeks. She was dressed in a pair of dark blue jeans that seemed to fit her too tightly and a nice pullover blouse with cowgirl's fringes swinging as she walked alongside Dolores. Dolores, also dressed in jeans that were washed out, and a sweatshirt on which was printed the thunder hawk and the words "Indian Power," was chatting amiably with the waitress as they walked up the sidewalk toward the preacher and his family.

"Good morning, Pastor," Dolores said. "This is Jenny Craig. She waits tables up in Kadoka. I invited her to attend church with me some day, and this is the day." Dolores smiled enthusiastically as Lark and Jenny eyed one another.

With Fran at his side, Lark reached a hand toward the waitress and said, "Welcome, Miss Craig."

Fran reached out toward the young woman and introduced

herself as their children walked around all of them and went into the church building.

"I'm Fran Wilson," Fran said warmly, "Lark's wife."

Jenny shook Fran's hand and replied, "Nice to meet you both."

Within a minute, all four were inside the church building. The silence of the sanctuary dominated all seven people as they waited to see if anyone else was going to attend. Dolores and Jenny sat on the west side of the sanctuary while Fran and the children sat on the opposite side. Lark was sorting papers on the lectern when the door opened and Percy and Ethan scuffled into the sanctuary and took their seats in front of Dolores and her guest.

Lark glanced at his congregation this morning. Then he looked at his watch. *Eleven fifteen isn't bad for Indian country*, he thought to himself. Just as he was about to speak, the door opened anew and Angus quickly walked into the sanctuary and sat down beside Dolores. Only Fran and the visitor in church looked at Lark, he noted. Both smiled at him as he began to speak.

"Welcome to our church this morning. We gather in the name of the Lord to offer our praise and thanksgiving to God."

Silence.

"As we come before the Great Spirit this Sunday, let's sing our 'Dakota Hymn.'"

The worshipers rose to their feet, opened the Dakota Odowan and, with Lark's strong voice leading with a slow beat, not unlike a drum beating in the distance, began to sing the hymn a cappella.

"Wakan tanka . . ."

Lark had already begun to learn Dakota and, with Angus' help, had translated this beautiful hymn for his family. Angus explained to him that these were the very words sung by Dacotah men, who were ordered hanged to death near New Ulm, Minnesota, by President Abraham Lincoln following the so-called Great Sioux Uprising, a rebellion by Dacotah people, who were motivated by hunger.

After the hymn, Lark prayed that the "Star-abiding One" would be with them all on this beautiful Sunday morning in

Longvalley. Then after the congregation was reseated, Lark read the scriptures for the day, including the Psalm on which he would base his sermon. He chuckled to himself earlier in the week, as he prepared the message for this Lord's Day, when he wondered what colleagues back East might think of his rewrite of Thomas Aquinas' *Summa Theologica* in a sermon to Native Americans in South Dakota!

"Friends," Lark began his message, "this morning, we read the words of the Psalmist, where he said, 'a fool says in his heart, there is no God.' Well, God must love fools for we all know there are many people in our time who might say the same thing. There is no god. People say that whenever they question why certain things happen in our world, why certain people suffer, why certain people never seem to get a break in life."

He paused. All eyes except Fran's and Jenny's were focused on the floor.

"I have learned that God's existence might be proven, or explained, in the following ways. These are ways which always made sense to your ancestors and to mine."

Jenny's head turned down toward the floor. Now, only Fran encouraged Lark by her smile from the pew.

"The Dacotah people noted the movement of sun and moon, seasons and buffalo. More than this, they sensed movement within themselves as they lived upon the earth. *Wakan Tanka* is the Great Spirit who moves herds and people, sun and moon and stars, they taught. For anything to move, there was need for the Great Spirit to move it.

"The Great Spirit caused the buffalo to wonder close to Dacotah people. The Great Spirit caused the winds and snows to blow. The Great Spirit caused the movement of the sun not only from east to west, but south to north and back again.

"Dacotah people learned from nature that there is an order or rhythm to life marked by certain directions and times. They believed, as did people around the earth, that this is not accidental but intentional. Cause and effect dawned upon the consciousness of humanity in many places and times. That cause to which

everything seems to point, humanity has named God, Allah, Great
Spirit, Father, Mother, Almighty, on and on.

"Dacotah people, like all people on earth, have noted that
birth, life, and death is the cycle that brings every part of creation
into being. But if this is only a cycle, who or what existed before
this began? Not one of us created ourselves. Nor did our parents.
Nor their parents. It is impossible for any of us to create ourselves.
Therefore, we can come to no other conclusion except that which
suggests that at one point in the history of the universe, there
was One who simply caused all other things to be. The Bible says
simply, 'And God said . . . and it was so.'

"There is human experience of growth in understanding and
love. I suspect that if all of us lived long enough, we might reach
a point in life where we would sense our very beings as most
loving, forgiving, and gracious as humanly possible."

Lark paused as Jenny Craig's head lifted and she looked
directly at him. For an instant, he could not take his eyes from
her face. The way she looked at him sent a shiver through his
body. Regaining his composure, Lark continued the sermon.

"Finally, as we journey through this life, we take note that
even inanimate nature herself, which so far as we know does not
possess knowledge such as we, acts toward an end, which is
always good for the earth and its creatures. It is plain this is no
accident. It is the Great Spirit living within nature somehow so as
to achieve the best for all. Like the arrow that flies from the strength
and aim of the hunter, finding its way to the heart of the buffalo
so that the tribe can eat, so nature moves in the direction God
aims in order that the earth is cared for and flourishes. We know
from human experience in the world that some intelligent being
exists by whom all natural things are directed to their proper
end, and this being we call God, *Wakan Tanka*.

"Now, we can understand why the psalmist wrote, 'The fool,
in his heart, says there is no God.' But we are not fools. We are
faithful people. We know there is no higher good than God. We
know, and we believe. Hence, we live to seek to learn more about

God every day we are alive. May God, the Great Spirit, keep your hearts and minds this day and every day. Amen."

Lark sat down behind the pulpit and every eye in the church now looked at the floor. The Dacotah people always practiced thinking after anyone spoke, for they sensed the need to reflect upon the words of another, especially one to whom they endeavored to show respect. They were no different in church. Silence followed the sermon as sure as spring follows winter.

Lark waited for almost five minutes and not a body stirred. Finally, when he felt he had waited long enough, he arose from his seat and asked if there were any prayer needs the people wanted to express.

No one spoke.

Lark proceeded to offer the morning prayer and, at its conclusion, the people joined him in saying the Lord's Prayer. Lark then announced that the offering would be received. Ethan and Percy stood up and walked forward to receive the offering plate from Lark, then turned and walked slowly back toward the rear of the church, offering each worshiper the opportunity to give something.

When they reached the back chairs, they turned and slowly walked forward to where Lark was standing, waiting for the plate.

"God," he prayed, "bless the givers and these gifts that they may be used for your purposes in Christ's name. Amen."

Percy and Ethan walked back to their chairs as Lark led the entire standing congregation in singing the doxology a capella.

After this, Lark announced the closing hymn, "God, The Almighty One," number three fifty-two in the white man's hymnal, which had been given them by the Congregational Church in Pierre. The Dacotah people sang this hymn less enthusiastically than the first, but they did their best to keep up with Lark as he sang.

Soon after the benediction closed the service, the room was turned into a dining hall as chairs were arranged around four folding tables while non-worshipping guests were arriving with pots of food to be shared with all.

Everything had to be carried into the church building. Hot coffee was brought in two pots by a young couple who lived a block from the church. Cold chicken and fry bread were carried in by Percy and Ethan from their house up the street. Hard-boiled eggs sat waiting in a basket brought by an older lady who actually had come into the church during the singing of the closing hymn. Cans of baked beans were opened and poured into a baking dish. An angel food cake was cut into twenty pieces so each guest would have a piece. A thermos of lemonade stood on the table, brought most likely by Dolores. Paper cups, plates, and napkins were placed beside plastic forks, spoons and knives. Within minutes, the luncheon was prepared and ready on one of the folding tables. Lark was asked to offer thanks for the food, after which he, Fran, and their children were invited to the head of the line to start the buffet procession.

The Wilsons and Jenny found themselves sitting at one table while every other guest sat themselves at the other two folding tables and chatted with one another like long-lost friends who had just been reunited following an undetermined absence from one another.

"It's nice of you to invite me to eat with you," Jenny Craig said as she sat down.

"No problem," Lark said good-naturedly.

"We enjoy meeting new people," Fran said sincerely.

"Yes, we see so few here in Longvalley," Lark added.

"We never see anybody," Saul said derisively with a glare in his father's direction.

"Well, thank you," Jenny said and smiled at both of them.

As they ate, Lark explained to Jenny that they had recently come to Longvalley from Pennsylvania. Fran added that their presence was experimental. The children ate in silence.

"My husband has been out of ministry for a while," Fran concluded.

"Oh," Jenny said, pretending to be surprised by this bit of information. "You preach so well. I can't imagine why you'd not be wanted anywhere a church needed a pastor," Jenny said genuinely.

"Thank you," Lark said as he stared at her once more. "Fran and I had some trouble for a while."

The Wilson children suddenly excused themselves and left the three adults at the table to continue their conversation.

"Don't go anywhere," Lark said to them as they were about to exit the church, "we'll be home shortly and then take a nice afternoon ride."

Jenny sat pensively as she awaited more information regarding Lark's meaning a few minutes before the children got up and left the meal.

"What my husband was trying to say is that we were separated for some time."

"Oh," Jenny said as she turned to look at Fran.

"It was a difficult time for both of us," Fran said as she lifted a bite of food to her mouth. "The children left, I assume, because they are tired of speaking of that time."

"I met this woman in New York," Lark quietly confided. "She was not who she pretended to be."

"I see," Jacqueline said as she lay her fork on the table and stared first at Lark and then at Fran. "It was an impediment to your relationship."

When she used the word "impediment," Lark paid closer attention to the waitress from Kadoka. There was something about the way she said it.

"You could say that again," Fran laughed, not noticing that Lark and Jacqueline's eyes now locked onto one another.

"I lost my church and nearly lost my family," Lark said as he tried to duck beneath the insistent gaze of their guest.

"I'm sorry," Jacqueline said. And she truly meant it.

"We're here to see if we can put the pieces back together," Fran said a bit nervously as she noted that Lark was now looking at the floor.

Silence fell over the three of them as each awaited either a way out of this impasse or a rescue from one of the Native American members chatting noisily with one another. It was Jacqueline who broke the silence.

"I'm that woman," she said in a hushed voice as she reached for Fran's arm.

"What?" Fran drew back from her and looked at her in utter disbelief.

Lark stood up, his face growing redder by the second as he looked at Jacqueline.

"Preposterous," Fran said rather loudly as everyone in the room stopped talking and turned their attention upon the three *waicesas* at the other table.

"It's true," Jacqueline continued as softly as she could and still be heard. "That is why I came here today. I want to apologize to you both."

"You're out of your mind," Fran, now on her feet, said very loudly. She turned and started to leave the table.

"Please," Jacqueline said to her, "stay and hear me out."

Lark stood as if he were a man suddenly conscious of the possibility that lightning might strike him, his face contorted and solidly opposed to what he was hearing.

"If you are who you say you are," Fran said sternly, "you owe us more than an apology!"

"I know," Jacqueline said directly to Fran as Lark stood motionless and soundless, all eyes in the room now intently watching the drama unfold before them. "When I saw you all a few weeks ago, I knew I had to come here and tell you how very sorry I am."

"STOP!" Lark screamed like a man in a bad dream.

The members of the church and community were now getting up, cleaning up their places, throwing paper plates and eating utensils in the waste can in the corner, gathering the various pots and pans on the serving table, and walking determinedly toward the doorway of the church.

Fran leaned forward, both hands on the table, looking Jacqueline directly in the face with a hatred in her eyes that spelled deep trouble ahead for their guest.

"You get the hell out of here," she said privately to Jacqueline, "and leave my husband alone. Haven't you done enough damage to our family already?"

"Fran, I had no idea it would turn out the way it did for you," Jacqueline tried to calm Lark's wife a bit. "I was so ashamed of what I did to your husband, I stopped playing those games with men after that."

"You," Lark was speaking now, but in hesitant and choppy syllables, "don't . . . look . . . like . . . Jennifer."

Jacqueline looked at him and pity overtook her. Maybe this had been a mistake. She could have simply left Kadoka without this scene.

Fran sat down as Dolores approached the table.

"I'll be outside," Dolores said to Jacqueline as cheerfully as she could and she turned to walk away from the trio, leaving them as the only people remaining in the church building.

"Thanks," Jacqueline said to her friend from the hardware store. "I'll only be a little while longer."

"It's alright," Dolores said as she closed the door to the church.

Lark remained standing, his body beginning to quiver a bit as he looked first at Fran, and then at Jacqueline.

"I thought I was working for the government," Jacqueline said. "The people who hired me called me a patriot."

"Some patriot," Fran sneered.

"Yes," Jacqueline continued, "I should have known that I was into something dirty. But the pay was good and the job was fun at first."

"Some fun," Fran fumed.

"Then I met you, Lark," she said as she turned her gaze upon him. "You were different."

"I bet he was," Fran said sarcastically as she shot a glance at her husband.

"No," Jacqueline said now to Fran alone, "he was truly a wonderful teacher. I felt terrible giving him that drug in my apartment."

"Oh," Fran said, now listening more carefully than before.

"Yes, didn't you know?"

"Nothing definite."

"I gave him too much. We had a tough time waking him up."

"I see," Fran said, "go on."

Lark, still standing, was now shaking like a man out in the cold, his mind distancing himself from the women's conversation.

"Yes, we had to give him an upper. I forced it down his throat after we were certain he wasn't going to wake up on his own."

"And the pictures," Fran asked about the photographs she'd seen in Lark's office the following day. "They were fake?"

"Oh yes," Jacqueline assured Lark's wife. "None of that ever happened."

"God damn you!" Fran was once more on her feet.

"GOD DAMN YOU!" Fran screamed at the top of her voice. She turned and walked toward the doorway of the church.

"GET OUT OF HERE AND NEVER COME BACK!" Fran slammed the door of the church, leaving Lark still standing at the table and Jacqueline sitting with her mouth agape.

Jacqueline arose and walked around the table toward Lark. He cringed as she approached him. She gently took him into her arms and held him close.

"Please believe me," she whispered to him as she ran her fingers through his hair, trying to get him to stop shaking. Like a mother calming her child, Jacqueline stroked his hair and spoke very softly to him. "Lark, I never meant to hurt you or Fran. For God's sake, forgive me."

He stared straight ahead, his body beginning to still in her arms.

"I've got to leave. They know where I am. I've got to leave," she said as she sensed his body soften.

"Why?" he murmured.

"It was just a job," Jacqueline said. "I knew after I left Lancaster that morning that I could never do that again to any one. I felt so awful."

"Who were you working for?" he whispered as he fought to regain his composure.

"I really don't know," she said, and it was the truth. "The

FBI wasn't even certain."

"Did they?" he hesitated.

"Yes," she said softly as she held him now in both arms and looked directly into his eyes, "go on. What do you want to know?"

"You don't look like Jennifer," he said as he stared at her, studying her face and body.

"I know," she said as she dropped her arms at her side. "It's all part of the act. The guys up in Kadoka think I'm queer."

"I just can't believe you are Jennifer," Lark said. "This is some kind of joke."

"Do you remember what Lou said to us that day in Lou's Corner Deli?"

He looked at her. He remembered. Only Jennifer would remember.

"Yes," he said.

Jacqueline smiled.

"I was Jennifer then," Jacqueline said. "Who knows who I will be wherever I go? My life has been one long charade. I'm rather tired of it."

They both sat, side by side. Jacqueline put her arm around Lark as they sat now, just the two of them.

"Lark," she said as she held him tightly and looked straight ahead, "I am so glad you and your family are back together again."

"Yes," he said, "so am I."

"If you don't know anything else about me," Jacqueline said with a conviction that could never be doubted by him, "please know that you saved me from everything I was before I met you, and I can never thank you enough for that. I have peace now in ways I haven't since I was a tiny girl."

"I'm glad to hear that, Jennifer," he said as he turned and looked at her face once more.

"Jacqueline," she said, correcting him, "my real name is Jacqueline Frontierre."

"I know," Lark said, smiling now for the first time since Jacqueline began her confession.

"You do?" She was surprised

"Yes," he said. "A good friend told me."

"Well, I'll be," she said as she also smiled at him. "I guess you know I was a hooker in New Orleans then."

"Yep," he smiled. "I heard that, too."

"I guess you really hated me," she said, looking down at the table.

"I loathed you!"

Silence engulfed them as each waited for some way to turn the conversation away from the past.

"But eventually," Lark continued, "I forgave you."

Jacqueline began to cry. She sobbed and leaned toward him as he put his arm around her shoulder.

"You," she hesitated, "forgave me?"

"Yes," Lark said quietly, "as I got my life back together and my family decided to give me another chance, I forgave you, Jacqueline."

She turned her face toward him, tears now freely flowing down her cheeks.

"You are a good man, Lark Wilson," she said. "I will never forget you."

"Nor I you," Lark said. "You were part of God's way of getting my attention."

They each smiled. Jacqueline leaned forward and gently kissed him on the cheek.

"Thank you," she said. "I'd better be going."

As she stood, she put her arms around Lark's shoulders and hugged him to her bosom. "Goodbye, Lark," she said and quickly walked from the room and his life.

Lark sat alone in the church building. He heard Dolores's truck start up outside shortly after two doors slammed. He heard a few crickets chirping in the recesses of the church building. He heard his kids next door talking loudly with one another. And he could have sworn he heard the voice of God say ever so quietly to his soul, *It is well. It is well.*

Lark walked to the front of the church and knelt at the communion table. In silence, he prayed, thanking God for this reconciliation. *So this is why I'm here*, he said to the Almighty. *You sure have a strange way of doing things!* Peace swept over him as he knelt there in the little wooden church building. It was a peace he didn't pretend to understand. It was a peace he could only receive, knowing all the while that he had done nothing to deserve it.

When his knees began to hurt him, Lark arose, gathered himself a bit, and walked out of the church building, across the dying grass, and into the parsonage.

"Fran," he called.

"I'm in here," she answered from the bedroom, her voice not as strong as earlier at the church.

When Lark walked into the little room, he was startled to see Fran packing two suitcases.

"What's this?" he asked.

"We've got to leave," she said confidently. "We can't stay here with that woman only fifty miles away."

"She's leaving, Fran," Lark pleaded with her. "She came today just to say goodbye."

Fran shot her husband a glance that he hadn't seen in a while but easily interpreted nonetheless. A lecture was coming his way.

"Fran," he said earnestly, "don't do this to us again."

"Wake up, Lark," she said sarcastically as she threw the last things into the second suitcase and began to fasten it shut. "This place is no place for us. Your ministry isn't going that well. The kids aren't happy. And now, Jennifer, or whatever the hell her name is, comes back into the picture."

"Fran, please," he said, but he could tell it was to no avail. "We'll never see her again. She is leaving the area."

"It makes no difference, Lark," Fran sat on the end of the bed and looked at her husband as she spoke. "This is a mistake. You don't know it yet. But it sure is apparent to the rest of us."

"You don't mean that," Lark said as he sat beside her. "You're just upset. We both are."

"No," Fran said as she got up and stood over him now. "I'm

a realist. You're a dreamer. You don't belong here. You just don't realize it yet. Harry Sawyer led you down a garden path on this. You'll see that eventually"

"Fran," he looked up at her face and could tell she was deeply hurt, "you don't mean this. You're upset. Give it time. Trust me."

"Lark," she tried to say now as strongly as anything she had ever said to him during their marriage, "I can't do this. I've tried. But I know today, as sure as I'm standing here, that I can't do it. It's not fair to the children or to me. And I don't believe it's what you ought to be doing with your life either."

"Fran . . . ," Lark objected. He could tell, by the tone of her voice, that she wasn't quite convinced of what she was now saying.

"No," she continued, "when your mother died, I thought we could make it way out here in South Dakota, out here away from everything that went wrong for us in the East. I thought we could start anew. I thought we'd be one big, happy family again."

"We are, Fran," Lark pleaded with her. "We are!"

"We were," she said, composing her sentences now like a teacher of small children. "But now, I'm not sure."

"I know you aren't, Fran," Lark said as he stood and extended his arms toward her. "But don't give up on me again."

She fell into his arms, now sobbing quietly into his shoulder.

"I've got to go," she said. "And the kids have decided to go with me."

"Where?" Lark said as terror began to envelope him. "Where are you going?"

"Oh," she hesitated, "maybe we'll just go for a little vacation before school starts. I don't know."

"That's a good idea," Lark said as he squeezed his wife once more and then looked into her wet eyes. "You all go ahead and I'll join you in Rapid City in a day or two."

"We thought we'd go to Chamberlain," Fran corrected him. "The kids want to explore the river."

"Good idea," Lark said, smiling. "I'll be there early Tuesday morning. I'll borrow Ethan's pickup."

"I may just keep on driving," she said as her face darkened once more.

"And . . . ," Lark said, as he studied his wife's demeanor.

"I don't know, Lark," she said as she slumped into the chair in the corner, "I just don't know."

Lark walked toward his wife, stood behind the chair and bent, putting his arms around her. As he did, he noted that she was shivering.

"Fran," he said quietly as he rubbed his hands up and down her bare arms, "are you all right?"

"I am so damned afraid," she whispered. "Something's not right about this place, Lark. I'm afraid for you, the children, and our family."

Lark walked around the chair in front of his wife, taking her hands in his as he knelt in front of her. The two stared at one another in silence, each trying to read the other at this moment.

"Fran," Lark finally said, "could you be more specific? This is different for all of us. I'm not sure what you are afraid of, hon."

"I can't say," Fran repeated, "I just know that fear is eating away at me. I've never felt this way in my life."

"Maybe it's just the change in everything so quickly," he tried to reassure her. "If it truly doesn't work out, you know we'll leave. I'm not stupid, Fran."

"No," she smiled for the first time in the conversation, "you're stubborn, not stupid."

"There," he said, relaxing as he saw her smile, "that's the girl I fell in love with not long ago."

Fran was on her feet in a flash, walking toward the closed bedroom door. Lark turned toward her and asked, "Fran, what's wrong?"

She turned to face him anew, her eyes ablaze with emotion and her body drawing up as though she were prepared to deliver a karate blow to the mid-section of her opponent.

"NO!" she screamed at him.

"Fran . . . ," Lark called after her as she opened the door and walked out of the bedroom. He got to his feet and followed her into the living room, where all three children had ceased whatever activity had engaged them and were now looking first at their mother, and then at their father.

Fran sat upon the couch and her body began to shake anew.

"What's wrong, Mom?" asked Walt.

"Did he hurt you, Mom?" Saul asked.

"He's hurt all of us," Lark, disbelieving his ears, heard his wife in answer to their younger son's question, as Leigh Ann began to cry. "We're all out here in the middle of nowhere and your father can't see the danger we're in at the moment."

"Mom . . . ," Walt said in a consoling manner as he sat beside her on the couch and glanced at his startled father.

"Kids," Lark said, "your mom is just a little upset with me right now. She is going to take you to Chamberlain for a little vacation. I'll join you on Tuesday."

Fran, regaining some composure, gathered herself and assured the children that she and their father just had a disagreement. She apologized sincerely to every one in the room for her outburst. Leigh Ann wiped her eyes as her mother stood up, walked to her father, and kissed him lightly upon the cheek. Then, walking as if in a dream, Fran went to the bedroom and came back with her suitcases in hand. Within minutes, she and the children were in the family car and driving away from the parsonage, as Lark watched them slowly leave Longvalley.

When his family was out of sight, Lark turned to go back into the parsonage, where the air conditioner was noisily producing air ten degrees cooler than that which moved around the little house on the outside. Slumping onto the couch, Lark recounted the events of this Lord's Day. As he thought about Fran's fear, an emotion he rarely had witnessed in her, the preacher's Sunday afternoon gift crept across his consciousness and he fell soundly asleep.

Chapter 11

Ta'ku On Wan Koda

The truck pulled hard up each incline and seemed to roll freely down each decline, belching blue-white smoke behind it as its doors rattled and dashboard knobs shook over each bump. Dolores held the steering wheel so tightly her knuckles lightened atop because of the pressure her fingers applied to the task. The radio was tuned to a country-and-western music station. Each woman sat in silence for nearly twenty miles. Dolores finally bridged the distance between her and her guest by asking a question.

"What was going on between you and the preacher's wife back there?"

"Oh, not much," Jacqueline answered nonchalantly.

"It sure looked like you were having quite an argument."

"We weren't arguing," Jacqueline retorted, getting defensive.

"Some of us were thinking of bringing you folk a peace pipe," Dolores quipped and chuckled at the thought.

"Cute," Jacqueline said as she too began to chuckle.

"Seriously, Jenny," Dolores asked, "what was going on back there?"

Jacqueline pondered her response. How could she explain the history of the three white people who had engaged in the scene in the church? She could make something up. She was good at that. But her respect for Dolores forbade a lie. She could

159

tell the truth. But how? Dolores might understand truth better than a lie at this point. Jacqueline prepared her response carefully as silence separated the riders anew.

"You don't have to answer that question," Dolores said finally. "We're friends. I can trust you with your secrets."

Jacqueline was moved by Dolores' simple way of addressing life. This Indian woman possessed a spirit which was larger than most persons Jacqueline had ever known. Certainly, she, of all people in Kadoka, could be trusted with the truth.

"I knew the Wilson family back East," Jacqueline heard herself confess as Dolores geared the truck down so it could climb yet another hill toward Kadoka.

"I thought so," Dolores said as she gunned the engine. "Mrs. Wilson doesn't like you. But I guess you know that already."

"Yes, she has good reason not to like me. Don't be too hard on her, Dolores."

"None of us have ever seen that side of her. She sure was angry with you. What did you do?"

"I told them I was sorry."

"What?"

"I apologized for messing up their lives sometime ago."

"Oh," Dolores said as she shifted into high gear and the truck rolled freely downhill, leaving a fog of smoke in its wake. "I don't understand."

It was quiet in the truck once more as both women peered through the windshield out onto the unchanging prairie. The singer on the radio was singing "Your Cheatin' Heart" and doing a very poor imitation of Hank Williams as he sang.

Jacqueline quietly began to tell her friend how she had responded to an ad in a newspaper and soon found herself involved in an operation aimed at undermining the peace movement leaders back East. She explained that, from the beginning, she had misgivings about seducing leaders of the anti-war movement and playing a role in ruining their credibility in their communities. But the pay was the best she'd ever seen and the risks were less than anything she'd done in her life. She was never sure how any of these men's lives were ruined after their brief encounters with her. That was always handled by others. Her role was to simply seduce politicians, educators, and religious leaders and get them into embarrassing situations. Then she would disappear and let others work out the messy details.

"Pardon me, Jenny," Dolores interrupted, "but you don't look to me like the type of woman who could do this work very effectively." She chuckled to herself.

"Appearances can be deceiving," Jacqueline said with quiet conviction. "I was different then."

"Oh," Dolores said as she turned to eye her riding partner while turning the volume down on the pickup's radio. "I'm interested. Go on."

Jacqueline continued with her story. She told Dolores how things worked well for her, until she met Lark Wilson. There was something about him that she admired. Maybe it was his sincerity, or trust, or faith. She wasn't sure. All she knew was that, as she seduced him and set him up for failure in a town back East called Lancaster, she began, for the first time, to feel bad about her well-paying job. She even thought of leaving the city before the task was done. She came close to telling Lark what she was up to but couldn't bring herself to do it. Afterward, she subscribed to the Lancaster newspapers for a month to see if her feigned tryst had worked one more time, all the while hoping that it didn't. She read where Lark had resigned his parish. The papers reported that he had taken a leave of absence, that he was estranged from his wife and family. She felt awful.

Jacqueline told Dolores that she turned herself in to the FBI shortly afterward and that their investigators had helped her relocate and re-establish herself in South Dakota. She shared nothing else, except that she was certain this was the reason Mrs. Wilson hated her. She told Dolores that she tried to apologize to them both when she realized that Lark was beginning to recognize her. The apology failed. A scene ensued. That was all there was to what Dolores and the others had witnessed this day in church.

Shortly before their arrival in Kadoka, Dolores asked her, "What are you going to do now?"

"I don't know," Jacqueline said quietly. "Who would have dreamed that I would run into that family here in South Dakota? It's just all so unreal."

"Yea, I know what you mean," Dolores said. "The world's a big place. What are the odds?"

"I guess I'll have to move on," Jacqueline said, just barely above the drone of the engine. Dolores did not respond.

When they pulled in front of the hardware store, Jacqueline got out of the truck and then stuck her head through the open door window to say a few last words to Dolores.

"I'd really appreciate it if what we shared together stays with us," Jacqueline said as Dolores stared straight ahead. "I need time to work this all out."

"You got it," Dolores responded as she shifted the truck into gear and began to pull away from the curb. "Anything for a friend!"

Dolores wheeled the truck into a U-turn and headed back south toward the interstate. Jacqueline watched her drive away, and then walked into her apartment and bounded up the stairs. With each step, her legs seemed heavier but nothing in all of physics could match the heaviness in her heart at this moment.

Once inside the apartment, Jacqueline went straight to the bedroom, threw herself across the bed, and wept for several minutes before falling into a deep sleep.

Three hours later, the ringing of the telephone awakened her. As she arose, the mid-afternoon sun was streaming brightly across her apartment floor, its brilliance assaulting her dreary irises. She reached the phone and lifted the receiver.

"Hello," she said groggily.

"Jenny," the voice responded, "were you sleeping?"

"Yes," she said, "who is this?"

"It's me, Max," he answered, just as she recognized his voice.

"Oh, Max," she said, now beginning to be more cognizant of the world around her. "What's up?"

"Well, I'm over here at the café, trying to fix the vent and light above the stove. Steve wants this done by tomorrow and I'm having trouble. I thought maybe you could help me."

"Yeah," she reluctantly replied, "I guess I could. Give me a few minutes and I'll be over there."

"Gee, thanks, kid," Max said cheerfully. He hung up.

Jacqueline went into the bathroom to freshen herself a bit. She still had her finer clothes on and they looked rather rumpled. Not knowing what Max needed of her, she quickly changed her clothes. She dressed in a pair of blue jeans and a shift blouse which hung loosely over the top of her jeans. She applied some makeup to hide the redness of her eyes and face. After brushing her teeth, she raced down the steps and across the street to the café.

Jacqueline let herself into the locked front door of the café with the key Steve had given her during her first month of work. She could hear the radio blaring in the kitchen and she spied Max, standing atop the stove in the kitchen, sweat stains clearly visible on the back of his trousers and shirt. He was reaching above his head for something, cursing to himself as he struggled. She walked into the kitchen.

"What the hell are you into?" she asked him in a loud voice so as to be heard above the radio by the sink, which was tuned to some country station.

"Heh," Max turned to face her, his wet belly sticking out over the top of his pants. "I guess I'm not quite tall enough for this job or something," he yelled over the country-and-western song and the late-afternoon static which accompanied every A.M. station in Western South Dakota in the summer time.

"Oh," she joked, "I thought you were practicing dancing on table tops!"

"Yeah, fat chance!" Max laughed. "I could use your help."

"What's wrong?" she asked him.

"Well, there's a screw up here that I can't reach. It needs to be loosened so I can take the vent fan down to clean it and then replace the light. I thought maybe you could reach it for me." He looked at her with hope.

"And that's what you need my help for?" she said incredulously. "Why didn't you stand on a box or something?"

"I hate to admit this, Jenny," Max said sheepishly, pointing to the ladder next to the stove, "but I'm afraid of heights. This is about as high as I go."

She noted the stepladder, upon which Max's shortsleeved jacket hung, standing by the stove. Something in the scene bothered her for an instant but she dismissed it with her usual act.

"Men," Jacqueline said in her best imitation of a man-hater to date. "What good are you guys, anyway?"

Max carefully climbed down from the stovetop using the stepladder and then he handed her the seven-inch screw driver he had held in his right hand, sweat now pouring down his face.

"Max, you sure look like you've been working hard," she smiled as she spoke.

"I've been here for an hour or so," he said as he looked up into her face. "It's about time for a beer. What you say you climb up there and loosen that last screw for me and then I'll get you and me some cold ones?"

"Okay," Jacqueline said, "but you'll have to tell me where it is because I've never done this kind of work in my life."

"That's surprising," Max said in a voice that was almost disturbingly quiet, "I always thought even your kind of girl knew more about screwing than us guys!"

"Bullshit," she said as she hitched up onto the stove without using the ladder. "Now, where is this screw you can't reach?"

"Reach right up above your head there, kid, and you'll feel it."

Jacqueline reached above her head and began to feel around for a screw head into which to place the screwdriver. She had to stretch a bit to feel the bottom of the vent fan and she could sense her shift blouse moving up with her arms so as to expose her belly. She stretched some more.

"Pardon my midriff, Max. I can't feel anything up here," she said as she looked now at the bottom of the vent fan and moved her hand around it.

"Oh, you will," Max said softly as he reached behind him

and grabbed a meat blade from the table and swung it up hard in the direction of her hyperextended belly.

The blade smacked hard, making the sound of a jack-o-lantern carving knife as it invaded her unsuspecting body, cutting smoothly through her abdominal muscles, its point racing toward her diaphragm, stopping only when the handle reached the exterior of her milky-white skin.

"Oh," was all Jacqueline could say as the unendurable pain radiated throughout her mid-section. Her arms fell to her side and with them, the screwdriver fell and bounced off the stovetop onto the floor. She glanced downward, standing very still, still on tiptoe upon the stovetop. She could see the handle of a knife blade resting snugly against her abdomen, moving only so slightly up and down as she tried to catch her breath. The pain was so sharp, so sudden. She was stunned. She was confused. She was shocked.

She looked next at Max, who now stood as if frozen beneath her, gazing at her puzzled look. He seemed to be watching her very intently, more interested in what she might do next than he was in helping her. A slight smile crossed his otherwise unreadable face.

"Max," she managed to gasp, "what have you done?"

He said nothing. He just stared at her as though he was trying to think of what to say or do next. His face now showed some degree of concern.

Her blood was beginning to bubble around the knife handle. Jacqueline, still adjusting to the reality that this man had just stabbed her, now found herself struggling to keep her legs under her as they began to shake beneath her. She feared to move for the pain was building incredibly in her belly. She didn't want to do anything to make it worse. She felt faint, fearing she was losing consciousness.

Suddenly, without warning, her legs gave way beneath her and her body moved as though she were preparing to sit down atop the stove. Blood now began to roll from the knife's entry into her body and down into and around her navel, rolling on to form rivulets at the top of her jeans.

As she staggered and fell, Max caught her in his arms, her head resting over his shoulder as he held her upright.

"I'm sorry, Jacqueline," he said quietly to her as she seemed to fight to remain conscious in his arms while tears began to form in her eyes. "This is nothing personal, just business. I'm sorry. Here, let me help you."

Jacqueline squirmed a bit in his arms, making what he felt necessary to do a bit more difficult to accomplish. She hadn't much strength left, he could tell. But she seemed to be suffering and this was something he didn't wish to see her do.

"Momma," Jacqueline faintly said as he held her extremely tense but relaxing body upright in his arms.

"That's right," Max said to her as he grasped the handle of the knife. "Nothing can harm you now, sweetheart. You call your momma."

"Maria," she whispered softly.

"Yes, darlin'," Max said as he held her in his strong left arm, "you go ahead and pray to Mother Mary. You'll be seeing her soon."

Max grasped the knife handle firmly just as Jacqueline's arms began to raise in what appeared to be a pleading motion. He gave the handle one very quick and excruciating turn to the right while thrusting its blade more deeply into her at the same time. Jacqueline gasped anew and collapsed immediately and heavily into his arms.

The river was roiling before her in the darkness. She could hear it and knew immediately where she was. She was alone and frightened, for this was not where she expected to be at this time.

Dawn was just breaking and the ground was barely visible. She lay face down, arms and legs akimbo, feeling filthy and alone. Just another discarded heap of this world's refuse, she thought to herself.

Jacqueline began to cry, at first a sob, and then a wretched, tear-filled cry building into a loud wail.

Why had she always had to struggle so hard in life just to survive? Why couldn't she have had the kind of life described in movie magazines and books? Why had she been selected for an existence no one in her right mind would have volunteered for in life?

Sorrow for herself built until she loathed the very life she'd been given. It wasn't worth the time and place it took in this world. It would have been better had she died in childbirth and her sister lived, she told herself as she lay there by the river, shivering and cold.

Drowning would be the solution to all her problems, she told herself. She struggled to crawl toward the river, the sound of its waters gathering angrily and threateningly close to her.

Breathing became more difficult as she struggled to the edge of the river. The best she could do, she surmised, would be to simply roll down into the waters and never be heard from again. This was it. This was how it would end. She would die now and it would all be over.

Suddenly, she heard a voice above the water's roar. She didn't recognize it at first. It had been so long since she had heard it. Raising her head, she looked across the river. There on the other side, in the first light of the new day, she saw two forms, one larger than the other. They looked familiar. She couldn't be certain. One of them was speaking quietly to the other.

"Is she here, Mother?" the voice asked. "You said we would find her here."

"Yes," the other voice replied, "I know I did. I know she'll be here some day. That's why we come here to look for her every morning. She'll be here one day, Marie. We must be patient."

Jacqueline now recognized her mother and sister. Tears of joy filled her eyes as she watched them standing on the other side of the river, talking with one another. She wanted to cry out to them but could not muster the strength to do so. She hoped they would see her as she could see them.

She devised a plan. She would roll down the riverbank into the water and swim across to her mother and sister. Sensing this would not be easy to do, for the river was continuing to roil past at life-threatening speed, she steeled herself to try. Somehow, she would reach that other bank and be rejoined with her sister and mother.

Jacqueline rolled down the bank and fell into the swiftly moving current, her body sinking beneath the water. As she gave herself to the experience, the roiling around her ceased. Without effort, Jacqueline floated across the river to the other bank.

As she emerged from the water, she crawled up the bank with every ounce of energy she still possessed as the sun was rising behind her mother and sister's silhouettes.

"Momma," she cried out, "Marie!"

Her sister and mother looked up toward her and began to run down the bank to help her to her feet. The three of them embraced, arm in arm, tears coursing down each one's face as longing and loving glances moved first from one to the other.

"Welcome home," Jacqueline's mother said as she kissed her upon her forehead. "We've been waiting for you."

"Oh sister," Marie exclaimed, "it is so good to be with you again. I love you."

"I love you, too" Jacqueline said as she stood between them. "I have missed you dearly."

"Come along now, girls," Sadie said quietly as she placed an arm around each of them. "Let's be going. I want to introduce Jacqueline to her grandmother."

Jacqueline cried with joy to be reunited with the only two persons in the whole wide world she ever loved, and ever missed. She was home at last. She sensed they would never be parted from one another again.

Max watched as he simply let Jenny's body fall hard upon the stovetop after he had turned the knife blade so as to cut through her abdominal artery. Death seemed instantaneous for this woman whom his family had been searching for sometime. Her body fell hard and heavy upon her stomach, her face turned toward him, staring fearfully at first as he held her in his arm and wrenched the knife inside her gut, but then peacefully as she breathed her last breath, still in his arm. She only seemed to move a bit, as though she were trying to get off the stovetop, like a swimmer when first hitting the water. Then she was quiet, her eyes opened forever to whatever awaits us all.

Max reached out and checked her pulse. There was none. Blood was now filling one of the burner areas just beneath her belly. He knew he had to move swiftly.

It would look like an accident. Everything had been measured. The plan worked as though the whole scene had been rehearsed. He reached behind him once more and grabbed the two-quart cooking pot with the seven-inch long, stainless-steel handle which rested upon the table. He gently rolled Jenny's body over, placing her on her back, her eyes now staring beyond the ceiling. He extracted the knife from the oozing belly wound, turning it 360 degrees as it exited, the flesh tearing as he pulled it from her body. Now, a gaping hole angrily bled as he lifted the pot by its bottom and thrust the handle into the very wound the knife had originally created.

He gazed at her face. It was beginning to soften into its death mask and a bruise to her right forehead was only barely visible. This would need to be fixed. He rolled her upon her stomach once more, the pot now lifting her pelvis and abdomen only slightly above the stovetop while more blood flowed around the pot handle and trickled down onto the stove.

Grabbing her head by her hair, he lifted it above the stovetop and then slammed it as hard as he could, face down, toward the burner, on which it had rested a moment before. Just to make certain, he lifted Jacqueline's head once more. This time, he shoved her face into the burner tines so hard several of her teeth broke upon impact and pieces fell into the burner basin and onto the floor. *This would surely give her face the effect I wanted*, he thought to himself. He left her in that position, face down and pelvis lifted by the pot, with its handle now deep within her belly, at an angle toward her heart.

Max moved more quickly now, gathering up the knife and anything else which would appear to the investigators as though it didn't belong. Her blood was now running freely down the front of the stove. Once he was sure everything was just right, he walked into the bathroom, where fresh shoes and clothes awaited. He stripped and washed his body carefully so as to remove any trace of Jenny's blood from his body. He glanced at himself in the mirror. Having never killed a woman before, he thought he detected something in his face he had never seen. Pity.

After applying deodorant, Max dressed quickly, dumped the bloody clothes and shoes into a duffle bag and walked, carrying them, to his car in back of the café. He had a plan for discarding these later.

This task completed, Max walked back into the café from the rear, strolling calmly into the kitchen, like a man after his afternoon nap and glancing at Jenny's dead body atop the stove as though he were seeing it for the first time. "What a waste," he grunted to himself as he walked toward the phone.

He dialed Steve's number and waited for the owner to answer.

"Hello," Steve said indifferently, chewing on something as he spoke.

"Steve," Max said in a voice pretending to be scared to death.

"Yeah, what is it, Max?"

"You better come down to the café," Max screamed, "there's been an accident!"

"What?" Steve was attentive now. "What's wrong?"

"It's Jenny," Max said, now whimpering. "I think she's dead."

"My God," Steve said. "I'll be right there."

Sheriff Walthroup arrived at the café by seven in the evening after a tough afternoon of investigating a multiple injury accident on Highway 14, east of Cottonwood, which had resulted in three teenage deaths. Speed and alcohol were ruled the cause of yet another needless teenage tragedy.

"This seems to be my day for looking at dead bodies," was all he said to Steve as he walked into the café kitchen and glanced at Jenny's body, lying face-down atop the stove. He stepped upon a broken tooth piece on the floor as he moved to get a closer view of the body. "Can somebody tell me what the hell took place here?" he grunted as he bent to look more closely at the young woman's body.

"Max and she were trying to fix the exhaust vent over the stove," Steve said as Dale Walthroup now carefully rolled Jenny's body on her back and looked closely at the pot attached to her belly, just above her bruised and blood-swollen navel.

"Blood's coagulated," the sheriff, who had served the county for nearly twenty years, muttered to himself. "I guess she's been dead since about four o'clock. That right?" He took each of her hands gently in his and moved them up and down as he spoke, then laid them exactly at her side as he had found them. "*Wowicake*," Dale said to himself.

"Yes, sir," Max responded rather shyly to the man in uniform. "That's about when I found her."

"You say you found her?"

"Yeah," Max said carefully. "She had been helping me fix that damned vent and I had just stepped out to the alley to smoke a cigarette. Jenny didn't like people smoking around her."

"Yeah," Walthroup responded, interested in Max's story. He turned Jenny's body over once more and left her lay face down. "Then what?"

"I heard a scream, and then almost immediately a crash like everything in the kitchen had fallen."

"*Onahonwaste*" Walthroup said so softly it was barely heard by anyone else in the room. "And?"

"I stamped out my cigarette and ran in here and found her like that." Max pointed to the lifeless body atop the stove.

"Was she alive or dead?" the sheriff inquired.

"I don't know."

"You don't know?" Sheriff Walthroup stared intently at Max. "Didn't you bother to check? *Ecawitkotkoka*!"

Steve chuckled, recognizing the Dakota term being applied by the sheriff to his dishwasher.

"No, sir, I didn't," Max said, unaware that he had just been called an idiot by the man in uniform.

"How did she fall, do you suppose?"

"She must have slipped on something. I don't know. I wasn't in here at the time."

"Slipped, eh? On what?"

"Don't know," Max said with a little more authority. "She was standing on that ladder by the stove and stretching up to loosen the screw that holds the vent when I went out to the alley to smoke. She must have lost her balance and fell over on the stove. How the hell do I know how she fell?"

"Yeah," said the sheriff. "Then what?"

"She hit the stove pretty hard," Max explained, "I could hear the crash outside with the door shut. Must have knocked herself out because she never made a sound after I ran in here. She just lay there. I didn't notice anything at first, but then I saw the blood."

"Uh huh," the lawman said as he carefully lifted her head above the stovetop and studied the bruises on Jenny's forehead. "You say she fell off that ladder," Walthroup summarized as he gently placed her face down anew upon the stovetop. "*Woitonsni*," he whispered to himself.

"Yeah," Max said as he began to sense this sheriff was not a person with whom one ought to trifle. "I guess so."

Dale Walthroup was a Korean War veteran who survived the Chou Lai Reservoir encounters with the North Korean and Chinese communists. He had seen more than his share of death and dying. The inhumanity human beings subject one another to in life had hardened him by the time he was discharged in 1954. He came back to the county after the war, determined to take up ranching on his father's ranch, marry, settle down, and raise a family of his own.

Fate had a much more challenging life for this Dakotan, born of a Scandinavian father and a Sioux mother. Amy, his wife of three years, died in the Rapid City Regional Hospital as a result of a botched Caesarian-section process when the surgeon failed to tie off an artery, and his only child, born one month premature, succumbed to pneumonia three months afterward.

Dale's father escaped into alcoholism soon thereafter and

rolled his pickup five times end over end on a county-line correction curve near Kadoka late one night while returning from a local bar, leaving Dale to care for the ranch and his ailing mother at the very time he needed to rebuild his own life. Dale's mother died of stomach cancer exactly one month before the bank took possession of the ranch, which was failing miserably during the drought of 1957, leaving Dale without a family, a livelihood, or much hope.

When the county commissioners approached Dale in 1958 to run for sheriff, knowing that the job paid so little and was such a thankless job that he would face no opposition in the coming election, they found him eager to accept the challenge. He was just angry enough to do a good job as a peacekeeper in a place as sparsely populated and so acquainted with violence as this area of South Dakota.

Dale Walthroup was not a man to be trifled with at all. He possessed what the Sioux called *Woksape*. He didn't suffer fools at all. He was a heavy John Wayne, a hard-drinking Ward Bond, a no-nonsense cynic who lived by himself in a trailer on the west edge of Kadoka. Once in a while, people reported seeing him hunting or fishing near Chamberlain. But most of the time, the only people who saw him coming knew they were either on the wrong side of the law or about to receive bad news. He usually solved crimes in the county quickly, sometimes, in the Old West fashion by shooting first and asking questions afterward. Most times, by his keen powers of observation coupled with his compiled knowledge of humanity at its worst. *Woawacin*, the Sioux said of him. A wise observer, indeed.

Once every four years, Dale went out of his way to make public appearances as he ran for re-election. Then, as suddenly as he appeared in cafés, bars, fraternal organizations, and schools, he disappeared following each election. Unlike state troopers who frequented cafés across South Dakota and were easily spotted along major highways from day to day, Dale Walthroup was a near-invisible presence among the citizens of Kadoka and surrounding towns, except when he was called to quell a domestic or public disturbance, investigate a criminal scene, or oversee the report of an accident.

People of the county liked the kind of sheriff they had found in Dale Walthroup. He liked his job. He did it well. Then he got out of the way so folk could go on with their lives. There was nary a soul who doubted that he'd be sheriff until he died. He kept a clean house, in law enforcement lingo, and never took anything away. If he stayed on as sheriff until he could no longer see, drive, walk, or shoot, that would be just fine with the residents of the county. Both *Wasicun* and Dacotah respected the man.

Still, he was not a man to fool around. So when he had finished looking over Jacqueline's body and returned her body to its face-down position, he turned to Steve and asked, "Who's this helper of yours?" as though Max were not even in the room.

"He's been with me a little while now," Steve said.

"Yeah," Dale sputtered, "where'd he come from? Not around here, I can tell."

Max, for the first time since he stabbed Jacqueline, squirmed as the sheriff turned his head toward him and said, "*Iyekiya.*"

"He's from out East somewhere," Steve said a little more cautiously now, sensing the meaning of Dale's word.

Turning directly to Max, the sheriff took a step toward him and asked, "Where you from, Mister?"

"New Jersey," was all Max said as he stared into the sheriff's deep brown eyes, trying to discern if his physical presence was based on western bravado or something more threatening.

"That so?" Dale said, as though he didn't believe Max. "What did you do out there?"

"Odd jobs, mostly," Max lied. "I like to travel."

Taking another step forward, Dale's formidable body now stood no more than a foot away from Max. "You like to travel?" he said. "Why'd you come here?"

Silence filled the room and before Max could offer an answer, the front door of the café swung open and Lewis Davenport came rushing into the kitchen. He seemed more nervous than usual as he glanced, first at Jacqueline's body lying upon the stovetop, and then at the sheriff.

"Who called you already?" Sheriff Walthroup asked the undertaker before muttering to himself, "*Witkotkoka.*"

"I did," Steve said. "It was obvious to me when I got here that Jenny was dead. I figured you'd be needing Lewis here."

"I came as fast as I could," Davenport said to Steve. "Hello, Max"

"Hi," Max responded more pleasantly, as if speaking to an old friend.

"She's not officially dead until that damned preacher gets here, you know," shot the sheriff. "*Wahokonwicakiya!* Where the hell is he anyway? I had to wait an hour for him up at Cottonwood this afternoon before we could remove those bodies. I wish this county could either afford a real coroner or deputize me to do the duty."

"Oh," Steve remembered, "the preacher's wife said he'd be here at eight. They've got something for the youth going on at the Catholic Church until then."

"Christ Almighty," Dale exclaimed. "We have to wait half an hour for him then."

"I guess so," Steve said more carefully.

"I could make us some coffee," Max said, trying to lighten the mood of the room as Davenport walked to the stove and stared down at Jacqueline's body.

"You can turn her over and have a good look, if you want," the sheriff said in Davenport's direction. "Of course," he continued as if for emphasis, "I guess you guys get a good look at all of us in the end, don't you?"

Davenport stepped forward, as if he hadn't heard a word the sheriff said. He turned Jenny's body over onto her back and stared at her gaping mouth, missing teeth, and fully exposed, angry-looking belly wound with a cooking pot attached by its handle now stabbing deep within her lifeless body.

"Ugly way to die," he said to no one in particular. "How did this happen?" Davenport wanted to know.

"Ask Steve's new partner here," Sheriff Walthroup said sarcastically. "He's the only witness to the *wanuwoakipa*. 'Accident,' he says. And not a very damned good one at that."

Walthroup said the word "accident" so wickedly in both Dakota and English that everyone in the room turned and looked at him.

"What are you getting at?" Steve asked the sheriff.

"I don't know," the sheriff said. "It's just that I've met this young woman a few times since she came here. I've heard her tell about her life before she came to Kadoka, how she grew up on a ranch down in Texas. I just don't fancy her falling off no ladder. That's all."

"Now, you look here, Sheriff Wal . . ." Max started.

" . . . Throup," Dale finished, "It's Dale Walthroup. I don't believe I know your last name, Mister. *Iyekiya*"

Max slammed the coffee pot onto the base of the coffee maker.

"It's Long," said Max. "I'm Max Long. I'm a writer. I'm here researching a story I'm thinking of writing about the contemporary West and its racetracks."

Lewis Davenport looked in disbelief at the man who had recently become Steve's dishwasher at the café. A writer? Who would have guessed?

"It's true," Steve said to the sheriff, "I've got his résumé in my office at home. Mr. Long sent it to me two months ago and asked if he could work here for a month while he did some research for a novel."

"And you believed him?" Sheriff Walthroup asked Steve, a look of surprise upon his face. "*Itonsni*," he snarled at Steve.

"Yes," Steve quickly responded. "I thought it would be exciting to have someone like Max here for a while."

"I don't," the sheriff said matter-of-factly. "This *ka'ga* shows up one week and your waitress is dead the next. I don't find that exciting, as you say, Steve. I find it damned interesting."

Max's face reddened. He shouted at the sheriff, "Why don't you say what you have on your mind, Sheriff? Quit beating around the bush."

"Well, sure," Dale said as each man leaned forward to listen to the sheriff. "I've known women from the West for a lot longer time than you, Mr. Long, or whatever the hell your name is, and I can tell you that most of them were weaned from the saddle and cut their teeth on broncos. They just don't fall off of stepladders. I'm not buying what you're selling, Mr. Long."

The two men stepped toward one another, fists tightening, as if to come to blows. Steve stepped between them and looked directly at Dale.

"Look, Dale," Steve said, "Max will be here for another week or so. I'm sure you can talk with him any time you want. Let's cool down for now, Dale. You've had a heavy day and we're all kind of shook up right now. Okay?"

The two men looked around Steve and eyed one another for a moment until Max turned and walked back to the coffee pot. Lewis Davenport turned and looked at Jenny's dead body once more, experiencing sudden feelings of uneasiness on his part about this unexpected turn of events.

"Yeah," the sheriff finally said, "I guess you're right. No hard feelings, Mr. Long." He looked at Max across the room. "*Wookiye*," he said to Max, as though he meant it.

"No hard feelings," Max said and poured each man a cup of coffee.

"It just seems funny to me," Dale Walthroup said as he held his coffee cup after Max handed it to him, "how you can be standing there, watching this woman straining to reach whatever the hell it was she was reaching for, and not do anything to help her. It was then you got a sudden urge to light one up?"

Max faced the sheriff, coffee pot in hand, not moving a muscle.

"You know," the sheriff continued, never taking his eyes from the dishwasher, "there's another thing I don't understand about this *accident*."

"Yeah, what's that?" Max asked, a brief look of contempt crossing his otherwise unreadable countenance.

"Well," the sheriff began, "it's the cooking pot she impaled herself upon. There's not a dent or a scratch on it. You'd think that if someone hit that stove hard enough to knock herself cold and shove that pot handle into her gut and eventually kill herself, there'd a be a dent or scratch, or some sign of impact on that pot. Damned freaky, if you ask me."

Max said nothing. He simply stood before the sheriff and waited for him to continue his analysis of the scene which, in the mind of Dale Walthroup, it seemed, was one of a crime and not an accident.

Davenport carefully folded Jenny's dead body over on her face once more so the coroner would see her first, as everyone else apparently had since she fell.

"That damned preacher will be here soon and he'll most likely conclude this was an accidental death," Sheriff Walthroup continued. "And when he signs the death certificate and issues the coroner's papers and releases the body for Davenport here to take care of, I'll have one hell of a time convincing anybody that it just might not have been an accident. Do you see my dilemma, Mr. Long? *Wasicun iapi nayahon he?*"

"Look, Goddammit," Max's voiced hardened, "will you speak English!"

"That's what he just asked you, Max," Steve chuckled once more.

"I don't understand," Max said.

"The sheriff asked you in Dakota if you understand English."

The tension in the room reached its apex with the explanation of Dale's question. Neither man moved. Davenport had turned away from Jacqueline's body and walked to the stepladder by the stove. Steve simply leaned against the sink, to which he had walked after stepping between the two when it looked like the sheriff and Max might tangle.

"Dale," Steve interjected, "there will be an autopsy. There always is in cases like this. That'll prove this was an accident or something worse, won't it?"

"Ha," the sheriff laughed derisively, "those idiots up in Pierre will take one look at the preacher's preliminary reports on the death certificate and simply won't ask the hard questions."

"Come on, Dale," Steve said more softly, "you've had a tough day. Give Max a break. He's in shock, can't you tell that?"

Max still stood in the center of the room, holding the coffee pot and staring into space.

Sheriff Walthroup shrugged his shoulders, as if to give up trying to convince anyone in the kitchen that Jacqueline's death had occurred in any other way than that which Max described. He walked over to Davenport and leaned against the stepladder.

"*Hoksiyopa ceyapidan*," Dale muttered under his breath.

"If they do an autopsy on Jenny," the undertaker asked him, "when can I expect her body to be returned for burial?"

"Week or two," the sheriff grunted. "Just depends on how many cases they've got up there and who's on vacation right now."

Max stirred from whatever stupor had enveloped him before, turned and carried the coffee pot back to its resting place upon the base of the maker.

"I can't believe Jenny's dead," Steve said to everyone in the room. "She was such a refreshing presence here. The whole town is going to miss her."

"I was just getting to know her," Davenport said, eyeing Max as he walked out of the kitchen, retrieved a chair from the dining room, and carried it back to the kitchen and sat down heavily upon it.

"The kids in town really liked her," Steve continued speaking. "She knew how to handle them when they came in here for burgers and fries. They never acted up around her. She was sassy with them. They seemed to like that."

"Look at her there," Davenport pointed toward the stove, "teeth missing, face bruised and belly swollen around that pot handle, as though she were pregnant." He began to weep.

"She was so young," Steve said as tears built in his eyes. "Sometimes, life just isn't fair."

Everyone in the room, except Max, knew that Dale certainly agreed with Steve's last statement.

"Nobody said life is supposed to be fair," Max said without thinking.

"Yeah, I suppose they didn't," Dale spoke, "but you'd think that a benevolent force would even it out some."

"You believe in that stuff?" Max asked the sheriff directly.

"What stuff?" Dale glowered at him.

"God," Max said softly. "What you Indians call . . . what is it? Walking Tonka or something like that?"

"*Wakantanka*," Dale said with reverence for the name as he continued the conversation. "If I didn't believe in God, a God of justice, I'd have gone mad a long time ago."

"What do you mean?" Max asked him seriously.

"Look, Max," Dale said as both Steve and Davenport shuffled their feet nervously, "let's just say that I have some experience in this area of human suffering and pain. Some people seem to experience it more than others. I have a hunch that dead girl lying over there could tell you a thing or two about this subject."

"I don't understand," Max feigned sincerity. "What was so tough about her life?"

"I said it was a hunch," Dale said sternly. "Anyway, it can't be easy to be a sexual freak in this country, you know."

"You mean because she was a lesbian she suffered more than others?"

"Most likely," Dale said. "I don't believe anybody volunteers to be different from most folk. It just happens."

"But earlier, you said you thought a benevolent force would even things out so the suffering could be spread around and not fall so hard on some."

"I know what I said," Dale answered.

"Well," Max sprung forward and stood up on his feet like a debater about to draw his conclusion in a debate, "which is it Dale? Do you believe in a 'benevolent force,' as you put it, or God, as I stated it?"

"Yes, Max," Dale smiled for the first time since he arrived at the café, "I do. It's just that I really believe that we humans can foil God for a while. Maybe just go on kicking people around and making it hard for them. All the while, God watches and waits, making sure we get what's coming to us in the end. *Woowotanna* is perhaps another name for *Wakantanka*. Justice is due for some of us more than others."

"I see," Max said as he sat down once more on his chair.

"No, I suspect you don't," Dale said confidently, then added quietly, "I doubt any of us does."

Silence now filled the room as each man reflected by himself on whatever emotions stirred at the moment. Nothing more was said until a few minutes later, when the preacher arrived in a rush, carrying a clipboard.

"Sammy" Garcia was the new Methodist preacher in Kadoka. He was a Filipino, with a broad smile and firm handshake for everyone in town. Sammy and his wife, Manny, short for Emanuelle, came from Manila to Dayton, where he studied for ministry in the early 'sixties. Since his graduation, Sammy had been assigned three parishes prior to Kadoka by various Methodist bishops, each assignment lasting about three years.

Sammy possessed a certain rigidity beneath his learned exterior warmth. It didn't take congregations long to find it and soon, the immovable Sammy was revealed. Hence, his career path in the Methodist Church could best be described as one of downward spiraling mobility, bishops still assessing where they might place this man so that he would do the least harm to the institution

Sammy had enormous education debts both in the United States and the Philippines, and he had family back home who looked to him for no little monetary support. Being a pastor in Kadoka, or most anywhere else in the Dakotas where he might be assigned, simply didn't pay enough to meet Sammy's needs. Hence, he sought and acquired the post as county coroner within the first month after annual conference and his assignment to Kadoka.

Notoriously late to any death scene, just as he often was to Sunday morning worship, Sammy would not last long in this parish or in the job of county coroner. Everyone in Kadoka knew this except Sammy, however.

"I came as soon as I could," he said breathlessly but carefully so as to ease the tension between himself and the sheriff. He walked to the stove and checked Jenny's body for any sign of life. He rolled her onto her back and looked closely at the pot protruding from Jacqueline's upturned body, probing with his fingers around the edges of the wound, the pot moving slightly with each touch. Then he inspected her head, gently opening her mouth and checking for missing and broken teeth and other signs of bruising. He felt her head and peered at the bruises on it. He looked at her arms, now lying inanimately at her side. He then looked around the room at the three men who awaited his verdict.

"She's been dead about four hours, I'd say," the preacher announced. "Did she fall from that ladder?"

The sheriff grunted *"Ecawitkotkoka"* and walked away from the ladder toward Max. "Ask the dishwasher," he said sarcastically.

"Yes," Max replied quietly as he arose from his chair, "she was trying to help me fix that vent above the stove. She must have lost her balance and fell."

"Too bad. My mother always said, 'When your time comes, you go.' I guess Jenny's time had come," the preacher concluded.

"That's a pretty damned sorry theology there, Preacher," snapped the sheriff, "and an even sorrier deductive analysis. I saw lots of people 'go,' as you say, in Korea. They left because I sent them straight to Hell where they belonged and not because God called them."

"Well, Sheriff Walthroup," Sammy said more carefully, "that's your way of looking at it, I suppose."

"Yeah," the sheriff muttered. "Get on with it, we ain't got all night."

The preacher walked out of the kitchen and sat down at an empty table in the dining area and proceeded to fill out the papers attached to his clipboard. The three men in the kitchen waited quietly while he worked on his report. When he was finished, the preacher returned to the kitchen.

"Mr. Davenport," Sammy said to Lewis, "you can remove the

body any time you wish. You'll have to transport it to Pierre for an autopsy."

"Yes," Lewis said, "I'll do that first thing tomorrow."

"What did you write down as the cause of death?" Sheriff Walthroup asked him.

"I'm not sure," the preacher hesitated. "I simply wrote 'accidental death.' I prefaced that it was caused by a fall from a ladder."

"What aren't you sure about?" Steve asked him. "You don't sound that convinced."

"Well, I can't tell if the pot handle lacerated her vena cava or the fall fractured her skull, thereby causing her death," Sammy replied. "They'll sort that out in Pierre, I'm sure."

"Oh yeah," Walthroup snorted. "They're geniuses up there! Just like you!"

The preacher blushed. Steve chuckled. Lewis laughed aloud nervously. Max was expressionless.

"Well," Max suddenly said, coming to life, "if you don't need me anymore tonight, I'm going."

"Don't go too far, Mr. Long," Dale Walthroup said so sternly everyone in the room stood to attention. "I will want to talk with you some more about this *accident.*"

"Sure, Sheriff," was Max's reply, "I'll be here." He started to walk out the back door as Steve called after him.

"Max," Steve said, "I'll be short-handed now with Jenny gone. Can you give me a hand waiting tables this week?"

"Sure," Max said. "No problem."

"Be here early tomorrow."

"Okay," Max said, and he was gone.

"I'll go across the street and get the gurney," Lewis Davenport said as he turned to leave the kitchen.

"Will you need any help getting Jenny's body out of here?" Steve called after him.

"Yes, I'll be right back," Lewis said over his shoulder as he exited the café.

"You about done here, Preacher?" Sheriff Walthroup asked.

"I'm finished," Sammy replied. "I'll get a copy of this report to you in the morning, Sheriff."

"Thanks," Dale said as though he meant it. "I'll see you in the morning."

The preacher left by the front door of the café, leaving just Dale Walthroup and Steve in the kitchen with Jenny's dead body. It was Steve who broke the silence.

"Are you really convinced this wasn't an accident?" he asked the sheriff.

"As sure as God made little green apples and preachers from the Pacific," Dale answered.

"And you think Max might have killed Jenny?"

"Yep, only there's no 'might' about it, seeing he was the only one in here with her."

"Why? Why would Max kill Jenny?"

"That's what I don't know," Walthroup said to Steve confidentially. "I intend to find out."

"You don't think Max is who he said he is?"

"If that creep's a writer, I'm Ernest Hemingway," Dale said with a snicker.

"How can you be sure?" Steve asked, interested in learning more about how Dale's mind worked.

"Call it a hunch," Dale said now more quietly than before. "My mother's people were good trackers too, you know. I am about to *Owe atab ya*."

"A hunch?" Steve found Dale's statement incredulous. "Track a fox, heh?"

"Look, Steve, this has all the earmarks of a professional hit of some kind. Don't ask me why I feel this way. I just have a hunch."

"A lot of police work is based on leads and evidence," Steve said.

"Yes, and the best detective work is based on hunches," Dale interrupted.

"You have other things on your mind," Steve said, "I can tell."

"You bet I have," Dale replied. "Have you noticed how many

strangers have washed up here on the plains over the years? First, that damned undertaker and his wife who is never around, then Jenny, and now, your dishwasher."

"But we live on an interstate highway," Steve protested.

"I don't think this is a coincidence, Steve," Dale Walthroup now spoke as the lifelong friend he was to Steve. "I had my doubts about Davenport when he came. So I did some checking and ran into dead ends all over the place, trying to track his history. It's as though this guy didn't exist until he came here!"

"And his wife," asked Steve, "she's not a former starlet from Hollywood?"

"Hell, no," Dale said, "she's a hooker from Milwaukee. *Witkowen!* She might have done some visiting tricks in Hollywood but she's never had a screen test."

"What about Jenny?"

"I have known Jenny's identity was fake for some time. About a month ago, I started checking on her more seriously. I'd been curious about her from the beginning but I had some free time last month and just started fooling around."

"Yeah, what did you find on her?"

"Well, for starters, she was no lesbian."

"How do you know that?"

"Let's just say I did some church work that first year she was here."

"Yeah?"

"She was shacking up with that Methodist preacher up in Howes who wanted to be a boxer every weekend in Rapid City, until I told the bishop his suspicions were founded on fact and they moved him the hell out of South Dakota."

"I'll be damned," was all Steve could say. "So what did you find out about Jenny lately?"

"Same thing as the undertaker, my friend," Dale said. "Dead end."

"Then," Steve asked, "what do you think of this?"

"Well," Dale said, "I can't be one-hundred-percent certain of this, Steve, but all I can tell you is that somebody much higher up the food chain than me has gone to great lengths to conceal the identities of both Mr. Davenport and Ms Craig."

"Why?"

"Ever heard of WPP?"

"What?"

"Sorry," Dale apologized, "the Witness Protection Program."

"No," answered Steve, "what's that?"

"Well, when certain criminals are caught and the feds want somebody more important than them, they're sometimes convinced to turn state evidence for the promise of lifelong protection from their former employers."

"So?"

"Well, in order to grant the protection, the feds create a whole new identity for the squealers and set them up in a whole new life somewhere else in the country."

"I'll be damned," Steve said to himself. "You think both Lewis and Jenny are here for that reason?"

"Can't be sure," Dale said. "Never can be sure 'cause if the feds suspect someone's cover is blown, bang, they're gone in a heartbeat."

"Wow," Steve said, "imagine that! What are the odds that Kadoka would have two such persons in our midst?"

"Pretty damned high, I'd say," Dale laughed. "*Woyusinyaye!*"

"I see," Steve said, truly interested in his friend's powers of deduction. "Anything else?"

"Yes," continued Dale. "I had some time on my hands and got to thinking about Jenny a few days ago. So I decided to test my theory on her."

"What did you do?"

"I called her on the phone and pretended to know who she was and inquired about how things were going with her?"

"And?"

"I'm certain she was here under a false identity, this Jenny Craig of yours. I have no idea who she really was but you can be sure, because of what's happened to her today, somebody out there knows who she was and they came a-calling."

"You're certain?"

"Yes," Dale said, "I'm certain. I am only sorry she died before I had the chance to talk privately with her about whoever it is she was hiding from out here in South Dakota. I might have been able to protect her."

"What about Max?"

"I believe I'll have less trouble tracking your dishwasher," Dale said. "But I won't know that for sure until I get on the phone with some people I know around the country."

"So, you want him to hang around until you check all of this out some more," Steve surmised.

"If you can help me do that, I'd be obliged," Dale said.

"I'll try," Steve said. "I'm not sure he bought our act here today."

"I'm not sure, either," Dale replied. "You really can play 'good cop,' though. We'll have to wait and see."

"You think he'll bolt and run, then," Steve asked, "maybe as early as tonight?"

"It's possible," Dale answered, "I'll just have to keep an eye on him for a while."

The two men walked through the dining area to the front door, where they saw Davenport pushing the gurney across the street toward the café.

"When people see this, we'll have a crowd here in no time," Steve said as Dale helped Davenport lift the gurney across the threshold.

He and Dale followed Davenport into the kitchen and assisted in lifting Jenny's now heavy body onto the gurney. Before Davenport covered her face with the sheet he had prepared, Dale Walthroup reached for the pot and tugged it from her abdomen. He inspected the handle, then wrapped it in some saran wrap from a roll on a shelf near the stove.

"Be sure to take this pot with you to Pierre in the morning," Dale said to Lewis as he wheeled Jenny's body toward the front door of the café. "I doubt if there are any fingerprints on it except mine and Steve's, but you never know."

Lewis took the parcel and placed it upon the body. He and Steve wheeled Jenny's body across the street and into the mortuary as Dale Walthroup walked behind them.

In the preparatory room of the mortuary, the two men lifted Jenny's body up on a table built for the burial preparations. Under the light of this room, it was very evident that Jenny had expired. Her face was ashen, bruised and swollen, blood trickling from her right ear and ever so lightly at her lips.

"Look," the sheriff said to Lewis, "I don't want you to touch that body. Just take it as it is to Pierre in the morning. I want those guys up there to see it as we saw it."

"Sure," Lewis Davenport said to the sheriff. "I won't do a thing. I'll just keep this room cool and I'll run the air conditioner in the hearse tomorrow. It's the least I can do for a friend." He began to weep again.

The two men looked at one another, Dale's face not revealing the questions which raced through his mind at Davenport's phraseology and tendency to cry. This was a softness Dale had not seen in Davenport. It was one more factor Dale would add to his list of questions about this man's true identity.

"Good," Dale said to Davenport. "I guess that's it for now."

Dale and Steve bade Lewis Davenport goodnight and walked back across the street to the café. "Let's walk around back a moment," Dale suggested. The two men strolled to the rear of the café.

Dale walked slowly back and forth behind the café, eyes on the ground as though he were searching for something.

"Your dishwasher is a very careful man," Dale said and he bent down to retrieve something from the alley behind the café.

"What's that?" Steve asked his inquisitive friend.

"His alibi," Dale said as he showed Steve a snuffed cigarette. "Do you know what brand he smokes?"

"Winstons, I believe," Steve answered.

"It's his lucky day," Dale said as he pocketed the spent stub.

"You're not telling me everything," Steve said. He knew his friend too well.

"There is one thing the dishwasher didn't think of," Dale said with what sounded like absolute assurance.

"What's that?"

"Her wrists," Dale said.

"Her wrists?"

"It's human nature," Dale said. "Whenever any of us falls, we generally reach out to break our fall."

"So?"

"Often, when people fall as hard as Max said Jenny fell, they break or sprain their wrists. We see it all the time."

"And?"

"Jenny's wrists were fine—in perfect shape," Dale hesitated. "It's almost as if she didn't know she was falling . . ."

"Or?" Steve asked his friend.

"Or," said Dale Walthroup, "she was dead before she hit that stovetop."

"My God," Steve said, "I never thought of any of this."

"That's okay," Dale laughed, "you do the cookin' and I'll do the lookin'."

Steve laughed aloud as the two men walked back to the front of the café just as Dolores' pickup pulled up in front of the building.

She jumped from the driver's seat and ran to them. "Is it true?" she asked. "Is Jenny dead?"

"How the hell did you hear about this already?" Dale asked her. "I didn't know we were still using smoke signals!" The three friends laughed.

"My boss called me. I just can't believe it!" Dolores said. "Jenny's dead."

"There will be an autopsy," Steve said.

"Why?" Dolores asked.

"There always is whenever someone dies like she did," Dale said.

"So you don't know when the wake will be?" she asked them.

"Not at this time," Steve answered.

"Is there anything I can do?" Dolores asked sincerely.

"The thought occurs to me that someone will have to clean out her apartment," Dale said as he glanced in Dolores' direction. "Are you willing to do that?"

"I guess so," Dolores said quietly.

"Why don't you meet me tomorrow morning around ten or so?" Dale said to her. "I'd like to go with you when you enter her apartment."

"What's wrong, Sheriff?" Dolores asked, sensing there was something neither man was saying to her.

"Oh, nothing," Dale said. "I just think it's good we both enter the apartment at first. That way, nobody can accuse you or your boss of snooping around or taking anything that doesn't belong to either of you."

"Okay," Dolores said, "thanks." She walked slowly back toward her pickup. "Our preacher's family will take this pretty hard."

"Why's that?" Dale asked her.

"Well, I guess I shouldn't tell you this," she hesitated near the front of her truck. "Jenny and the Wilsons had quite an argument today at church."

"Oh," Dale asked as he shot a glance at Steve, "what about?"

"Don't know," Dolores lied. "I'll see you tomorrow, Sheriff. Goodnight, Steve."

Dale watched intently as Dolores gunned the engine of the pickup and, for the second time in seven hours, made a U-turn and drove southward toward the interstate.

"She knows more than she's saying," Dale said to Steve as they walked to the sheriff's car. Soon, Dale was driving away from the café in his 1964 Studebaker, which was a perfect, unmarked car for a county sheriff. Only Dale's mechanic and Steve knew that a 356-cubic-inch Chevy engine purred beneath the hood of his little car and no one ever questioned how it was that Dale could catch even the fastest cars of the counties whenever necessary.

As he watched the sheriff drive away, Steve reflected upon their lifetime friendship. Never had it seemed as important as tonight for these two men who, as boys, talked and dreamed together of leaving this godforsaken county and never coming back, and as adults, wouldn't trade the prairie life, with all of its freedom and space, for anything else on earth. If those who had come to Kadoka recently were not who they pretended to be, he and Dale would find them out. Living in a place where everybody knew who you were and never asked, where you were and never looked, what you did and never asked why, there was little tolerance for those who could dilute such pristine familiarity. *We'll have to have Dale for supper again real soon,* Steve thought to himself as Dale's car turned toward the corner and was gone.

Dale had confided in him this evening in ways they had not experienced in a while. Dale needed Steve's help to solve this crime, if indeed there was one. This friendship throughout their lifetimes had been a flowering tree under which each was protected from the heat of the day. Under that shelter, each had poured out his heart to the other so many times. There were few, if any, secrets anymore between them. Each was the brother the other never had. Each was the one person who could understand the intricacies of moods, good and bad, emotions, stormy or calm. They were like good music to one another; they could touch parts of each man's life without words.

Dale needed Steve right now as much as he had needed him when it seemed all was lost and there was no future. Steve could sense this in the way Dale functioned this night. Dale was never as certain as he pretended to be around the others. Dale was fishing in foreign waters.

Dale needed help from his friend. Steve knew this as surely as he knew the sun would rise in the morning. Whatever Dale asked for, whenever Dale asked, Steve would do it for his friend. Anything for his friend.

Chapter 12

Iyohi Hancokaya

The knock upon the parsonage door startled Lark from his first moments of sleep. He stretched and waited, hoping he was simply dreaming. But soon, he heard it anew, more insistent this time. Glancing at the clock atop the dresser, Lark noted it was nearly midnight. *Who could be wanting to see a pastor at this hour?* he wondered as he struggled to put on his pants and a T-shirt. He stumbled through the darkness of the living room, switching the light on as he reached the front door.

"Who's there?" he asked before opening the door.

There was no answer.

Lark unlocked the door and cautiously opened it. There in the darkness stood a man he did not know.

"What do you want?" Lark asked him.

"Are you the pastor?" the figure in the doorway asked him.

"Yes," Lark replied. "How may I help you?"

"Can I come in?" the man asked.

"It's late," Lark said as he studied the man's rather small frame in the doorway. Lark guessed his unexpected guest was merely five feet, four inches in height and fairly light in weight. He assumed the man was a Native American by the way he spoke. "I was already in bed. Can this wait until morning?"

"I can't sleep," the man said with more urgency in his voice. "I haven't slept for weeks. I've got to talk with someone."

Lark hesitated.

"All right," Lark said. "Come on in."

Lark opened the door and the Indian walked into the parsonage living room and glanced around. He was dressed very poorly and smelled as though he hadn't bathed in some time. His skin was leathery, his hair unkempt. The checkered shirt he wore was torn in several places and his jeans, which appeared to be several sizes too large for his frame, were muddied and frayed at the bottom.

"Sit down," Lark said. "Tell me who you are. Have I met you before?"

"No, we have never met," the man said quietly, seeming to adjust his eyes to the brightness of the room as he continued to glance around.

Lark watched his guest carefully as the two men sat in silence for moments on end. The man appeared very weary, his breathing labored. In the light of the parsonage living room, Lark noted several dark discolorations on the man's hands and face.

"I lived here once," the Indian said, breaking the silence of the room. "I was only ten years old. The pastor and his wife raised me after my family died in an accident out near Rapid."

"I see," Lark said, deciding to simply let this stranger speak his peace in his own good time and at his own pace while he himself fought sleep.

"That was thirty years ago," the man continued to Lark's amazement, for he appeared to be much older than forty. "It was right after my dad came home from the war. They were in Rapid celebrating. They never came home that night."

"So," Lark tried to learn more, "the pastor and his wife raised you?"

"Yes, until I graduated from St. Joseph's School over in Chamberlain."

"I see," Lark said, "then what did you do?"

"I went into the army for a couple of years and then came back here to the reservation," the man said as he stared at nothing in particular, while quietly adding "*Unktepi . . . wicunktepi.*"

"What?" Lark asked.

"Oh," the Indian laughed, "they kill us . . . we kill them."

"So," Lark continued, "you've been here since you got out of the army."

"More or less," the man replied as he leaned back into the chair on which he sat. "I move around a lot. *Tipi ota.*"

Lark yawned, missing the last two words spoken in Dakota as silence fell upon the two men once more.

"Would you like some coffee?" Lark asked him.

"Yes."

Lark arose and walked into the kitchen. As he prepared the coffee pot, he glanced from time to time into the room, where his guest now seemed to be napping while sitting upright. The man's head, which now lay nearly upon his chest, bobbed from side to side and his shoulders lifted and sagged in rhythm with each belabored breath he took.

"Do you like anything in your coffee?" Lark called from the kitchen.

No response.

Within minutes, Lark walked into the living room with two cups of black coffee in hand. The Indian roused himself and looked into Lark's eyes as he reached up for the cup of coffee.

"*Un te kta en,*" he said as he took the cup from Lark's hand. "They don't know what's taking me, but they're sure I'm dying. *Un wayazanke hin.*"

"I'm sorry," Lark said as he sat down across from his guest.

"*U Sni.* No need for sympathy," the man said as he took a sip of coffee. "I probably have it coming." Then he added in Dakota, "*Wiconte Akipa Ataya.*"

The words struck Lark like a sledgehammer.

"Is that why you wanted to talk with a pastor tonight?" Lark asked him.

"Yes," he said, taking another sip of coffee. "I don't know how much longer I have. I can tell it's getting close for I hardly have energy to walk anymore. But, *htayetu i'tokam,*" he hesitated again, "before I die, I have to tell someone what I know."

Lark did not respond. He waited for whatever it was that troubled the dying man's soul this night to be spoken. The two men drank their coffee in silence. When they had finished and Lark had offered to serve more, the Indian spoke more earnestly as he held a refilled cup in his shaking hand.

"I have done something terrible and another man is paying for it," he said. "*Wicawakte!*" he cried aloud. "I killed some men and another is in jail for life because of me." His voice quivered as he went on to speak about the uprising at Wounded Knee. His story of the events differed only slightly from what Lark had learned from those of his parish, until the Indian got to the shooting of the FBI men.

He had been with persons in the long line of cars who drove into the village of Wounded Knee on the night of February 27, 1973. It was clear and warm for a February night, he remembered. There were three hundred Dacotahs and two dozen leaders of the American Indian Movement, including Russell Means himself, to whom all looked for leadership. Among the group were Vietnam veterans, who soon began organizing defenses around the nearby Roman Catholic Church. What goals they had, he said, were focused primarily on the corruption within the BIA and the concern for open elections of leaders on the Pine Ridge Reservation.

Hardly any of them slept that first night. The radio the next morning reported the siege and rumors ran wild. Many talked of the probability of dying there as they huddled together that first frosty morning. They knew that the U.S. government would not tolerate what they had done. They believed there would be no negotiations. They formed a circle and prayed for the bravery to die a good death for their children and people. *Damakota,* they repeated to one another as they waited.

Later that day, an FBI agent arrived at a roadblock and was met by the president of the Oglala Sioux Civil Rights Organization and AIM's leader, Russell Means. He was presented with their demands that the 1868 Fort Laramie Treaty be enforced, granting national territory and sovereignty to their people, freedom to elect their own leaders, and the lifting of BIA oppression from their people.

It was reported that the agent screamed at them and mocked them, threatening them with annihilation unless they surrendered. This only strengthened their resolve to resist. *Damakota*, they said to one another in greeting as day faded into day during the siege. For seventy-one days, through three blizzards, they resisted and held on. *Damakota!*

Soon, media from around the world arrived to report this latest confrontation between Native Americans and the government of the United States. Night after night, it seemed, major TV networks reported on the impasse at Wounded Knee. The press was omnipresent. Flashbulbs and steno pads were evident everywhere in the village.

The Sioux feigned more firepower than they possessed by sharing rifles and painting pieces of stove pipe to pretend they were rocket launchers or bazookas. From day to day, firefights and skirmishes took place. World War II veterans crossed federal lines at night to bring in supplies and two pilots flew in medicine, food and ammunition. *Damakota!*

As the days wore on, two Sioux defenders were killed by federal bullets. A man named Frank Clearwater and a Vietnam vet named Buddy Lamont were found dead, victims of sniper fire. Fifteen others were wounded. Rumors spread within the village that FBI-trained death squads had been flown into South Dakota and were terrorizing the people throughout the reservation. AIM was identified as a terrorist organization and named by the FBI, along with the Black Panthers, as being one of the most dangerous groups in America, it was said on radio and television. *Damakota!*

When it became obvious to the leaders that they had no chance of gaining more support, they agreed to end the siege after seventy-one days. Little did any of them suspect at the time that none of their concerns would be addressed seriously, nor that mysterious deaths of many who had taken part in the uprising would follow. Sixty-six violent deaths in all. *Damakota!* Many unsolved murders. *Damakota!*

Then AIM again appeared on the Pine Ridge Reservation. They came back in 1975 and established a spiritual camp, much like the present one in the Black Hills, at the Jumping Bull Ranch. It was only a matter of time before the feds returned and confronted the Indian leaders anew. After a build-up of personnel on the reservation, the FBI supplemented its manpower by ordering special agents into South Dakota for a sixty-day period. The stage was set for tragedy once more.

He and another man were driving explosives into the reservation from Rapid City when they noted two late-model cars following them. They tried to elude the cars behind them, but to no avail. They avoided the road which led to the AIM encampment and decided to simply stop and confront the cars on their own. They stepped out of their pickup, carrying semi-automatic rifles in their hands. The two cars stopped and two men got out of them, walked to the rear of their cars, and removed rifles of their own from the trunks. One of them fired. The ensuing gunfight soon brought many Indians running to the scene and a blazing gunbattle took place. Cars were coming onto the scene, guns were firing in all directions at once. He and his partner jumped into their pickup and drove off to unload the explosives. When they returned to the scene, it was quiet. Word was that two FBI men had been wounded or killed. He walked down the hillside to make sure.

What happened next was pure instinct. As he approached, one of the wounded men arose and pointed his gun. Five shots rang out. The two FBI men, Run Williams and Jack Color, lay dead on the ground. He ran up the hill, jumped into the pickup, and in the confusion that followed, managed to drive off the reservation and simply fade into the Rapid City area.

"*Damakota,*" the man exclaimed as he concluded telling his story. "*Damakota!*"

Then silence filled the room once more. The two men sat looking intently at one another for what seemed an eternity.

"I am a Dachotan," the Indian said softly. "*Damakota.*"

Lark listened as this stranger recounted the killing of the

FBI agents once more. It was he, he claimed, who killed the government men. It was he, he claimed, who fired the fatal shots. It was his relatives, he claimed, who then cooperated with authorities and told them that others were responsible. It was he, he claimed, who now sat as one convicted by his own guilt, not of murder, for the killings were in self-defense, but of fear. And now, it was he who was dying due to his cowardice and shame.

Unlike those brave Sioux people who stood and died in the Massacre at Wounded Knee, he had hidden. He had run.

"They have the wrong man in prison," he concluded as his body convulsed with emotion. "I did it. I shot those two men."

"But how?" Lark asked. "How could you keep this secret so long? There were others involved. They know you did the shooting."

"Yes," the stranger continued. "The government wanted Peltier. We gave him to them. *Unktepi . . . wicunktepi.*"

"But," Lark said incredulously, "they had evidence and witnesses."

"Yes," the Indian continued, "all supplied by us."

"He is one of your own people!" Lark said more loudly.

"Black Elk said it long ago," the man continued to counter Lark's argument, "our nation's hoop is broken and scattered, there is no center any longer, and the sacred tree is dead."

The words were cold and revealed with what resolve this man and others on the reservation had determined to give the federal government what it wanted. Peltier, acquitted of attempted murder of a Milwaukee police officer only months before Lark's arrival at Longvalley and denied an appeal by the Eight Circuit Court, was rumored to be ready to ask the Supreme Court to review his case. Every member of the church had mentioned this to Lark at one time or another. Expectations were high on the reservation that Leonard Peltier, who had been captured in Canada nearly eight months after the shootout and extradited to the United States to stand trial for the murder of the two Special Agents of the FBI, would be granted by the Supreme Court what he could not obtain at the bench of Judge Paul Benson in Fargo in June 1977 nor in

St. Louis in December 1977, where one of the panel of judges hearing his appeal was William Webster, recently named by President Carter to head the FBI.

"The deck is stacked against Leonard Peltier," Lark said quietly.

"Unless . . ." the man started to say.

"Unless what?" Lark asked, interrupting him.

"Unless they can spring him from Lompoc," he said without emotion.

"What? You've got to be kidding. That's a high-security prison. He's not going anywhere."

"Stranger things have happened," the Indian said and for the first time during their late-night encounter, he smiled. "*Unwastepi Dacotah!*" he said with a sigh as he leaned back into the chair, "*Wanna mdustan.*"

"My friend," Lark said to him, "you look tired. I know I'm tired. It's almost one-thirty. Would you like to stay here tonight?"

"That is very kind of you, Pastor," the man replied.

"We can continue this conversation in the morning, if you like" Lark said.

"Okay." The Indian looked very tired, indeed. "*Heyakecinhan.*"

"Why don't you sleep in my bed?" Lark offered. "I can stretch out here in the living room or sleep in one of our kids' beds."

"Okay."

Lark's guest followed him into the bedroom and waited while Lark gathered some things he would need in the morning.

"You just make yourself comfortable," Lark said to him. "The bathroom is in the hallway to your right. I'll leave the night light on in it for you."

"Thank you," the man said as he looked around the small bedroom with its double bed, small dresser and nightstand alongside a meager closet whose door held several shirts and pants hanging on a makeshift hanger.

"It's not much," Lark apologized. "But my wife and I make it do for now."

"Our churches are poor," the Indian said, "and the clergy *tuwe on'sika*."

Lark had heard that phrase his first Sunday in Longvalley. He couldn't remember who said it to him but he remembered the meaning that was explained.

"Poor fellows" was an apt description for anyone who served Indian churches in the Dakotas. Lark could attest to that fact now that he had met all of his colleagues on the reservation. *Tuwe on'sika* indeed!

Nothing else was said. Lark returned to the living room and stretched a sheet that he had retrieved from the bathroom closet over the sofa. Turning out the light, he lay upon the sofa and thought of his conversation with his guest. Just before he fell asleep, Lark realized that he didn't even know his guest's name.

He arose and walked to the doorway of the bedroom. He listened to the deep and steady resonance of breathing. He was sure the man was asleep. They would formally introduce themselves to one another in a few hours, Lark decided.

He returned to the living room, lay down upon the couch, and immediately followed the lead of his guest into a deep and dreamless sleep.

The station wagon, its lights turned off for over a mile, crept down Main Street in Longvalley until its motor was cut near the parsonage. A lighted cigarette silhouetted figure sat inside. The figure, short and stocky, emerged eventually from the driver's side and retrieved two cans of liquid from the back seat. Then quietly, the cargo was carried around to the rear of the parsonage.

Eyes watched from a distance, listening for some indication of safety so he could edge closer to the car. Eyes sniffed the air for any trace of familiarity, but none save the town and its residents came forth. Eyes moved slowly toward the station wagon.

Suddenly, Eyes was aware of something or someone else in the shadows nearby. How could this have been missed, Eyes wondered? Eyes froze and turned enough to catch the scent of another man there near the house. Eyes could not see the man but instinctively knew he was there. Eyes walked around the side of the station wagon and listened.

Suddenly, the night air was alive with sounds and smells Eyes had seen before. Fire! Eyes walked to the front of the car and looked directly at the parsonage, now beginning to burn as the figure emerged from behind it and ran straight in Eyes' direction.

Soundless, Eyes beheld the events of the next few seconds as though in a dream. As the figure raced toward the station wagon, the hidden one emerged and overtook it. One arm reached across the mouth of the running figure, stopping it in mid-stride. The other arm swung across the figure's throat with a blade that faintly glinted against the ever-brightening yard.

Eyes backed away from the car as the hidden one dragged the body of the figure toward the waiting car. Quickly, the body of the figure was placed into the rear of the wagon. Then the hidden one slipped inside the wagon and urged its engine to start. As quietly as the wagon had arrived, it departed, carrying the figure and the hidden one to some unknown destination.

The sound of dry wood and old paper being consumed by rising flames beckoned Lark from his reverie. The air in the parsonage was extremely hot and smoke choked him as Lark, suddenly fully awake, leapt from the sofa and rubbed his painful eyes as he tried to make out what was happening. He knew in an instant that the house was succumbing to flames. They seemed to be particularly brilliant in the bedroom area.

Lark staggered toward the bedroom doorway, hoping he could rescue his guest from certain death. As he stood in the hallway, the sound of the fire, which now lapped at the ceiling of the bedroom, forming a fiery backdrop on the entire west wall of the parsonage, he could see the form of the Indian, still lying upon the bed, his arms outstretched to the heavens as though he were walking up a hill.

Realizing that he couldn't save the man, Lark turned and

instinctively sought to save himself as the smoke from the fire now filled the entire house. He reached the front door and tried to open it. Try as he might, the door would not open. Feeling himself starting to faint and gasping deeply for some soot-free air, Lark fell to the floor of the living room, where he discovered the air to be more breathable. He had but one strategy left if he were to save himself from the fate of his guest.

He crawled quickly in the direction of the bathroom as flames danced now across the ceiling above him. The heat was almost unendurable as he reached the threshold of the bathroom doorway, keeping as low to the floor as any forward progress allowed. He took a deep breath and stood to face what he believed to be the window. With all the energy he still possessed, he threw his body toward the window. A force like that of another one unseen, together with a deafening explosion, lifted and pushed him through the window and out of the house onto the ground, just a yard or so from the conflagration.

Lark lay on his back, gazing up at the blaze which now seemed to be consuming what was once his home. Sparks flew in all directions from the building as the roof collapsed into the center of the house.

He rolled onto his side and gathered strength to rise and walk away from the burning house. After a few hundred feet, he turned and faced the house once more. It crackled and burned. Small explosions, like miniature fireworks displays on a summer's night, erupted from varying places inside the now dying blaze. Two by fours glowed, giving but a hint of the structure which, only moments before, housed everything Lark and his family owned and offered to poor indigents a place to lay their heads for the night.

As he stood gazing into the flames, listening to them lick up like hungry dogs the last vestiges of life, he froze with fear. How could this happen? Why did it happen? What happens now?

He turned away from the fiery pillars of the parsonage once more and began to run. At first, his gait was not unlike that of a man at the end of a race: unsteady, weak and weary, stumbling, at best. With no light from the moonless sky engulfing the prairie, Lark's pace was halting at first. But once used to the taller grasses whipping at his bare legs and naked feet, he gained confidence in his footing and raced ever faster away from the scene.

Soon, the land began to rise beneath his feet and his breathing became more difficult with the exertion. Uphill he ran until his legs gave way beneath him and he stumbled to the ground.

The air felt good as it coursed through his recovering lungs. The night was neither too warm nor too cool. He sat up and gazed back toward the house which once was his.

The fire was beginning to die below, the sound of it no longer discernible from where he sat and watched. People stirred in the village below. Figures raced toward the house to help extinguish the blaze. No sirens broke the stillness of the night, signalling help was on its way. Nothing else changed below except the colors of the blaze itself. Yellow to orange to red to crimson to blue.

He gazed at the scene until he regained his strength. Then rising, he turned and ran once more. No particular direction beckoned save any place far away from what he had just experienced. On he ran, stopping to rest only when he could not breathe deeply. For hours he ran and rested, never noting that another ran with him.

Eyes halted each time the runner stopped and rested. Eyes crouched very low to the ground so as to remain unseen and unheard by the one who ran so hard. Eyes could do this forever. He was bred for it. He loved it. From time to time, Eyes wandered away from the pathway left by the runner to refresh at a stream or pond nearby. Then quickly picking up the scent of the trail, Eyes sauntered up behind the runner, never revealing a presence that might be disturbing or distracting.

On he ran until the first signs of dawn appeared on the horizon to the east. Looking around, he could not make out any landmarks he knew. Only a slight, early-morning breeze disturbed the grassy knolls around him. The rest was peaceful and still. Except for his stomach, which had begun to growl discernibly with each time of rest, only the breeze whispered in the stillness.

By early morning, he could run no more. He lay down upon the grass and looked up to the sky. It was going to be a beautiful day. Not a cloud in the sky. It seemed so peaceful here. Sleep, its arms open to caress the weary and heavy laden, gently held him in its grasp and all the fears of the night evaporated like the morning dew.

Chapter 13

To'ketu Oyakapi

The smell of burning wood and flesh greeted Sonny Firecloud when he stepped out of his Chevy pickup and began to survey the wreckage of the scene. The charred body was not hard to see in the midst of still-smoking ash. The shrunken figure lay atop still-warm, steel bed springs.

A small crowd stood nearby, quietly talking with one another as they watched the tribal policeman take notes on a small pad he always seemed to carry in his hip pocket. The concurrence of opinion focused on the assumed body of the pastor, now burned beyond recognition, arms stretched toward the sky, as though pleading with the Almighty one last time before death overtook him.

Some women in the crowd wept as they found it difficult to gaze upon what now remained of the church parsonage and the pastor. Some of the youth who played on the high school football team and some of the band members were now coming to the scene, walking on their way to the school bus stop, albeit using a circuitous route this morning.

Shortly after eight, Dale Walthroup arrived. The two lawmen eyed each other as Dale slowly got out of his car and approached Sonny.

"*To'ken yaun he*," Sonny asked Dale as he stretched forth his hand in greeting.

"I've had better days," Dale said gruffly.

"Where were you when I called?" Sonny asked his counterpart.

"Busy night," was all Dale said as he now walked toward the remains of the parsonage. "Couldn't sleep. So I just drove around."

"I see," Sonny smiled. "Who is she?"

"Dunno," shrugged Dale. "But I intend to find out."

"I see," Sonny looked at Dale quizzically.

"Oh," Dale said, realizing that Sonny knew nothing of the "accident" in Kadoka the preceding night. "I'm working on a mysterious death that took the life of a young woman up in Kadoka last night. I thought you meant . . ."

"No, man," Sonny interrupted, "I was only kidding you. Sorry."

"No problem," Dale said as he bent to get a closer look at the corpse. "Is this the preacher?" he asked Sonny.

"I assume it is," Sonny replied. "We're looking for the rest of his family right now. Nobody seems to know where they are."

Dale bent down, his back toward the corpse, which lay upon what was left of the bedspring. Something caught his eye and he reached for it in the ashes.

"Hey, Sheriff," Sonny shouted, "stop messing with the crime scene."

"*Wosice wopazo?*"

"Pretty obvious, isn't it?" Sonny asked.

"Well, look here," Dale said as he retrieved a wedding ring from the ashes and extended it toward Sonny. "Is it the pastor's ring?"

Sonny gazed inside the warm circle and spied the initials "LW" and "FW" and the word "Forever" still readable in the circle.

"This is the pastor's ring," Sonny said as he handed it to the sheriff. "His name was Lark Wilson and his wife's name is Fran."

"Too bad," Dale said as he gazed upon the ring. "Who would want to kill the pastor? And why?"

Sonny turned and looked toward the rising sun. "*Iyehantu*," Sonny said quietly.

"This is a case we need to work together," Dale said with authority.

"Why?" Sonny wanted to know.

"Well," Dale began hesitantly, "I came down here this morning to see this preacher and ask him a few questions about his knowledge of the woman who died in Kadoka last night. I had reason to believe he knew her and could shed some light on her background. Now, he's dead too. Damned curious coincidence, if you ask me."

"I see," Sonny replied, now very interested in everything Dale knew and wasn't saying at the moment. He had known Dale for twenty years. The two men didn't exactly trust one another, Sonny being the child of Sioux parents and Dale having only one parent who could claim the heritage. But each respected the other for his life's work made them brothers in ways neither one's heritage would allow.

Dale eyed Sonny for a brief moment as the two men stood in the midst of the ruin that hours before had been the parsonage. Then he told the story of the death of the waitress in Kadoka, the mysterious dishwasher who might have been the only eyewitness to her death, and the attempts he made during the night to gain information on both of them. He also shared that he had learned that the pastor and the young woman had been involved in some kind of argument just hours before her death. He explained that he learned this from a telephone call from a resident of Longvalley. He was awaiting calls from the FBI, he explained.

"So," Sonny said, "you think these deaths are related?"

"*Cetunhdapicasni*," Dale snorted.

Just then, a car raced down the main street toward the crowd and came to a screeching halt. Three children jumped from the back seat and raced toward the remains of the parsonage. An ashen-faced woman emerged from the driver's seat. As she walked toward Dale and Sonny and gazed at the scene, smoke still rising from where her house stood only yesterday, she staggered and collapsed upon the lawn, sobbing hysterically.

Dale reached her first, gently lifting her body in his arms and stroking her hair away from her wet eyes. "Are you Mrs. Wilson?" he asked her as he sought to comfort her in his supportive embrace.

"Yes," she sobbed. "I shouldn't have gone," she said through her convulsing shudders as she continued to weep. "We heard on the morning news that there had been a fire . . . the Longvalley church parsonage . . . oh my God!" She began to cry uncontrollably and buried her head in Dale's chest. "I'm sorry, Lark. I'm so sorry!" she wailed.

Sonny had now gathered the children together. The three stood in shock as they gazed upon the smoldering ruins of their home and their father's body lying in the middle of it.

"Daddy," Leigh Ann cried, "I love you."

Walt and Saul put their arms around her and fought back their tears while Sonny gently asked them where they had been during the night.

"We went to Chamberlain," Walt bravely responded to the police officer's inquiry. "We were going to do some school shopping and then Daddy was going to join us tomorrow for some fun."

"When did you leave for Chamberlain?" Sonny asked, still more gently.

"Yesterday afternoon," Walt said, his voice beginning to quiver, "just after lunch."

Sonny was going to pursue this line of inquiry when Saul said, "We like Chamberlain. You can rent boats there and ride on the lake."

"I see," Sonny replied, his inquisitive spirit now satisfied.

"When did this happen?" Walt wanted to know.

"As best we know," Sonny replied, "shortly after midnight. Folks here didn't even notice it until the fire was so bad no one could save the building."

Walt looked around at the now dispersing crowd and shook his head. Then he took his sister and brother and walked back to their mother, who was now sitting up upon the lawn, talking with Sheriff Walthroup.

"Your husband," Dale continued his interrogation carefully, "how old was he?"

Tears formed in Fran's eyes anew as she gazed far beyond the sheriff and the present moment.

"He was thirty-eight," she said quietly, seemingly coming to grips with the reality that she was now a widow. "He would have been thirty-nine in November."

Dale watched the children gather around their mother, seating themselves close to her upon the ground.

"And you folks came here to Longvalley this summer?"

"Yes, about three months ago," it was the oldest son who took up the conversation.

"Where did you move from?" Dale now intended to get as much information as he could from the stricken family while Sonny interviewed some of the few remaining villagers who stood nearby.

"Pennsylvania," Walt answered directly. "We moved from Lancaster, Pennsylvania."

"We don't like it much here," the younger lad interjected with surprising authority in his voice. "There's nothing to do and the kids here don't like us."

The older boy shot his brother a glance that spoke *That's enough for now*, while their sister nudged closer to Fran and began to sob.

"You haven't found any friends?" Dale asked.

"Yes," said Walt. "We have a few."

Saul raised his eyes and looked away as Fran began to speak once more.

"The children and I have had a hard time adjusting to South Dakota," she said quietly. "You'd have to know where we came from to begin to understand the immensity of this transition for us." The sentence was spoken with an obvious attention to the care one takes so as to not offend natives of a region to which one has just moved.

"I can imagine that this transition has been very difficult for you, Mrs. Wilson," Dale said kindly. "Not everyone is cut out for life on the prairie. Nor an Indian reservation, for that matter."

There, the word had been used. Reservation.

Mrs. Wilson gazed into the sheriff's eyes, as if looking for some clue as to how far this part of their conversation could go.

"Has your husband always worked with the disadvantaged?" Dale wanted to know just how new all of this was for the now fatherless and husbandless family.

"Lark always gravitated toward those who needed more than he could sometimes give." She was being careful to protect both her husband's reputation and her children's sensitivities.

"He served the poor in inner cities before coming here to South Dakota?"

"Let's say the middle class," Mrs. Wilson seemed to want to close this part of his inquiry. "Lark always had a fondness for the middle-class people and those who had a hard time making a living."

By this time, Sonny had joined the group and was seated nearby, listening to their conversation. He seemed to be scribbling something on his little note pad.

"I just don't know how this could happen," Fran spoke to both lawmen. "Lark was always so careful. How could he have died in such an accident?"

The children began to weep as Sonny glanced first at Dale and then at Mrs. Wilson, trying to think of a way to put to words what was on his mind. Silence except for the quiet sobs of the children overtook them.

"I don't believe this was an accident," Sonny said finally.

"What?" Fran was startled. "Then what happened here?"

"We don't know for sure," Dale took up the conversation anew. "We're going to need to send your husband's body to Pierre for an autopsy."

"Oh no," Fran sobbed anew. "I can't believe this. God wouldn't bring us all out here for Lark to be a victim of . . ." she couldn't finish.

"We don't know for sure," Sonny continued. "It's just a hunch, I have to be honest. I don't know anything for sure as yet. But if your husband is the victim of foul play of some kind, we'll know as soon as an autopsy is performed."

"I don't understand," Fran now was screaming at the sky. "Why?"

"Mrs. Wilson," Dale tried to calm her a bit as he reached and touched her arm, "there have been two *accidental* deaths in the past twenty-four hours that are under investigation."

"Two?" Fran stopped crying and now gazed only at Dale. "I don't understand what you are saying."

"We had a death up in Kadoka yesterday afternoon that I have some suspicion about and here, Sonny has some misgivings. We both are wondering if they are related in some way."

"I don't understand," was all Fran could say as she looked first at Dale and then Sonny.

"I have to ask you some questions, Mrs. Wilson," Dale continued. "You are under no obligation to answer them. But if you know anything, it might help us sort this out."

"Why don't I take the children down to the store and get something to eat?" Sonny offered. "We'll have to wait a while for Davenport to arrive and take your husband's body to Pierre."

"All right," Fran said numbly. "You children go with Sheriff . . ."

"Firecloud," Sonny said as he got to his feet and began to walk toward his car. The children soon followed him, leaving only Dale Walthroup and Fran Wilson seated upon the ground in front of what was, only hours before, the parsonage of the Longvalley Church.

As they sat looking at one another, it was Fran who spoke first.

"The death in Kadoka," she said with great hesitation, "was it a waitress?"

Dale Walthroup was seldom surprised but his heart skipped a beat with Fran's question. He was glad to know that Mrs. Wilson would be cooperative with his investigation.

"Yes," he said. "You folk knew her?"

"Lark did," Fran said, now with a hardened edge to her voice and a steely gaze into the sheriff's eyes. "They had been brief acquaintances in Lancaster."

"Go on," Dale urged.

Then Fran shared the entire story as she knew it. Lark had met the young woman in New York City on his way back to Lancaster from a denominational peace rally preparation meeting. She had pretended to be a professor at Franklin and Marshall College in Lancaster. She had pretended to be interested in the Peace Movement. Lark was attracted to her. One thing led to another until Lark was confronted with compromising pictures of the young woman and himself. Their marriage faltered immediately. His career as a senior minister in one of Lancaster's historical churches came to a crashing halt. The scandal had been heartbreaking for them both.

"Then what happened?" Dale needed to know.

"After a separation, we got our family back together. Lark was exonerated of all charges against him once it was discovered that he himself had been a victim of some kind of plot to embarrass Peace Movement leaders. He was really getting his life back together and was excited about this new opportunity to serve the church on the Pine Ridge Reservation."

"And you?"

"I'll admit it wasn't easy for me to give up my teaching job in Lancaster and come all the way out here to start anew. I felt sorry for our children. But I loved my husband. I loved what I saw in his eyes again as we made the decision to come here"

"Which was?"

"Lark was like he was when we left seminary. He had passion for his work once more. And let me tell you, there was never a better time between us than when Lark had that fire for ministry."

"What about the young woman?"

"We never knew what happened to her. She just seemed to vanish. One day she was there, messing up our lives. The next, she was gone without a trace."

"Did you or your husband ever learn anything about the plot to ruin his career in Lancaster?"

"Only that the pictures used to enrage the congregational leaders were professionally altered and the drug given to Lark the last night he saw Jennifer was an experimental one developed by the military."

"Jennifer?" Dale was curious about the name.

"That's what she called herself then," Fran said with disgust. She stopped and stared into space once more, tears began to form in her eyes.

"What do you mean *then?*" Dale pressed her.

"She's known as 'Jenny' now," Fran said with some disgust as her body convulsed involuntarily. "She was here yesterday in church! One of Lark's parishioners invited her."

"You recognized her?" Dale was truly curious.

"Yes and no," Fran said, regaining her emotions. "I saw her. Frankly, I couldn't see what attraction that woman could hold for Lark."

"Why is that?"

"She looked so different. She has let herself go something horrible since she was in Lancaster."

"She didn't look like herself?"

"No," Fran said with renewed disgust. "She was fairly beautiful when she was in Lancaster. But she wasn't very attractive yesterday. Her hair is darker and she has to be at least twenty to twenty-five pounds heavier."

"Then how do you know it was the same woman?" Dale needed to know everything Fran knew about Jenny.

"She told us," Fran said, as she shook anew. "And even if she hadn't, I knew that my husband somehow sensed he knew her from somewhere. All I could think of yesterday was, *Here we go again.*"

"You were angry?" Dale asked.

Fran started to weep again as she glanced over her shoulder at the lifeless remains of her husband in the still smoldering ruins of the parsonage. After a few brief moments, she gathered herself once more and looked straight at Dale.

"Yes," she said with conviction. "I confess that I was furious with her and Lark yesterday. I threatened to take the kids back to Lancaster. I am so sorry that I left Lark with that impression before he died." Her crying resumed.

Dale waited for Fran to regain her composure. When she did, she looked up at the sheriff and said, "You haven't answered some of my questions."

"You're very intuitive, Mrs. Wilson," Dale said as he tried to avoid her stare. "It was the young woman named Jenny who died yesterday afternoon."

"I somehow knew that, Sheriff," Fran continued. "What I don't know is why you used the word 'suspicious' with regard to her death, and the other policeman said my husband's death might also be something other than an accident. What are you two trying to tell me?"

"Only that neither death can be ruled accidental until we're sure," Dale lied.

"Look," Fran said hastily, "my kids are at the store. Tell me what you know."

"Well," Dale Walthroup wasn't used to people pressing him in investigations. The shoe was on the other foot. This woman wanted to know what he knew and he couldn't think of any reason not to tell her.

"I'm listening," Fran said with determination to learn more.

"Let's just say that I have reason to doubt that Jenny died the way it appeared she did in that café yesterday."

"And my husband?

"If Jenny's death wasn't accidental," Dale continued, "then that would cast a doubt upon what we're looking at here."

"Why?"

"Mrs. Wilson," Dale continued, "I'm fairly convinced that Jenny Craig, as she was known in Kadoka, was hiding from someone. It may be that she was discovered. Unfortunately, the person who discovered her may also have been aware that she contacted your husband yesterday. That would have placed his life in jeopardy."

"My God," Fran shouted. "What do you mean? Are my children in danger?"

"No," Dale now said with confidence. "I can assure you that your children are not in any danger."

Fran visibly relaxed. Then she quietly asked, "Am I?"

"I don't believe you are," Dale assured her. "But at this point, everything I'm working with is conjecture. I won't know for sure until I get some answers from people back East."

Fran sat up with a start. "What people?" she asked.

"Don't worry," Dale assured her anew. "I'm talking with FBI and other police sources. I don't believe you or your children are in immediate danger. Whoever did this, if it was a plot of some kind, is long gone from here by now."

Fran looked at the sheriff. He exuded a confidence at the moment that she sensed she could trust. She decided to take whatever advice this man would offer her.

"Mrs. Wilson," Dale asked Fran another question, "how tall was your husband?"

Fran was startled back to reality by Dale's use of the past tense with regard to her husband. She began to cry once more.

"Mrs. Wilson?" Dale pressed her.

"I'm sorry," she said between renewed sobs. "Lark was six-three. Why do you ask?"

Dale turned to look at the corpse in the ruins once more. Then he turned toward Fran and said, "Just a thought. Do you mind if I ask you a couple more questions about your husband?"

"No," Fran said as she regained her composure.

"Did your husband ever break any major bones?"

"Not that I ever knew of," Fran said, now sensing the direction in which Dale's inquiry was leading.

"Who was your husband's dentist?"

"I'll get that information for you later today," Fran said. "Do you think this body is someone other than my husband?"

"In cases like these, we always have to make sure," Dale said comfortingly. "Thanks, Mrs. Wilson. You have been a terrific help to us."

"It's Fran," she said with a smile.

"Thanks, Fran."

The two got to their feet as Sonny drove up with the children.

A hearse trailed the tribal policeman's car. When the vehicles came to a rest, Sonny and the children got out and walked to Fran and Dale while the undertaker walked around behind the hearse and retrieved a gurney and started to push it toward the body in the ruins.

"You'll need some help with the body, Lewis," Dale called to him. "We're going to send it straight to Pierre, right, Sonny?"

"Yes," Sonny replied, "I'll get the papers from my car."

Lewis shrugged and waited for Sonny and Dale to help him lift the body carefully from the bedsprings and place it onto the gurney. After they had rolled the body into the back of the hearse alongside that of Jacqueline's, all three men walked toward Fran and the children.

"Full house," joked Sonny as they approached Fran. "Was that the body of the waitress?"

"Yeah," Lewis said, not appreciating Sonny's attempt at light conversation in the wake of two mysterious deaths in less than twenty-four hours.

"Thanks, Lewis," Dale said as the undertaker walked away from the two lawmen and went toward Fran Wilson.

"Mrs. Wilson," Lewis Davenport stammered, "I'm so sorry for your loss. I'm Lewis Davenport, the undertaker in Kadoka."

"Thank you," Fran said as she began to weep once more. "There is nothing more here for us. The children and I will drive back to Chamberlain. May we follow you?"

"Yes, ma'am," Lewis said quietly. "That would be fine."

Fran turned to shake Dale's hand. "Thank you," she said as she gave his hand a gentle squeeze. "You've been very kind."

"You're welcome," Dale said, not quite sure how to respond to this preacher's widow. "I'll be in touch."

"We'll both be in touch," Sonny Firecloud repeated as he extended his hand toward Fran and as she took it he continued, "Let me know where you'll be staying in Chamberlain."

"Al's Oasis Motel," Fran said. "We never checked out today. Lark was going to join us tomorrow in Chamberlain."

Both lawmen stared at the ground. Fran and the children walked back to their car, got in, and drove slowly away behind Lewis Davenport's hearse.

"What did you learn?" Sonny asked Dale as the two lawmen found themselves to be the only people left at the scene.

"*Waditaka Winohinca*," Dale said as if to himself.

"What?" Sonny insisted.

"She is a brave woman," Dale said even more quietly. "I'll call you when I get back to Kadoka. I've got some paperwork to fill out. And I'm expecting some phone calls from Washington," he concluded with a lie.

"Okay," Sonny said. "In the meantime, what do I do?"

"Serve and protect," Dale said with a smirk, "just serve and protect."

"Yeah," Sonny replied with derision, "you and I sure seem to be doing a lot of that lately."

Dale got into his Studebaker and headed toward Highway 73, just behind Mrs. Wilson's car. He wondered to himself as he turned the car north toward Kadoka how he might have saved the victim's life in Longvalley if only the call from Washington had come sooner the evening before.

"Hello," Dale said quietly as he answered the phone on its fourth ring, a habit with him that bordered on superstition. "Dale Walthroup here."

The clock that ticked incessantly on his desk read 10:30 P.M. The air in his little abode was stuffy and warm for this late evening.

"Dale," the voice on the other end said with some insistence to be heard, "this is Jorgerson. Hal told me you called earlier this evening and I just got in from the Kennedy Center."

"Oh," Dale mumbled, "what was going on there tonight?"

"An absolutely beautiful performance of 'Aida,'" Jorgerson said with appreciation of the arts evident in his voice.

"Must have been nice," Dale continued, "but then, besides the Saturday Texaco show, we don't get much opera out our way."

The two men laughed.

"From the description Hal left with my assistant," Jorgerson continued, "I'd say you have a member of the De Angelis family visiting you. In fact, you have one of their more notorious members, if I have my facts straight."

"How's that?" Dale asked.

"Matty Fratello," the man on the other end continued, or "Max or Jimmy or Pop. These are all names by which this character is known out here. He is one very mean and dangerous hit man who works for his uncle's family out of Hoboken, New Jersey. Actually, we've been looking for this guy for just about four years. We've got the goods on him for a hit in New York City eight years ago. The family was tipped off and we thought they'd sent him out of the country or something."

"Being in South Dakota," Dale said with meaning, "especially this part of South Dakota, is like being 'out of the country.'"

The two men laughed again. They had known one another in the armed forces and had always gotten along well.

"You say he's pretending to be a writer or a dishwasher out there?"

"Yeah," Dale slurred his response, "pretending is a good way of putting it."

"Well," the voice continued, "if this is who I think it is, you don't have to worry for yourself, but you do have to look out for anyone else this character is after for it isn't like these persons to hang around after they've killed someone."

"Do you mean . . ." Dale started to ask a question of his FBI friend.

"Yes," Jorgerson interrupted, "there must be another target, if I am right about who you have on your hands. Got any ideas?"

"Uhm," Dale mused, "only hunches."

"Go on," Jorgerson said, "maybe I can help."

"We have an undertaker here who I've always had some questions in my mind about."

"What's his name?"

"Lewis Davenport."

"Doesn't ring a bell at the moment," Jorgerson said. "It's not *like us to place two persons in the same community. Especially a community as small as yours."*

"I see," Dale said quietly.

"Anyone else?"

"Do you ever place preachers?"

"What the hell?"

"Preachers," Dale said more insistently than before. "We've got a new preacher down the road from Kadoka and I have reason to believe that the waitress and he knew one another."

"I'm sure we've got some preachers in the program, Dale," Jorgerson said with authority. "But I'd have to research that one for you. What's the preacher's name and what church does he serve?"

"His name is Wilson, I'm told. Lark is his first name."

"Interesting," Jorgerson said. "How long has he been there?"

"About three months," Dale replied.

"What denomination?"

"Is that important?

"Might be."

"I'll check it out," Dale said. "I'm really not sure. All we have in this town are Catholics and Methodists."

"Well," Jorgerson went on, "I recall from my U.S. History and Culture classes that the Congress gave certain Indian tribes to certain denominations way back in the nineteenth century. What are the tribes in your area?"

"Sioux," Dale said. "Dacotah, Yankton, Lakota and Teton," he specified.

"I think the Catholics, Congregationalists, Episcopalians and Presbyterians were assigned to those tribes originally. But I guess Indians are fair game for any religious persuasion these days."

"Kitanna waste," Dale said without thinking.

"What was that?" Jorgerson wanted to know. He suddenly remembered that Dale often muttered to himself in his mother's native tongue.

"Nothing," Dale said. "You're right. Everybody's here now, from Catholics to Pentecostals. Hell, even the Mormons are unto a 'lost tribe.'"

"Yes," Jorgerson was interested in learning about South Dakota. "I hear there has been a resurrection of some native religions, with AIM operating in your area now."

"Yeah," Dale said derisively, "they'll resurrect the Sioux's interpretation of Paiute prophecy, for it serves their more radically militant stance."

"How's that?" Jorgerson, truly interested now, seemed willing to talk with his old friend all night long.

"Well," Dale hesitated, "you see, Wovoka taught that the Indian dead would be raised, the white man would disappear as result of various natural calamities, and Indians would live on the plains once more, free of death, disease, and misery."

"Beautiful prophecy," Jorgerson said, "if you're an Indian."

"Yes," joked Dale, "I'm not worried."

Again, the two friends laughed.

"I don't see anything in this that AIM couldn't completely incorporate in their political strategies," Jorgerson said as the conversation continued.

"Well," Dale renewed the history lesson for his white friend from the nation's capital, "the disappearance of the white man was not envisioned by Wovoka or by most of his followers as the consequence of Indian arms or wars."

"Oh," Jorgerson said, now getting the point of Dale's earlier judgement of AIM.

"Indeed," Dale continued, "Wovoka wanted the warriors to give up fighting and to live in peace with all men, doing justice to all. Wowicake."

"What?"

"Justice," was Dale's only reply.

"My God," Jorgerson said, "when was this Wovoka alive?"

"In the eighteen-seventies," Dale replied. "His doctrine was perhaps the most revolutionary of his time."

"And the Sioux would have nothing to do with it?"

"The Sioux believed that Wakantanka sent the white race to punish them for their sins."

"Yes."

"And they believed that their sins were now expiated and they would be delivered from their oppression and bondage . . ."

"I remember now," Jorgerson interrupted, "you're talking about the Ghost Religion and Dance."

"Yes," Dale said, "Wanagi Wowaci. It was easy that winter to raise the specter of shirts impervious to the white man's bullets by dancing in them to the drums of days that will never return to our land."

Silence fell between the two men. While Jorgerson saw primitive dancers around campfires, caught up in spasmodic action and physical exhaustion in his mind's eye, Dale was preoccupied with a more contemporary scene: a young waitress lying on a café stovetop, serving as a reminder to all who stopped to see the brevity and unpredictability of life.

"Dale," Jorgerson said more earnestly. "You be careful with this 'Max' character. If he's the man you've described and you have an inexplicable death on your hands anywhere near him, he's very dangerous. He's a killer, pure and simple. He won't care who's in his way. Keep an eye on him until we're sure. But keep your distance. You understand?"

"Wicakte," Dale said as to himself alone. Then to Jorgerson, he replied, "Yeah, I'll be very careful. I come from a people who follow from a distance very well."

They concluded their conversation with jolly goodbyes.

Dale went to the bathroom and rubbed cold water on his face. Then he opened the medicine cabinet, removing face blackener and some earth tone pigments. Within minutes, he was prepared, except for a change of shirts, to spend the night watching and following, if need be, the dishwasher from the Kadoka Café.

He retrieved the ancient cloth from his clothes closet in the hallway. Its fringes were now frayed and many a stringlet was missing. The deerskin slipped begrudgingly over his head and rested snugly across his chest and back, its ancient handpainted symbols now faded by the years but still discernible to native eyes.

"Wanagise wicaunpi," he said quietly as he gazed at himself in the bathroom mirror. Then he did something no one in Kadoka

*had ever witnessed him doing. He smiled. Dale Walthroup smiled
as he lifted the burning pipe in his hand, puffed, and then exhaled
the smoke, cupping it in his hand and wafting it over his forehead.
"Wowicake," he said to the figure that stared back at him from
the mirror. "Kazuzzupi iyehantu."*

*Dale Walthroup, county sheriff, son of a Dacotah mother who
named him 'Woope Yuha,' left his home, got into his Studebaker
and rode his trusted steed into the night, now fully committed to
tracking every step of Max Long.*

Chapter 14

Wowiyukean Ohna

Eyes watched the runner arise from sleep, stand and stretch, looking first to the east where Eyes crouched low so as to not be seen, then the west, then the south, and finally, the north. The runner held his stomach, as if feeling cold and hungry. Then ever so slowly, he began to run toward the north. Eyes ran just a hundred steps or so to his right, staying always in the direction of the sun, slightly behind him so as to go continually unnoticed.

The morning air was warm and a slight breeze flowed from the south, aiding both as they ran. As if by instinct, the runner headed due north. Eyes followed and watched as from time to time, the man stopped to catch his breath, bending forward, resting his hands on his knees. Then, as if he were an entrant in a double marathon, the man resumed running northward. Uphill and downhill, through tall grasses and jumping across muddied rills, they ran. Eyes ran, unnoticed by the one he followed so carefully.

As he ran, his heart beat within his chest like an ancient drum, its rhythm matching the cadence of his steps. His legs seemed to regain strength with each rest stop. He renewed his pace, lengthening his stride downhill and shortening them uphill, as his cousin had taught him many years before. *Fast pace downhill, steady pace uphill*, his cousin had said as they ran cross-country for their schools. His lungs never felt so clear as they did this morning. He couldn't remember when he last felt as alive and free as he did this day.

As he came to the top of the next hill, the land stretched before him like a vast tabletop in all directions. He could barely make out the signs of civilization on the northern horizon. Between him and that small town in the distance crossed the interstate. He noted a small variety of trucks, camper vans, and cars going in both directions. *That must be Kadoka,* he thought to himself as he paused. *I will call from there.*

He ran again, quickening his pace with the slight downhill run in front of him. "Thank you," he said aloud as he eased into his stride. "Thank you."

Glancing to his left, he saw a small car driving northward. It was his first awareness that he had been running parallel with Highway 73. Somehow, in his running, he had worked his way toward the highway. His heart skipped a beat. He knew he would soon be safe.

Dale Walthroup eased back on the accelerator as he headed down the final hill toward Kadoka, which was still nearly three miles away. He thought of the last twenty-four hours and began to put the pieces of the mystery together in his own mind. There was only one thing that still puzzled him.

Dale had seen many bodies burned beyond recognition. In wartime Korea, he had helped pull charred remains from tank carcasses. In his duty as sheriff, he had witnessed rescue units pull what was left of people from burned-out vehicles and house fires. He was no stranger to the scene he had witnessed earlier this day.

It was Fran's description of her husband that puzzled Dale most. He knew that though bodies may burn to indescribable degrees, generally speaking, the skeletal frames with darkened and shrunken skin upon them still retained the height and girth of those who died in such horrible ways. Dale knew that the body Lewis Davenport pulled from the ruins of the Longvalley parsonage was not that of the preacher. He would stake his life on that claim.

But if it were not the preacher's body, then whose? And where in God's name is the preacher? These were the questions that were running through Dale's mind as he glanced right and saw a man running in the high grass not more than two hundred yards from the road.

Dale stopped the car alongside the highway and stepped out to get a better view of the running man. He called to the man, "Hello!"

The man kept on running, as if he had neither seen nor heard Dale.

"You there!" Dale yelled louder as the man now ran past him in the grass, roughly two hundred yards to the east. "What are you doing?"

No response. The man kept running. Soon, he was a few hundred yards further down the way toward Kadoka.

Dale decided to follow him in the car. He stepped into his car and put the car in first gear and slowly crept forward. He decided the man must be training for some kind of road race. Yet this was an odd way to do it. Off-road. Without shoes!

Then Dale noticed another figure running slightly behind the runner, low to the ground, bounding over small rises of grass as it moved, gracefully keeping pace with the runner.

"*Sunka*," Dale muttered to himself at the sight. "*Inyanka duzahe.*"

Then shaking his head as though clearing it from cobwebs, Dale realized who this might be running toward the interstate.

"*Wahosiye!*" he shouted as he revved the engine, swiftly changing gears so as to quickly overtake the runner and the one who ran behind him. Turning the steering wheel to a hard right, Dale's car was soon spinning across the grassy prairie toward the runner. As he passed the runner, he blew his horn and then turned directly in front of the man, bringing his run to an abrupt halt.

Dale jumped from the car and walked briskly toward the

runner.

"No," the runner screamed. "Don't hurt me! Leave me alone!"

As Dale reached the astonished runner, whose face now was ashen and whose body was near collapse, Eyes leapt from a clump of grass toward Dale's outstretched arm, snarling, teeth bared, ready for a fight.

Dale ducked as Eyes sailed over his head and tumbled in the grass nearby. With one swift motion, Dale removed his revolver from its holster on his right hip and fired one warning shot in the direction of Eyes, missing him and as he darted away.

Turning toward where the runner stood only seconds before, Dale saw no one for now the runner was in his car, driving erratically toward the roadway. Dale chased after his car, then stood and aimed a shot at the rear of the car.

The sound of the gun and the explosion of the right rear tire happened almost simultaneously as the car spun out of control and nearly rolled onto its right side before coming to a halt just short of the highway.

Dale ran toward the car, no longer doubting who it was he had tried to stop from running. He approached the car from the passenger side, noting that the driver was now slumped across the steering wheel.

"Pastor Wilson," Dale called out when he was but three steps from the rear of his car. "Pastor Wilson, are you all right?"

No response. The figure in the car did not move. Dale raced toward it and opened the passenger-side door. He reached into the car just as a searing pained engulfed his right ankle. He knew what it was.

Eyes held his ankle in a death grip, unwilling to let go until he knew his friend was not harmed. Blood oozed from Dale's ankle and onto the ground as Eyes simply refused to let go.

Like a wild animal in a steel trap, Dale Walthroup could not move without further damaging his leg. Dale could feel himself starting to slip from consciousness when the man behind the wheel roused from stupor and gazed into the sheriff's eyes.

"Are you Lark Wilson?" the sheriff meekly asked.

"Yes," said the runner.

"I am Sheriff Walthroup," Dale said as the pain now raced up the back of his leg toward his spine. "Please call your dog off of me."

"What?" Lark was confused. "I thought you were going to kill me."

"No," Dale said, grimacing in pain as he spoke. "Actually, I was going to look for you today. I'm glad you are all right."

Lark glanced over Dale's shoulder and into the eyes of the dog. Eyes acknowledged his friend's glance with a growl, then released his jaws and Dale's ankle fell limply over the running board.

"We've got to get you to the hospital," Lark said to the sheriff. "Let me help you get into the car."

Lark stepped out and walked around to the passenger side of the vehicle. Dale's ankle looked rather ugly through bloodied sock and pants leg. As gently as he could, Lark lifted the wounded sheriff's body into the car, Dale howling in pain with each jostle of his leg.

Eyes watched as Lark walked around to the trunk and lifted it, retrieving a spare tire and jack. Within minutes, the car's right rear end was lifted high enough to remove the useless tire and replace it with the spare. Once in place, Lark threw the tire and jack into the trunk, then walked toward the driver's side of the car and got in.

Eyes watched the car drive out of the grass and onto the highway, gaining speed as it drove away from him toward the north. Eyes sat in the grass until the car was out of sight. Then turning south, Eyes sniffed the air for a scent of anything to eat and loped back uphill toward Longvalley.

What served as a hospital in Kadoka stood conveniently near the interstate, just beyond the ramp for Wall and Rapid City to the west. It was a clinic operated by Rapid City's regional hospital and staffed by two nurses, one aide, and a doctor one afternoon a week, usually Thursday. The clinic had no beds but only a waiting room and an examining room. When doctors were not present, the nurses were instructed to treat wounds and make preliminary diagnoses, which were then telephoned to Rapid City, where a decision would be made regarding emergency transportation. Some persons actually expired at the clinic while awaiting treatment for gunshot wounds, various accidents, overdoses, heart attacks and strokes. But they were pronounced dead in Rapid City after being carried there either by ambulance or helicopter.

Dale would live! That was the assessment of the nurse who bound his ankle after generously applying Merthiolate and giving him a tetanus shot.

"If you start frothing at the mouth, we'll have to give you a series of rabies shots, or just shoot you!" she joked as she wrapped tape atop the gauze bandage.

Dale just stared at her as she smiled. They had been an item once. Betty and Dale were the talk of the town shortly after his wife died. The two of them were seen frequenting bars and motels from Kadoka to Rapid City. Then, as fierce as their passion had been, it cooled. Now, they were not even friends. *"Familiarity breeds contempt,"* Betty had confided to one of her friends who could not stop from sharing the Shakespearean quote until everyone in Kadoka had heard it, including Dale!

"You're a damned lucky man, Dale Walthroup," Betty confided as she finished wrapping his ankle. "I just don't understand how a dog can bite you that hard in that area of your leg and not destroy your Achilles tendon."

"Not that bad, then?" Dale wanted to know.

"Hell, no," the nurse fired back, "You'll just have to keep your leg elevated the rest of today and not put any weight on it until the doctor sees it on Thursday. You'll be back out there chasing down speeders and drunks before you know it."

"What do I owe you?" was all Dale could muster as Betty handed him a pair of worn-out crutches once they were adjusted to his height.

"Not a goddamned thing," she said sarcastically as she shoved the crutches into his hands. "You of all people in this godforsaken burg should know that!"

"Thanks anyway," Dale said as he lifted himself from the table. "The county will be settling up with you on this."

"Next time," Betty snarled over her shoulder as she left the room, "you'd better look out for those dogs they have down on the reservation. The next one may not know you, Chief!"

The way she said the last word revealed to Dale that Betty had never quite forgiven him for keeping his heritage a secret from her until one of her friends embarrassed her in front of everyone in the bar by asking her how many "little papooses" she and Dale were planning to produce.

Dale rolled down what remained of his pants leg and struggled out of the examining room into the waiting area. Lark Wilson sat waiting for him.

"Where do you live, Sheriff?" Lark wanted to know. "I'll drive you home. The nurse says you have to keep your leg up for a while."

"Thanks," Dale said. "I'd be much obliged."

The two men left the clinic and Lark drove to Dale's place. Once inside, Dale took a seat on the lone chair in the living room while Lark retrieved a stool from the corner and a chair from his study.

"How are you going to do your job until that heals?" Lark asked as he sat down after helping Dale adjust his leg onto the stool.

"That's the county's problem," Dale said.

"Is that so?" Lark asked Dale.

"Yeah," Dale continued, "I doubt if anything very exciting is going to happen here in the next three days or so. And if it does, well, they'll just have to figure it out."

"Is this the first time you've been laid up, Sheriff?"

"Yeah," Dale lied, leaving out the time he was shot by a drunk outside a house from which a frantic woman had called for help during a domestic disturbance. That time, Dale was laid up for two weeks.

"You're lucky then," Lark continued to engage him in

conversation while trying to decide when he could safely leave this man on his own.

"About as lucky as you, Preacher," Dale said now, more seriously than any word that had been spoken between them. "Why don't you tell me what you know about our little waitress here in Kadoka?"

Lark was stunned. "I don't know what you mean." Lark stalled for time in order to think about the sheriff's question.

"Come on, Preacher," Dale said impatiently. "I want to know everything you know about Jenny."

Lark hesitated. Then he shared every detail which he was aware of concerning Jacqueline Frontierre. He concluded by telling the sheriff how startled he was to find her living here in South Dakota.

"She's no longer living here," the sheriff said quietly.

"What are you saying?"

"She's dead."

"What!"

"She died yesterday afternoon," Dale said as he looked deeply into Lark's eyes for any signs of equivocation. "She died shortly after her argument with you at your church."

Lark shuddered.

"Her death was made to look like an accident," Dale continued, "by the same person who tried to do the same to you last night."

Lark's body shook with terror at the sheriff's words. "I don't know what to say," Lark finally managed to say as his teeth chattered involuntarily. "I can't believe she's dead."

"Well, your wife believes you are dead," Dale continued to inform Lark of the circumstances surrounding these mysterious deaths. "I guess we need to call her and let her know the good news."

"Yes," Lark said. "We need to call Fran and the kids. They're in Chamberlain at . . ."

"Al's Oasis Motel," Dale finished Lark's sentence for him. "I know. What I don't know is who that was who died in your house last night."

"Oh God," Lark cried out. "I am so sorry I could not save him."

"Who was it?" Dale insisted.

"I don't really know," Lark confided in the sheriff. Then he told Dale, in every detail but one, all that happened the night before until he was thrust out of the window in his attempt to escape the burning parsonage and ran for his life.

Dale looked at Lark intently, seemingly wanting to ask more questions. Then he shrugged his shoulders and said to himself, "*Wahosiye.*"

"May I call Fran?" Lark asked.

"You'd better let me do it," Dale said. "I am accustomed to giving people bad news. I'd like to try my hand at the other side for a change."

Lark helped Dale to his feet and the sheriff struggled with the crutches until he was seated in his chair in his office. Lark, stool in hand, helped Dale prop up his leg once more. Then Dale called the motel and asked for Mrs. Wilson.

"Hello," Fran answered with a voice as weary as any Dale had heard.

"Mrs. Wilson," Dale said carefully, "we've found your husband."

"What?"

"We found your husband, Mrs. Wilson. He is all right."

Silence

"Mrs. Wilson," Dale continued slowly as though talking to a child, "your husband is alive. He is with me here in Kadoka."

Silence. Then quiet sobs.

"You may come to pick him up, or I'll have Steve drive him down from here," Dale continued speaking very slowly, trying not to startle Fran while trying to picture her in his mind's eye.

More sobs, audibly growing out of control.

"Mrs. Wilson," Dale said a bit more command in his voice. "Do you hear what I am saying?"

"Yes," She said between sobs while a voice in the background asked "What's wrong, Mom?"

"Good," Dale continued more cautiously, now that he knew there was a semblance of cognizance at the other end of the line. "That body in the parsonage was not your husband's. I knew that the minute you told me how tall your husband is. We don't know yet who that was. But we know your husband is alive."

"Oh, thank God!"

"Mommy, what is it?" a child's voice asked in the background.

"It's your father," Fran said as though speaking from a church chancel. "He is alive!"

Squeals of delight were audible even to Lark who sat across the desk from the sheriff. Then silence anew at the other end of the line.

"Mrs. Wilson," Dale said, "are you there?"

"Sorry," Fran said hastily, "the children and I will be there as soon as we can make it."

Quickly explaining to Fran how she would find his home, Dale then wanted to know if she wished to speak with Lark.

"Oh, may I?"

"Here he is," Dale said, almost beaming as he extended the phone to Lark.

"Fran," Lark said.

"It is so wonderful to hear your voice, Lark. Thanks be to God."

"Yes," Lark said quietly to his wife, "thanks be to God!"

"I'll be there soon," she said as the children clamored in the background to speak with their father.

When Lark returned to Dale's place with two burgers and fries, the sheriff was on the phone, speaking animatedly with whoever was on the other end of the line.

"I don't know who the hell he was," Dale exclaimed. "John Doe, as far as I know!"

Dale motioned for Lark to put his burger and fries in front of him on the desk as he listened to the person on the phone speak. He motioned for Lark to go to the kitchen and get them something to drink. Lark walked into the kitchen and opened the refrigerator as Dale resumed speaking on the phone.

"All I can tell you is that whoever that poor bastard is, he isn't the preacher from Longvalley, unless ghosts can go to the café and bring me back a great hamburger for supper!"

Lark peered into the refrigerator. It was pretty bare except for several packages of cheese, some condiment bottles, and ten cool ones lined up on one side, as though they were ordered to make room for more. He grabbed two of the beers and closed the door. After Lark searched for an opener for a minute, Dale called to him from his office.

"The opener's on the doorway here," Dale called and then continued talking on the phone.

Lark saw the opener, attached to the wooden doorway between the kitchen and Dale's office. He opened the bottles and carried them into the sheriff's office.

"Yeah," Dale was concluding his conversation while he chomped on his burger, "I'll talk with you tomorrow about later, Lewis. Goodnight."

"That was the undertaker?" Lark asked.

"Yeah," Dale said as he shoved the last bit of his hamburger into his mouth. "Damned good food Steve cooks up down there at the café."

"Not bad," Lark said as he began to eat his hamburger and noticed that his hunger now grew with each bite.

The two men finished their meals in silence, each weary from the events of their day.

"Tell me, Reverend," Dale said as he finished his beer and tossed the bottle into the wastebasket near his desk, "what are you going to do now?"

"I don't know," Lark said honestly. "I know Fran and the kids aren't really happy here. I was hoping they'd give it more of a try."

"What about you?" the sheriff asked. "Are you happy here in South Dakota?"

"I'm not sure," Lark said.

The phone rang. Dale picked up the receiver and grunted, "Sheriff Walthroup here."

As he listened, he looked at Lark and began to smile. "Yes, he's right here.

It's for you." He handed the receiver to Lark.

"Hello," Lark said tentatively.

"Lark," a familiar voice began, "I'm so glad to learn you are alive. Fran called me earlier today to say that you had died in a fire. Then about an hour ago, she called to tell me it was a mistake . . . that you are alive. I just had to hear your voice for myself."

"I'm alive, all right," Lark said. "It is nice of you to call me, Harry"

Then to Dale, Lark said, holding his hand over the mouthpiece, "It's my former denominational minister from back East."

"My God, Lark, if I had known that Jacqueline Frontierre was there, I never would have recommended that you and Fran move to South Dakota," Harry Sawyer said. "I can hardly believe any of this that Fran has told me today."

"It's not anybody's fault," Lark assured the older man. "How could anyone foresee this?"

"Are you going to stay, Lark?" Harry asked him.

"I'm not sure," Lark responded. "I need some time . . ."

"Of course you do," Harry interrupted. "Anybody would need time after what you've been through."

"Thanks," Lark replied. "I appreciate your concern."

"Look, Lark," Harry Sawyer now adopted his church leader's tone of voice. "If there is anything you or Fran need, you just give me a call. You hear me? I got you folk into this. It's the least I can do to help you through it now."

"Thank you, Doctor Sawyer," Lark said with conviction. "That is very kind of you."

"I'll try to reach you in a couple of days," Harry Sawyer assured him. "I'll call you at the motel in . . . what was the name of the place?"

"Chamberlain," Lark answered. "That will be fine. I guess we'll be there for a while."

"Now get some rest, my friend," Harry said as he prepared to hang up. "God has kept you around for a reason, you know. I'll be in touch."

"Goodnight," Lark said. "And thanks again, Harry."

"You're welcome," Harry Sawyer concluded. "Goodnight."

The sheriff eyed Lark as the preacher handed the receiver back to him.

"An old friend?" Dale asked.

"Yes," Lark smiled. "I think he is."

The men would have talked more but suddenly, the front door of Dale's house swung open and Fran and the children rushed inside. Lark arose and turned to see his family walking toward him through the living room. The children rushed against their father and held him tight, each one trying to talk at once.

"Daddy," Leigh Anne cried. "We thought you were dead."

"Dad," Saul asked, "where were you?"

"Dad," Walt said, "we love you."

"That goes for me, too," Fran smiled as she gazed adoringly at her husband's face. Then she saw the sheriff with his bandaged leg sitting behind his desk.

"What happened to you?" she asked Dale.

"It's a long story," Dale said to the preacher's wife. "Your husband there can fill you in with the details as you folk drive back to Chamberlain."

Fran shot a glance at Lark and then got herself into the family hug which was taking place in Dale's office. After thanking Dale for his hospitality and being assured by the sheriff that he would be all right for the rest of the night by himself, Lark and his family left around eight-thirty for Chamberlain and the Oasis Motel.

An hour after the Wilsons departed, there was a knock on the sheriff's door.

"Come on in," Dale yelled as he lifted his head from the

desk, where he had fallen asleep sometime before. "I'm in my office."

It was Lewis Davenport, as Dale had never seen him: unshaven, unkempt, and obviously under the influence.

"Sheriff . . ." Lewis slurred as he staggered through the doorway to Dale's office.

"Sit down before you fall down, Lewis," Dale commanded as he recognized the symptoms he'd encountered on many a late-night drive through the county. "What the hell have you been doing to yourself?"

"It's the girl . . . and the preacher, or whoever that was in the preacher's house," Lewis tried to explain. "I'm afraid."

"Of what?"

"I might be next."

"I don't think so," Dale tried to calm the agitated little man a bit.

"You don't understand," Lewis insisted, "I'm not . . ."

"You're not who you pretend to be," Dale interrupted.

"That's right," Lewis said, shocked by Dale's insight.

"I've known that for some time," Dale lied, trying to encourage Lewis to talk about himself by acting sympathetic.

"Then you know . . . ," Lewis hesitated, "I'm gay."

Dale sat upright in his chair and studied the undertaker with more interest. He shook his head to indicate he knew Lewis' secret.

"And," Lewis continued, "you know my marriage is a farce?"

"Yep," Dale lied through his teeth, for even in his wildest hunch, he never suspected that Lewis was not married to his elusive mate, Muriel.

"You probably know why I'm here pretending to be someone I'm not," Lewis said as he seemed to gain some composure.

"No," Dale confessed, "I don't have a clue. And how might all this be related to Jenny and the victim in Longvalley?"

"My family and a New Jersey family had a little problem a while back," Lewis began to embellish the truth exactly as he had rehearsed it while downing nearly a fifth of Scotch. "It was what you might call a business disagreement."

"How's that?"

"You might say," Lewis continued haltingly, "that our family thwarted an unfriendly takeover by the family in New Jersey."

"I see," Dale said. "Your family kept them from coming in and taking over your business."

"That's it," Lewis Davenport said, delighted that he was communicating so well with the only man in the county he now thought he could trust. "We simply kept them from taking over our business."

"Funeral business?" Dale asked, struggling to keep from laughing as he did so.

"More or less," Davenport slurred less enthusiastically.

"But this doesn't explain why you are now afraid, as you say," Dale said more sympathetically. "And it doesn't tell me why you are living here in Kadoka.

I guess you'll have to tell me more, Lewis."

As Lewis Davenport tried to explain by saying there had been a strong disagreement and unfortunate misunderstanding which led to an untimely death of a member of the family from New Jersey, Dale put the pieces together well enough to know why his contact in Washington didn't know anything about the undertaker. Lewis was now hiding out in Kadoka in order to protect himself from retribution at the hands of some underworld family in New Jersey. This had been an act of his own volition and not something Lewis had been handed by the feds. Dale's respect for Lewis Davenport rose just a bit as he listened to the undertaker's woeful tale of deception and sensed his guest's weariness with the ruse.

"And so, you think that someone killed Jenny," Dale sought to summarize, "then tried to kill the preacher because he knew Jenny from out East."

"Yes," Lewis said in a low voice. "I believe I'm next."

"You think it may be the same family operation you faced before," Dale encouraged his guest to share more.

"I think it is," Lewis Davenport lied with well-rehearsed

conviction. "I called Chicago tonight and my family agrees that this might be the case."

"For the record," Dale said strongly, "just who do you believe the hit man might be?"

Davenport shifted uneasily in his chair. He glanced at the large clock on Dale's desk. Then he looked around the room and noted several sheets of newsprint, barely visible in the slightly darkened office, taped to the west wall, each sheet holding a name of a person of importance to this very case: Jenny Craig, Max Long, Lark Wilson, Lewis Davenport! Each sheet contained notes which Lewis could not quite decipher beneath the names on them. Three of the names had large check marks beside them. Only the one that read Lewis Davenport was unchecked!

"Lewis?" The sheriff prodded. "Who do you believe the murderer is?"

Lewis stared now solely at the sheet of paper that contained his name at the top. He squinted to read the small notations written beneath his name. Try as he did, he could only be sure of one word: "phony."

Lewis turned and faced the sheriff once more. "I think it might be Max," he said and then sat back in his chair, resting his head on one hand as he seemed to relax.

Dale did not respond. He moved a bit in his chair, trying to find a more comfortable position for his leg, for it was now starting to ache much more than he'd expected.

The two men simply sat and looked at one another, until Dale asked, "So, what's your plan, Lewis?"

"I think I'll be leaving tonight, Sheriff," Lewis said now in a voice filled with resignation. "I'm going to try to get as far away from here as I can so they can't find me."

"I don't think you are in any shape to be driving, Lewis," Dale said like a mother to her child. "Why don't you just stay here tonight with me? I don't believe the killer knows you're here. Even if he does, I doubt he'd try anything at my house."

"You don't know these people," Lewis Davenport said as the terror he had held in check until now filled his eyes.

"Maybe you are wrong about this," Dale said, endeavoring to soothe the frightened little man who sat in his office.

"Have you seen Max today?" Lewis asked sincerely.

"Not today," Dale said. "Come to think of it, I haven't seen him anywhere today. I assume he worked in the café today. I'll call Steve first thing in the morning to see if Max showed up for work today."

"You're watching him, aren't you, Sheriff?"

"Sort of," Dale said. "I've had a busy day and this unfortunate run-in with a mangy cur just south of town." Dale pointed to his ankle. He told Lewis about finding the preacher running on the prairie. He told him about the dog's attack and the need to get fixed up at the clinic. He shared brief details about the joyful Wilson family reunion. He said nothing about anything Lark had shared with him regarding the victim. Davenport seemed to relax as Dale spoke of the events of the day. Whatever it was that Dale said, it was enough to convince Davenport of the wisdom of staying the night. They agreed that Dale could sleep sitting up in the living room with his leg propped up and Lewis could have the bedroom, as long as he didn't mind sleeping in an unmade bed.

"Well," Lewis Davenport said in a voice that revealed to Dale that alcohol was truly bringing this conversation to a close, "I guess you're right, Sheriff. I'm in no condition to go anywhere tonight. If you don't mind, I'll just go to the bathroom and then go to bed."

"Not at all," Dale said, still comfortingly. "Make yourself at home."

Lewis Davenport struggled to his feet and staggered through the living room, into the hallway and to the bathroom. Turning on the light, Lewis saw a strange shirt hanging over the shower curtain rod. It had recently been washed, he surmised. He reached out to touch the garment and noted that it was made of the thinnest deerskin he had ever seen. It felt smooth to the touch, much like a damp chamois cloth one might use to dry an auto after washing it. There were markings on it, many of which were so faded they were only barely visible. As Lewis surveyed it, he saw what looked like newly applied paints in various places. They looked as though they had been spattered on the cloth by an artist taking a brush, dipping it in deep red paint and simply throwing the hue from a short distance.

Lewis relieved himself, washed his hands, looked at his face in the mirror, noting for the first time today that he hadn't shaved. Then he carefully found his way to the bedroom, where he simply threw himself across the bed with its oddly shaped pillows and beautiful star blanket. Shortly before sleep overtook him, Lewis decided he would inquire about Dale's shirt in the morning.

After all was quiet in his house, Dale lifted himself to his feet with the help of his crutches and thumped through the living room and into the bathroom. "*Yasica*," he muttered when he saw the shirt. He took it from the rod over the tub and stuffed it under his right arm. After relieving himself, Dale nervously went out through the living room and left the house.

When he got to his car, he opened the trunk and threw the shirt into it. Slamming the trunk he knew would not awaken Lewis Davenport. He hobbled back toward the house and through the front door. Quickly, he settled into the big chair after pushing the stool from his office to a place just in front of it so that he could maneuver his legs atop it. With all the energy he could summon, he reached for his wounded leg and carefully lifted it by holding tight to the pant's knee. Then he simply lifted his other leg and tried to relax.

It took a while. But as sleep came to Dale Walthroup this night, he rejoiced in its stuporous advance. If he dreamed, he would not remember. If he did not remember, he could function another day.

Chapter 15

Owaste Ihanke

Parked cars and pickups lined the dusty street. People had come from all corners of South Dakota to celebrate the dedication of the new church building and pastor's home adjacent to it. Every reservation was represented in the glorious procession just starting to take shape on the main street as Lark and his family exited their new home, to be greeted by smiles and waves from every direction.

Larked kissed Fran on the cheek and bade her and the children to go to the church. Then he quickly walked to the head of the procession line, where Harry Sawyer, deep in conversation with Ethan, awaited his arrival.

"Lark," Harry said as they turned in line to face the church building, "Ethan told me that his dog saved you that horrible night."

"Is that so?" Lark asked as he glanced over his shoulder and into Ethan's beaming face. "Did you ask him what the dog's name is?"

Ethan's head lowered at the question.

"It didn't occur to me to ask," Harry said seriously just as the drums began to play and the four men who sat pounding them so earnestly began to chant along to the beat.

Every person in the line gave their attention to the drummers as they played and sang. It was the call to worship, being issued in a way neither Harry Sawyer nor any of his ancestors had ever heard. Every fourth beat of the drum struck the head harder than the previous three until the rhythm seemed to match that of an expectant heart.

"When they conclude their song," Lark whispered to Harry, "I will try to start our processional hymn in the right key."

Harry did not respond. He was mesmerized by the cascading drum beat and the almost counter-tenor pitch to the drummer's voices.

"What are they singing?" Harry asked softly as he kept focused on the drummers, who sat in a circle by the church entryway.

"They are calling to the four directions," Lark summarized quietly. "They are asking that four spirits come together now: God, Universe, Man and Self. This way, the gathering will be blessed."

The two men stood at the head of the procession line until, as suddenly as they had begun, the drummers ceased their drumming and singing. In the silence, a meadowlark could be heard finishing its song in the high grass behind the church.

Lark started the processional song in Dakota and immediately, everyone in the procession except Harry was singing:

> *"Wo-a-hta-ni on te-hi—ya*
> *Nis du-kan-pi he-cin-han,*
> *Je-sus Christ e-kta ho-ye—ya,*
> *Qa wa-cin-yan un mi-ye:*
> *Je-sus i—ye, Je-sus i—ye*
> *To-na si-ca on-si-da,*
> *Je-sus i—ye, Je-sus i—ye,*
> *To-na si-ca on-si-da"*

The tune was familiar to Harry. Hence, he hummed it as the pastor beside him, the people behind him in the procession, and those unseen from within the church, could all be heard singing

William Bradford's 19th-century hymn in a language only fully familiar to Stone Age persons from the prairies. *Yes,* thought Harry as he walked beside Lark toward the church doors, *Savior: like a shepherd lead us!*

As they entered the recently completed church building that now stood where once the parsonage was located, Lark could not believe his eyes. Every seat was taken. People stood along both aisles and filled the newly built fellowship hall.

Loudly, they sang with him:

> *"Wanna wokakije nica,*
> *Iye to ekta yanke,*
> *Qa wiconte he ohiya,*
> *On wacinyanpi waste:*
> *Jesus iye,*
> *Wowakan unqupi kte!"*

When Lark and Harry reached the chancel, they ascended the three steps and each took a seat on either side of the communion table, while the other ministers, who had walked in the procession along with their lay leaders from each church of the association, filled the front pews.

Silence filled the room and was only broken by a flute playing at some distance from the church outside. Softly yet distinctively, each note floated through the building as though riding upon the fairest wings of a butterfly, never quite stopping at any place in the sanctuary but simply passing through in such a way as once it was gone, it was sorely missed.

When the flute had stopped and a moment of silence had passed, Lark arose and walked to the center of the chancel, facing the people.

"Surely, the Lord is in this place," he said quietly, almost as if to himself alone.

The people responded with a resounding, "Thanks be to God!" They then stood upon their feet as one to sing the doxology:

"Praise God from Whom all blessings flow,
Praise God all creatures here below,
Praise God above the heavenly hosts,
Praise Father, Son and Holy Ghost!
Amen."

The worshippers at Longvalley Community Church were then led in worship by singing groups from each of the twelve churches of the association and words of praise and best wishes from each of the eight pastors who served them, all men, every one of them a Native American except Kerry Wong, who was a South Korean.

Finally, after what seemed like an eternity, Lark stood again to read the biblical text for Harry's dedicatory sermon. Harry had decided to preach on Deuteronomy. After Lark read Chapter 4, verses 32-40, he reread verse 39: "Acknowledge and take to heart this day that the Lord is God in heaven above and on the earth below." After giving a few introductory remarks about Harry, Lark took his seat and, like every one else in the church, listened intently to Harry Sawyer's sermon.

It was a beautifully crafted sermon which brought together the ancient wisdom of the text and the recent events in the lives of the pastor and the congregation. Obstacle after obstacle had been faced, summarized Harry, with an assurance written deep within the hearts of every member that God would have the final say in the lives of pastor and people. Uncharacteristically yet graciously, the Native American people in the sanctuary never lowered their heads while this easterner, new to South Dakota and to them, endeavored to bring God's word to them in such a way as to encompass all that they and their pastor and his family had experience in the year they had been together.

Lark glanced at Fran from time to time, then at his children, who seemed to be growing up very fast now on the prairie. No longer the children they were only a year before, each one seemed to be adopting to the land and the people as their own now, and this decision was somehow being communicated in their daily demeanor. Fran smiled as his eye caught hers. They were here to stay, Lark sensed as he saw the peace and pride on each face of his family.

Looking at the gathered congregation, Lark was pleased to see that every one of the members of the church was there, sitting among family and friends from other churches and towns. Ethan and Percy, Angus and Dolores, new members, Mona Lisa and Wayne, Henry and Violet, and all of their children were present at various places among the crowd that filled the room. He noted that even Dale Walthroup was present in the back of the room!

The moderator of the association led the congregation in the dedication of the new church building and the pastor's home following Harry's sermon. When it was time for the offering, Walt, Leigh Ann, and Saul, along with Louise, Phyllis and Paul arose and came forward to receive the six baskets. After they had gone through the congregation, baskets in hands, they returned to the foot of the chancel, where Lark and Harry received the offering and placed it on the table.

Lark turned toward the congregation and said, "Let us pray as Jesus taught his disciples to pray."

In one voice, the congregation prayed:

> "Ateunyanpi Mahpiya ekta nanke cin, Nicaje wakandapi
>   kte:
> Nitokiconze u kte.
> Nitawacin maka akan econpi nunwe; Mahpiya ekta
>   iyececca.
> Anpetu kin de anpetu woyute unqu po.
> Qa waunhtanipi unkicicajuju miye; tona sicaya
>   ecaunkiconpi wicunkicicajujupi kin iyececa.
> Qa taku wawiyutan en unkayapi sni ye: tuka sice cin
>   etanhan eunyaku po.
> Wokiconze kin he Niye nitawa, qa wowasake kin, qa
>   wowitan kin, owihanke wanica. Amen."

As if functioning on some pre-arranged cue, the drummers and singers immediately began after the congregation concluded the prayer, while people in the church building began to move toward the exits. What followed would have made an army envious, for without any sign of a leader, the people set up tables and dinner was ready outside the church building in a mere ten minutes.

Soon, people stood in lines on both sides of the serving tables, plates in hand, taking samples of each and every dish that had been prepared for the feast. As Harry glanced around, he noted little groups of people, no doubt each from their own congregations, now gathered about on the lawn between the church building and the pastor's home, sitting upon blankets with numerous forms of decorations, eating and joking with one another, and obviously enjoying themselves. Fran spread a beautiful star blanket that had been a gift to her in honor of Lark's installation as pastor the previous winter, for her family and their distinguished guest to sit upon for lunch.

After all had gone through the line and were seated, Ethan asked everyone to bow their heads in prayer. He prayed that God would be pleased to be present as these people feasted upon the goodness of the earth and in the midst of loving families and friends. Even Dale Walthroup, who now sat on a blanket next to Sonny Firecloud and his family, could be heard to say a loud "Amen" after Ethan's prayer.

"This is really quite an astonishing day," Harry Sawyer said as he bit into a fried chicken leg.

"Indeed," Lark agreed. "We have people here from all over the state! It's quite a tribute to our little church."

"Oh no," Fran interjected, "It's a tribute to you, Lark."

"How so?" Lark asked his wife.

"I think I can answer that," Harry said quickly before Fran, who was wiping some berry pudding from her chin, could respond. "It's a tribute to your courage and faith. You have stayed with your people, instead of leaving them, when no one would have blamed you for doing so. It's like Jesus' story of the good shepherd."

Lark smiled, for he was deeply touched by Harry's insightful support of his decision to stay.

"Harry's right, dear," Fran added, "these people are here

today to honor you as much as they are to assist in the dedication of our new church and parsonage. I know I and the kids are proud of you. So are all of these people."

"I love you," was all Lark could say as he looked at Fran, choking back tears of joy.

"I love you," Fran returned the compliment. "These people love you. I can't tell you how glad I am to be here with you on this day."

"Thank you, Fran," Lark now said, regaining his composure. "I couldn't have done any of this without you and the children."

"Neither of you can imagine how all of us feel back in Pennsylvania when we read of your work in South Dakota," Harry interrupted. "Do your ears burn from time to time?"

Both Lark and Fran laughed at Harry's question while Saul asked, "What does that mean? Do our ears burn? I don't get it."

"It's an old saying," Harry assured the lad. "It means that when your ears burn, someone in the world is talking about you."

"Oh," Saul said as he began to chuckle. "Good or bad?"

"Yes," it was Walt's turn to play the sage, "good or bad."

"Dr. Sawyer means that people back East are speaking positively about us," Leigh Ann assured her younger brother.

"That's correct," Harry concurred. "In light of today's events, how could we do otherwise?"

"Look at them," Dale was saying to Sonny and his wife, Juanita, "who would have thought those people would stay after what happened last summer?"

"I know a few who felt they'd never see them again after that fire," Sonny said.

"All but Ethan, I heard," Juanita added. "He called the pastor three days after the fire and told him the church would rebuild the house and create a new sanctuary if he would come back to be their pastor."

"Yes," Sonny continued, "the story is that the pastor and Ethan prayed together for a week up on Bear Butte before Lark made his decision to stay."

"Is that so?" Dale quipped.

"Fran almost didn't come back with him," Juanita said to the two lawmen.

"I heard she and the children went back East for a month while she made up her mind."

"*Wasaka*," Dale said as he glanced in the pastor's direction. "*Wacinyepica*."

"He sure is," Sonny agreed as all three now turned to Lark, caught his eye, and waved a greeting in his direction.

Dale got up from the ground and stretched his frame. He shook his legs and arms a bit, as if to move the blood more easily through his aging body.

"I guess I'd better get back to Kadoka," he said. "Never know what's awaiting me up there."

"Can't you stay for the gifting ceremony?" Sonny asked earnestly.

"Oh, I don't know . . ." Dale started to say.

"Of course he can," Juanita said with a smile. "It won't take long."

As soon as every person had finished eating, Ethan asked the body to form a circle and join hands. When they were together, Ethan prayed again.

"Great Spirit," he began, "receive our thanks for one another gathered here today. Make our hearts grateful for everything you give us in life: family, friends, church, and community. Teach us that no matter how strong the wrong done to us, you are working your purpose for our lives, that purpose first enlivened with our first breath. 'The wrong shall fail, the right prevail,' is the foundation of our faith in you, Creator God. May we never forget it or neglect to teach it to our children. Amen."

"Amen," resounded throughout the circle.

"Now," Ethan went on, "I know that many of you have long roads to travel today before you get home, so we won't take too long with this, but we want to give our pastor, his family, and his friend, Dr. Sawyer, some gifts of gratitude today. So be patient with us, please."

One by one, each member family of the congregation came forward with blankets for the Wilsons and for Harry Sawyer. Then, a representative from each of the twelve congregations of the association gave a gift. Before most people could count the brief speeches that preceded the gifts to the Wilsons and Dr. Sawyer, the ground in front of the honored pastor and his friend was strewn with gifts of all kinds.

"I will need to rent a trailer," Harry Sawyer said quietly to Lark at one point in the ceremony.

When it seemed that the gifting ceremony was ended, Lark stepped into the circle and thanked all persons present for their graciousness to him and his family. Harry Sawyer followed with deep appreciation for their kindness shown to him during his visit and on this day.

"Wait a minute," Sonny Firecloud shouted just as people began to stir and break the circle. "I have a gift for Sheriff Walthroup."

Astonished, Dale turned around and stood, facing the circle once more.

"Dale," Sonny began to say, "I know how you love hunting and fishing. More than this . . ."

"What's this all about?" Dale interrupted Sonny.

"More than this," Sonny started to speak again, "I know how important your role has been in solving some of the crimes that have afflicted our reservation and the county you serve."

"Come on," Dale said anew, "what's going on?"

"This isn't a joke," Sonny said seriously. "You are as important to the people of the reservation as you are to the people north of here."

Dale blushed and glanced at the ground in front of him.

"And," Sonny said, "I heard that you lost your good deer-skinning knife a while back . . ."

Dale's head rose quickly and he stared at Sonny in disbelief and shock!

"So," Sonny concluded, "I want to give you this gift in my appreciation for all you have done for all of us in this circle."

Sonny reached behind him and took the bag Juanita held proudly in her hand. He handed it to Dale, whose face now began to turn from beet red to ashen white.

Dale opened the bag just enough to assure himself that his knife was indeed in the bag. He looked intently at Sonny, who now stood side by side with Juanita, a huge smile upon his face.

Dale reached into the bag, knowing that everyone in the circle would want to see the gift Sonny had given him, and withdrew the knife from it and held it up for all to see. Applause, which enabled him to regain his composure, greeted his gesture.

"Thank you, Sonny," was all Dale could manage as he quickly returned the knife to the bag.

After most people shook hands and bid farewell to one another, the women of the congregation began to clean up the tables, after which the men carried them back into the church building. The Wilsons, along with Dr. Sawyer, retreated to the newly built parsonage, which stood just north of where the old church building once stood.

Dale walked toward Sonny's car and waited until those who were gathered around the tribal policeman had said their farewells and driven away.

"I guess you want to know where I found it," Sonny said to Dale as the two men stood side by side, watching the last visitor's car drive away toward Highway 73.

"I'm more interested in when you found it," Dale said. "I think I know where you found it."

"You do?" Sonny seemed to ask sincerely.

"Come on," Dale was impatient.

"If you're so sure about where I found it, why don't you tell me?"

"I asked you first," Dale said as he turned now and faced Sonny.

"Fair enough," the younger man said. "You aren't going to believe this but that damned dog of Ethan's came walking into town two days after the parsonage fire with it in his mouth!"

"What?" Dale couldn't believe his ears.

"That's what everybody here told me," Sonny said with a grin. "I wasn't here, you know. I was out doing my duty: serving and protecting!"

"Well," said Dale, "I'll be damned. That knife must have fallen out of my car in that little fracas when I found the pastor running toward Kadoka."

"That's what I figured, too," Sonny went on. "You know, he's a pretty smart dog."

"Yeah," Dale agreed, "and he bites like a surgeon!"

"Uh huh," Sonny said as he inhaled. "You never found that dishwasher who killed the waitress up there in Kadoka, did you?"

"Nope," Dale said more cautiously as he stared into Sonny's eyes. "I told my friends at the bureau to pass the word along to that sonofabitch's family that if I ever saw him out here again, I'd arrest him for murder."

"Yeah," Sonny seemed disinterested as he dragged the toe of his boot through the dust at their feet, "I guess that will keep him away from us from now on."

"You bet," Dale said confidently.

"Whatever became of that undertaker? What was his name?"

"Davenport," Dale answered. "He went back to Chicago after they split up."

"That wife of his found herself a better man, I suppose," Sonny said with a smile.

"Uh huh," Dale responded, sensing that this conversation was not quite completed.

"You know," Sonny said now, a little more earnestly, "I found a station wagon down in a draw about thirty miles west of here, not more than a month after all this excitement here in Longvalley. It had no licensed plates, no identification of any kind. Just a couple of empty gasoline cans that I couldn't trace to any stations around here."

"What about it?" Dale pretended interest in the direction Sonny was taking him. "Just another stolen car?"

"No," Sonny said as he stopped smiling. "This one had a dead body in it."

Dale never blinked but stared intently at Sonny.

"An old guy, kind of heavy," Sonny went on. "He had almost lost his head when that car rolled into that draw. Damndest thing you ever did see. Yes, sir, somehow, his head was all but severed in that crash."

"You don't suppose . . ." Dale started to say.

"I thought about calling you," Sonny interrupted. "But then, you got enough to do without helping me deal with a 'John Doe' death down here. We just buried him out there where we found him after I couldn't find anything about him. I don't know who he was."

"Well, I'll be damned," Dale said. "Strange things happen out here all the time, don't they?"

Sonny stretched his hand toward Dale and said, more earnestly than before, "Thanks."

"Thank you," Dale said as the two men shook hands.

"You take good care of yourself," Sonny called after him as Dale walked toward his Studebaker.

"You do the same," Dale said as he stepped into his car.

Eyes watched from a distance as the two men parted company. Then, losing interest, Eyes turned and walked slowly in the direction of the new parsonage. The grass was totally deserted, save for crumbs from the dinner to harvest. Suddenly noting a piece of fry bread that was all but hidden from the human eye, Eyes loped to its resting place and grabbed it. It was good. It promised more. Like a note of certain dues, this savory grace called his senses to the hunt. He would forage this afternoon and be satisfied with whatever was left behind.

Edwards Brothers Malloy
Thorofare, NJ USA
December 7, 2012